THE MAUSER

I sat in the gloomy living room and snapped a clip into the Mauser. I hate guns. I hate their look and their cold oily smell and their weight. I hate the sick thrill of power they give to weaklings. I hate the high-caliber pieces with the walnut grips that open up gaps you can put your hand through, and I hate the shiny little purse jobs that make a nickel-sized red and black hole. I hate guns because they remind me of things that should never have happened. But mainly I hate them because they scare the hell out of me.

A gun is just a bad idea waiting for its time.

KYD
FOR HIRE

Timothy Harris

A Dell Book

Published by
Dell Publishing Co., Inc.
1 Dag Hammarskjold Plaza
New York, New York 10017

Published in Great Britain by Victor Gollancz Ltd.
with the author using the pseudonym Hyde Harris.

Dell ® TM 681510, Dell Publishing Co., Inc.

ISBN: 0-440-11670-8

Printed in the United States of America
First U.S.A. printing—February 1978
Second U.S.A. printing—May 1981

"No one ever keeps a secret so well as a child."

—VICTOR HUGO

KYD
FOR HIRE

Chapter ONE

The phone was ringing as I let myself from the waiting room into my office.

"Thomas Kyd?" a voice asked.

"Speaking."

"My name is Joe Elevel. I want to talk to you." It was an aggressive, deep voice that crowded in your ear.

"I'm in my office, Mr. Elevel." I reached for my appointment book. "When would you like to come in?"

"I'll be there in twenty-five minutes." He hung up.

That's how the nightmare started. Just a stranger's voice over the phone. A stranger in a hurry, who talked with the staccato urgency of a telegram.

I put the phone down and pulled up the venetian blinds. Usually I could see the Hollywood Hills but that morning they were lost in layers of yellow and brown smog. According to the radio, Los Angeles was in line to break one of its heat-wave records. With luck, it might experience the hottest, most unpleasant July day since 1956. Already the local landmarks were receding into the chemical haze. The bronze pimp on the corner of Hollywood Boulevard and Western was barely visible from fifty yards, and the air smelled like a couple of cars had been burned to death.

My end of Hollywood was the seamier section, many blocks east of where the stars' names were in the pavement. Despite the heat, business on the street was going on as usual. All along the block the girls had taken up positions in the doorways of the clubs and massage joints, and the porn movie houses and adult bookstores were getting their first customers. At that hour it was a landscape of hung-over derelicts, tired hustlers, and neon signs with no magic.

It wasn't much of a neighborhood but it was mine that year, and I liked my office better than the modern cubicle I'd had with the Beverly Hills outfit. The building was fifty years old, which in the Los Angeles time warp gave it the dignity of a classical artifact. The ceiling was very high, with an elegantly carved wooden cornice that went well with the polished wooden floors. The previous tenant had been a psychiatrist, and I'd inherited his furniture and the out-of-date magazines on the waiting-room table. I'd tacked a few photographs around the walls, put my criminology degree and my license from the Bureau of Collective and Investigative Services in prominent positions, and left everything else unchanged.

From the window I watched a bearded derelict pushing a supermarket cart of old newspapers past the hookers on the pavement. Whatever the weather he always wore a heavy overcoat buttoned up to the neck. Today his face looked like melted red candle wax.

I went into the alcove and took a bottle of Beefeater's gin out of the fridge and poured a short one over some ice cubes. I was celebrating the city's latest heat wave. After a few sips, I took off my damp shirt and washed myself at the sink with cold water. In the mirror I made one of those critical appraisals which become more frequent once you pass thirty. I sucked in my gut, took a deep breath, and tried to look manly in a nonchalant way. There wasn't an ounce of spare flesh on my rugged frame—there were about ten pounds. For a guy of thirty-three who spent a lot of his life glued to a chair or in a car, I was pretty sure you would still think twice about kicking sand in my face. I was six foot two and 190 pounds of overworked insomnia, spicy takeout food, and expensive gin. I needed a haircut, about a week's sleep, and a fat case to pay the rent on my office. Maybe Joe Elevel was my man. I put on a clean shirt for him, wound up my wrist watch, and stepped back into the office.

Most of the ice in my glass had melted. I sat down, lit a Gauloise, and looked down on Hollywood Boulevard.

A few minutes later a gray, short-wheel-base Bentley drew to a stop across the street. A Mexican chauffeur in a navy blue suit and cap opened the door and a man stepped out. The Bentley's windows were dark tinted glass and the man had stepped out into harsh sunlight but he didn't stop to adjust his eyes. He didn't even look at the hustlers who were calling to him. He walked straight across the four lanes of traffic, through squealing brakes and blaring horns, toward my building.

There was something straight-backed, single-minded, and doomed about the way Joe Elevel crossed that street. It remainded me of a commanding officer I'd served under in the Tet offensive of '68. He used to walk across a field under mortar bombardment like a man looking for his wife in a crowded department store. Watching his behavior under fire you started to believe he had some private line to the higher sources and they'd guaranteed him protection so long as he never showed fear. Joe Elevel had that same way of walking; he was wound up like one of those mechanical toys that can only go in one direction.

I hid my half-finished drink in a desk drawer and walked around to open the connecting door to the waiting room.

Some clients enter tentatively, like children taking their first step into a dentist's office. Others slide in furtively and hang back against the wall. A few barge in like they own the place and have dropped around to collect the rent.

Joe Elevel walked in fast. I didn't have time to get out of my seat before he was leaning over my desk, shaking my hand. He was a thin, erect man in his early fifties with a stern, haggard face. His clothes were black, very expensive, and there was a silk mourning band on his arm. On his right hand he wore something like five thousand dollars' worth of jewelry in the form of a gold Cartier watch and a diamond pinky ring. He had bright blue eyes with pouches that stood out like they'd been put on with a palette knife. He led with his jaw and kept his face twisted to the side, which gave him a tough suspicious look until you noticed that one side of his face didn't move. It had been paralyzed by a stroke.

"You found Gil Heller's wife," he said. "I hear you found her in three hours. I want you to find someone for me."

"Have a seat, Mr. Elevel."

"Some neighborhood you work in. Gil said you were good. If you're so good, what're you doing on this side of the tracks?"

"You said you wanted someone found."

"I asked you a question," he said.

I said, "If you think you have a better chance with the big agencies in Beverly Hills, you ought to see them. Wall-to-wall carpets and receptionists don't find missing people, Mr. Elevel. But there're some good detectives with the larger agencies. I used to work with them."

"So?" he said. "Why'd you quit?"

"I keep the confidences of my clients, Mr. Elevel."

"What's that supposed to mean?"

"It means if I don't talk about my clients, I'm not going to talk about myself."

He brooded sullenly for several moments, trying my answer on for size. He wasn't used to those kinds of replies, even if they were true. He ran his eyes around the room like a shopper picking up and discarding merchandise for sale; there was no concentration to his scrutiny. It was as if he hoped he could detect something in my office, an omen, a secret sign, that would help him decide that this was where he ought to be. He reminded me of an out-of-luck gambler who's blown all his reserves and is making bets on crazy, fatal whims like whether the woman opposite him smiles when he puts his chips on red. He glanced at the Persian carpets and the dusty venetian blinds and finally his eyes found the framed photograph of me and several friends in front of a Saigon whorehouse. We were in uniform in the picture, and the whorehouse looked like a government building, which it had been before the French pulled out. For some reason clients trust investigators with war records. They assume you're going to be methodical and tough. I didn't see any reason to tell Joe Elevel that of the four soldiers in the picture, one had an oil-burning junk habit, one had been court-martialed for black market activities, another was now in a Mexican jail for drug possession, and the fourth, whose name was Thomas Kyd, had spent a month under psychiatric observation in a military hospital. I didn't tell him that it had taken me over three years to get out of the habit of throwing myself flat on the street when I heard a car backfiring. Was it the picture of me with a crew cut and in officer's uniform that decided him? I'll never know. He frowned at it a long time, then slid a color Polaroid snapshot across the desk.

"That's Charlotte, my daughter. She disappeared two days ago."

The girl in the photograph was a type that California used to know how to produce better than any place in the world. She was about twenty, with sun-bleached hair, and peeling, freckled skin. Her eyes were blue and focused on something no one would ever touch with his hands. Her expression, with its childishly tremulous smile, had a spaced-out look that told me she believed in flying saucers, macrobiotic rice, and the humanizing effect of grass and acid. She was naïve, mystical, and ready to believe in anything beautiful so long as it didn't include pain. She was a bland, sweet acid baby, and I wondered if she still had that wide, ethereal gaze. It was the way a lot of girls had looked when I was twenty and dope was going to change the human race and people thought you could stop a war by sitting down and singing folk songs to the National Guard. She wore a sheer

Indian gown over a bikini that showed every curve of a body that was still half puppy-fat. Behind her was a cove of white sand and an ocean that looked like her eyes—clear, limpid, and too friendly for words. To be frank, she didn't interest me a hell of a lot.

"That picture was taken a month ago in Bermuda," he said.

"Why did she vanish?"

"My wife killed herself two nights ago. Charlotte left the house just before it happened. I don't know why my wife killed herself. I don't know why Charlotte's run away. I don't know where this craziness is coming from." He spoke in a bitter, deadened monotone, piling up the things he didn't know as if counting them were a way of making sense out of them. "My wife left this note. I don't know what that means either." He slid a piece of pale gray stationery across the desk. A lot of suicide notes run on like bad novels. This one had the brevity of a telegram.

"Charlotte knows. Soon you'll all know. It's unspeakable.

"I don't want to live any more. Forgive me."

There had not been enough ego left for the dying woman to sign her name. Probably no desire even to leave a note. A last flicker of obligation had prompted the message.

"Overdose?" I asked.

"The coroner's report isn't out yet but I've heard unofficially. Sleeping pills." He ground his teeth together. "Lots and lots of sleeping pills."

"And you have no idea why . . ."

"I have no idea why *anything!*" he shouted. "Nothing! My wife was a happy woman. We were happily married. My daughter was happy. Happy! God! She lived with us." He stared vacantly at his shoes, breathing noisily through his nose. Then he threw me a look that was almost like hatred. "These are all the questions the police asked me. They don't get anywhere. There are no answers to them. Wouldn't I know if I was living in a nightmare?"

"Sometimes there's no way of knowing until it starts, Mr. Elevel."

"Tell me!" he snorted.

"Where would Charlotte be likely to go if she was upset?"

"Calvin's been phoning everyone she knew. He's drawn a complete blank."

"Calvin?" I asked.

"My assistant, Calvin Moonhurst. I'm a businessman, Mr. Kyd. I own Elevel Office and Home Furniture. Does that ring any bells?"

"Should it?" I lit a cigarette and tried to look impassive.

"Well, everything in your office was made in one of my factories. You're sitting on one of my chairs." He rolled his eyes in impatience at my ignorance. It didn't say much, I suppose, for my powers of observation.

"I charge one hundred dollars a day," I said flatly, "plus expenses. I start by asking a two-hundred-dollar retainer. If I complete the job in one day I return the second hundred dollars."

"I'll give you five hundred dollars if you find Charlotte in the next twenty-four hours." He looked at his watch. "Starting now."

"Bonuses don't raise my batting average, Mr. Elevel. I said I worked for a hundred dollars a day."

He reddened slightly and wrote out a check for two hundred dollars. It occurred to me that he might be more sensitive than I'd originally thought. I was also certain, from his attitude toward money, that there hadn't been much around when he was growing up.

"Where do we start?" he said.

"Your home."

"You can follow me." He stood up, tapping his left hand against his leg. "I'm parked outside."

"I'm going to make a few inquiries by phone, Mr. Elevel. Then I'll be right over."

"You'll never find it," he said impatiently. "You don't know where I live."

"The address is on your check." I stayed in my seat, looking up at him.

"It's very difficult to find. You'll be driving around Bel Air for hours. This could be a matter of life or death."

I glanced at the check on my desk and then stood up, holding out my hand to him. "I used to live on Saratoga Drive." I smiled encouragingly. "It's fifty yards from your house. I'll find it."

Joe Elevel left off-balance and on the defensive, which didn't displease me at all.

Chapter TWO

Sipping the last of the nearly warm gin, I watched him from my window as he drove away. Something bothered me. He'd repeatedly emphasized that he knew absolutely nothing about his daughter's disappearance. Then he'd said it might be a matter of life or death. How did he know? Or was that just a manner of speaking? Probably. It was natural for clients to be hysterical, to wildly dramatize their problems. A client was almost always in some kind of distress he or she had never faced before. A lot of the things I heard in that room probably weren't very different from what the psychiatrist had listened to when the office was his. Joe Elevel, however, didn't strike me as the kind of client who would want a shoulder to cry on. He carried his own troubles and kept them to himself. Considering he'd just buried a wife and temporarily lost his daughter, I thought he was holding up pretty well.

I took his check to the Bank of America at the end of the block and deposited half of it. I'd already had two clients stop payment on checks to me that month, and I was getting tired of wasting time recovering my fees at the small claims court.

The smoothly paved roads of Bel Air were dead still in the noonday heat. Most of the houses were hidden behind high walls, or so camouflaged with trees and flowering shrubbery that you couldn't see them. I drove fast, from memory, taking in the gorgeously planted gardens, and only slowing as I passed the grove of eucalyptus trees near the top, where a Bel Air prowl car always played dead for speeders. They were there, drawn off the road under the green shade of the trees. Two young cops, fresh out of the Academy, with handlebar mustaches, long sideburns, and expensive aviator sunglasses. They wore their thick hair as long as they could without breaking the regulations. Off duty they wanted to look like everyone else. In Los Angeles everything had finally merged; even traffic cops wanted to look like coke dealers and rock stars.

The Elevel place was at the end of a long, leafy street; it marked the spot where the developers had decided to call it quits against the resistance of the hilly chaparral behind. A wrought-iron gate hung between two white marble pillars. From the tops of the pillars two closed-circuit television cameras stared down, a glowing red dot in the center of each dark lens. I honked my horn and after a moment a Mexican gardener opened the gate by pushing a button.

"Mr. Elevel's expecting me," I offered.

The gardener looked away without answering. He was tall for a Mexican, with ungainly limbs and a shock of black hair falling over his sullen face. He wasn't out to win any charm prizes.

"You speak English?" I asked.

He scowled and turned his back to close the gate. He was wearing work clothes but his shoes were brand-new, gaudy yellow patent leather boots. They didn't look right for gardening. They didn't look right for anywhere. He had an acned, pouting face with a scar across the cheek that looked like it had been made with the dull side of a butter knife. He seemed awfully discouraged about something. I didn't know whether he had something on his mind, or just didn't have one. I didn't like him. I told him in Spanish to come up to the house because the patron and I wanted to talk to him. The kid was probably an illegal alien and afraid the police investigation was going to uncover his phony papers. Maybe he was Charles Manson's younger brother. How did I know?

The driveway meandered through lush gardens of palm trees and banana plants and then opened up into a stretch of blacktop wide enough to accommodate half a dozen city buses. It was a lot of real estate to be found in a city like Los Angeles, where the only undeveloped land belongs to golf clubs and cemeteries. I counted nine cars parked in front of the house.

The house itself was big on principle. The architect had obviously been a plagiarist with a changeable temperament. He'd designed a building that moved from French Chateau into Spanish Colonial without drawing breath, and digressed briefly into Greek temple on one of the wings. To liven things up he'd thrown in a Japanese pagoda at the bottom of the garden, which you reached by walking down a stone path flanked with two chorus lines of marble angels spitting water at each other. There were sundials and gurgling fountains and fish pools filled with ornamental carp, the very old Japanese variety that costs a small fortune. There was also a bronze horse with a cowboy twirling a rope, rearing up out of some tulip beds. It was quite a spread. The Elevel swimming pool looked like a nice place for a sperm whale to grow up in. Beyond the pool, set at the edge of the rising chaparral, were three bungalows with broad porches supported by wooden buttresses. But it was the main house that compelled attention with its combination of turrets, spires, and leaded windows, Doric columns and Mediteranncan tiled roofs, flying buttresses and American tract-house stucco. I had a horrible feeling the whole place was going to be crammed to the ceiling with Elevel office and home furniture.

There was a young man waiting at the top of the steps into the house. He had a pale, determined face, thin lips, and very short curly blond hair. He was dressed in a black tropical suit, a white silk shirt, black tie, and black Gucci loafers with the mandatory gold chain. His eyes were hidden by dark sunglasses that made a shocking contrast to his white skin and pale hair. He wasn't big but he looked the way boxers and football players sometimes do when they wear suits; the clothes appeared unnatural on him. Up close I got a better look at his face. The left side wasn't all his; someone had done a cut-rate plastic job on the cheekbone and moved his nose around a little. Sunlight caught the scalpel marks and shiny areas of scar tissue, drawing the eye to them. It wasn't a major deformity but in that kind of light it stood out. There was an unlit pipe in his hand, which he pointed at me as I mounted the steps.

"You're Kyd," he drawled precisely. "Mr. Elevel is ready to see you. He's in his wife's bedroom."

"You must be Calvin Moonhurst." I extended my hand. He hesitated, frowning, then shook it very quickly as if it might be hot or contaminated. Maybe it was my imagination but I had a feeling he didn't think someone in his position should shake hands with someone in mine. I gave him a big smile, noticing that his teeth were crooked and that quite a few tough street vowels lurked under his suavely sophisticated drawl. You got teeth like that from not being able to afford to have them fixed as a kid; they belonged to another period, when he'd had another accent.

"Before I talk to Elevel," I said, "maybe I could clear up a few things. You've been trying to locate his daughter."

"That's correct." He started to say something else but his voice was drowned out by the high-pitched scream of an engine being fired up around the back of the house. It sounded like a highly tuned racing motor with no muffler. Someone was giving it gas, lots of it, and it made a powerful shrieking sound that echoed back from the foothills. It went on for about five deafening seconds and then sputtered, backfired, and stopped.

I glanced at Calvin but he didn't offer any explanation.

"You said *Mrs*. Elevel's bedroom before." I paused. "Have they always had separate bedrooms?"

"Yes, I think so." He stiffened. "I don't see what that

has to do with anything, though. The Elevels had an almost perfect marriage."

"That's what Mr. Elevel said." I shook my head. "You kind of wonder why she would kill herself if things were that good."

"The main thing now is Charlotte." He looked at his watch. He liked good things; it was a gold Bueche-Girod with a fancy platinum mesh band.

"Charlotte." I nodded. "She's twenty-three. Any special reason why she still lives at home?"

"I've been here almost four years and she's always lived at home."

"What about boyfriends?"

"She's never been very interested in men. Nor was her mother." He said it rather proudly. "Mrs. Elevel spent most of her time doing charity work for certain orphanages. She was devoted to helping the underprivileged."

"That was nice of her."

"Are you trying to be funny?"

"Hell no. I'm just trying to figure out why this family is having so much trouble." I lit a cigarette and repeated Mrs. Elevel's suicide note. *"Charlotte knows. Soon you'll all know. It's unspeakable.* That's a pretty heavy goodbye."

"I don't see how you can take seriously anything written by someone unbalanced enough to take her own life." He clenched his pipe between his teeth.

"Well, that's true, but people don't get unbalanced in a vacuum. Even if the note was an exaggeration, her death is real. People don't kill themselves for no reason."

"I realize it would help you if I could come up with some unsavory gossip about Mrs. Elevel, but unfortunately I don't happen to know any. I don't know anyone who does."

He couldn't quite bring off that sort of remark. It came out awkward and stilted. There was just a little too much unrefined street aggression there. To be good at that kind of thing you have to sound bored when you put the knife in. He didn't sound bored. He sounded like an insecure prig.

The next thing that happened surprised me. He moved toward the open door, started to stand aside to let me through, and then decided he ought to be the one to enter first. As I followed behind him, he stumbled over the entrance and had to grab the door frame to get his balance. Just for a second I thought he was going to fall flat. The strangest thing was that it looked as if he'd lost his balance *before* he'd ever stumbled.

We walked in silence down a corridor over a fluffy electric blue rug that resembled a thirty-yard bath mat. The walls were hung with the kind of oil paintings that banks and large office buildings rent by the month: big canvases in gilt frames that are churned out ten at a time by hack painters. Storm-tossed waves shattering against lonely lighthouses, wild horses contemplating desert sunsets, endless still lifes of fruit, flowers, and sleeping cats and dogs. Intermixed with all this pablum was a series of family portraits executed in pastel and obviously copied from photographs. Farther along there were framed photographs of the family together at a nightclub. These I bothered to stop and look at. They were taken by the club photographer: Mr. and Mrs. Elevel dancing, the whole family sitting at a table laden with food, Charlotte and her father dancing cheek to cheek. At the end of the row there was a shot of Calvin and Mrs. Elevel dancing. There was a good foot and a half between their bodies. Calvin had an artificial smile but his eyes were flat with boredom. Mrs. Elevel wore a polite, pleasant expression of indifference which went with her trim, unglamorous dress and flat shoes. Not a woman who cared about her appearance. She dressed herself, you felt, in the same spirit that she brushed her teeth and washed behind her ears. She was going through the motions of having a good time. I thought she looked like someone who had spent most of her life going through the motions of one thing or another. Too bad you can't go through the motions of death.

"They don't really do her justice," Calvin said gruffly. "She didn't like going out much. She just did it to please Joe and Charlotte."

"And you made up the foursome." I said. "Pretty dull work for a young guy."

"I'm just not going to get riled when you say things like that. I suppose you're one of those smart people who think it's unnatural for families to stick together. Oh sure, I can see the way your mind works. Well, you're wrong. They did all love each other. And I've had some of the best times of my life with them. We had great times. Terrific times." He was talking himself into a state of emotional excitement. "This country would be in a lot better shape if there were more families like the Elevels, I can tell you that."

"Plenty are trying." I said. "I can think of plenty on welfare who'd be happy to move in here tomorrow."

"That's not what I meant." He scowled. "I think welfare's very bad."

"You're right. The checks never come on time." I was getting tired of his remarks and even more bored with my own. "Tell me," I said, "when Charlotte wasn't painting the town red with her folks, what did she do?"

"She studied acting and dancing. But I've called her school. That was the first place I called. They haven't heard from her. And she didn't paint the town red. She couldn't drink anything. She had a very sensitive stomach."

"Puked a lot, huh?"

"Well, she had a tendency to nausea if she got upset."

"Upset? What did she get upset about?"

"I don't know. Her acting. She felt sometimes she wasn't making enough progress."

"What did you think?"

"We all went to see her once, the whole family. It was a play the drama school was doing. I'm sure she would have been very good."

"What happened?" I asked.

"Her stomach acted up. It was just nerves."

"Have the cops verified Mrs. Elevel's suicide note?"

"Gee, I really don't know." He had suddenly assumed a kind of dumb innocence. "As you can imagine, Joe was pretty devastated, and the police probably didn't bother with it. I mean, they know she swallowed all those pills. It all got handled very fast. Actually,"— he sniffed—"the police were pretty wonderful. You hear so many terrible things about them these days but all in all they couldn't have been more understanding."

The police in such a situation were capable of very sensitive behavior toward people in distress, and the aura of money in the house would have insured plenty of respectful understanding. But when Calvin said it, the words sounded as hollow and pat as a politician's after-dinner rhetoric.

"Have the police been notified of Charlotte's disappearance?"

"I really think the police have enough to do. There are a lot of people who can't afford to take care of these things privately. It only seems fair to go the private route, since the Elevels are well off."

I was beginning to think I was talking to someone with a big future in politics; Calvin knew how to gloss over things as smoothly and maddeningly as a presidential press secretary.

We took the corridor around an L turn. Joe was waiting near the end of the hall. He'd changed into a black silk robe and bedroom slippers and was puffing dispiritedly on a pipe. It was a long-stemmed pipe with a small ivory bowl, and Calvin had an exact duplicate of it in his hand. I wondered if he owned copies of his boss's dressing gown and bedroom slippers too.

"I want to go through this now," Joe said, a remark

that came out as if it had been stored up for a while. "I don't want to have to go through it twice."

He ushered me into his late wife's bedroom. It was a long room with high recessed windows looking down on the swimming pool. The ceiling was painted in light blue enamel to match the baby-blue curtains and bedspread. There were lots of soft fluffy chairs and hassocks, touches of pink and white, and two stuffed animals, a monkey and an elephant, on the bed. It was the bedroom of a woman in search of the colors and soothing textures of a child's nursery. Only the rolltop desk filling an alcove at one end of the room suggested that Mrs. Elevel had engaged in anything more arduous than playing with dolls.

"I understand the police haven't been notified of Charlotte's disappearance," I said.

Joe looked at Calvin. "That's right."

"Any particular reason?" I started to light a cigarette and then thought better of it. He might not like my smoking in his wife's bedroom.

"No particular reason, but a general one." He smiled sadly at Calvin. "I'm an intensely private person. We all are. And Charlotte is that way too. There's been nothing in the papers about my wife. I don't want Charlotte traumatized by some uniformed policeman."

I looked at the two men. They were standing close together and I was aware of a silent bond of sympathy uniting them, from which I was excluded.

"Charlotte knew something, Mr. Elevel," I said. "Whatever it was, your wife knew it too. It was the kind of thing she couldn't live with. I imagine Charlotte's having trouble living with it now. You've employed me to find Charlotte. I may not be able to find her without touching on some sensitive areas."

"What are you trying to say?" Joe's weary face had a nauseated cast.

"I think you should have your attorney retain me, Mr. Elevel, rather than your hiring me yourself. As long as I'm representing your attorney I'm legally in a position where I can refuse to divulge information to the police."

"I don't see where the police come into it."

"Your wife found out something. She preferred death to facing it. Charlotte found it out too. She preferred running away. Something *unspeakable*. It's a strong word, Mr. Elevel. I think you understand that perfectly well or you'd have taken the matter to the police yesterday."

"I think he may well be right on this one," Calvin said. "I'd say he's got a definite point.

Joe Elevel lifted his hand and squeezed his forehead. There was a long silence while we waited for him to say something. He let his hand drop and glanced, with a look of shame, at both of us. His eyes were dazed and empty. The mental machinery for sifting alternatives and making decisions had ground to a halt. I had a feeling that if I'd told him the best thing for him was to go to the window and jump out, he would have done it without ever losing that dazed, empty look.

"Why don't I just get your attorney on the phone?" Calvin said softly. "He can be here in half an hour."

"What?" Joe asked. He was blinking slowly.

"I'll get him to come over, Joe. It's the smart thing." Calvin gave me a troubled smile and left the room.

Joe Elevel was succumbing to fatigue and delayed shock. His face had suddenly turned a kind of grayish green. I got him a chair. He sat down without a word and put his head down between his legs. His whole body seemed to be humming on a sick high note.

I stood behind him for a moment with my hand resting on his shoulder, and after a while the trembling stopped. But he kept his head down so I couldn't see his face and I figured he didn't want to show his grief to a stranger.

Quietly I walked over to the rolltop desk. Opening it made a rattling noise that thundered in the silent bedroom. The drawers were filled with neatly stacked piles of correspondence involving Mrs. Elevel's orphanage work. There were several books of used check stubs, which I took, along with a photograph of her. I found her purse hanging on a hook in the closet and took from it a Moroccan leather address book and matching wallet, a set of keys, and a half-used checkbook. She had made some interesting cash withdrawals in the past two weeks.

When I turned around, Joe was staring at me through red-rimmed eyes. His half-paralyzed face was slack and unnaturally still.

"Can you do something for me?" I asked gently.

"Yeah." His voice was coming from high in his throat as if he were on the verge of tears.

"I need your authorization to look at the last few months' phone bills for the house and all the bungalows."

"Anything else?" He got the words out with difficulty.

"I also want permission to question all the staff and look around, and I'm probably going to have to co-opt another investigation service for legwork. That could mean more money."

"Anything," he said.

I thought I might as well get as much out of him as I could while he was in this broken condition.

"I also want access to all pertinent information from your attorney concerning your will, from your accountant concerning your wife's finances, and from your doctor concerning her health. Her check stubs show three separate withdrawals over the past two weeks. Cash withdrawals of four, six, and eight thousand dollars. Do you have any idea what that cash was used for?"

"I don't." He cleared his throat. "No, not like her to do that."

"I'm going to check Charlotte's room, Mr. Elevel." I

walked out, leaving him slumped in his chair, his silver hair and drained gray skin lit up by a shaft of sunlight.

Outside in the corridor I met someone coming from the opposite direction. He was a tall, extremely obese man with a tight-mouthed expression. He wore an expensive light-checked suit with a matching vest and a yellow knit tie. Fat as he was, the suit hung on him like an oversized pup tent. He had a broad glistening brow. His whole face had an unhealthy sheen to it; the flesh looked soft and malleable, as if you could leave a depression in it with your thumb. A thick square mustache obliterated his upper lip. He reminded me of a pompous bloodhound, with his drooping jowls and mournful bloodshot eyes. The climb up the stairs had winded him. As he approached he was preceded by a smell of sweat and too-sweet cologne.

"Are you Mr. Elevel's attorney?" I asked him.

"I am Dr. Lester." His voice was hoarse and full of breathing noises. He looked at me with a baleful, inquiring gaze. "You must be the investigator Calvin mentioned." He had an unreal British accent. "I'm looking for Mr. Elevel."

"Thomas Kyd." I held out my hand. He frowned at it as if it were a scalpel a nurse had dropped and was attempting to return unsterilized. I kept it there and finally he took it. He had a grip like a piece of steamed fish.

"I'd like to ask you some questions, doctor."

He didn't say anything.

"Was Mrs. Elevel your patient?"

"Everyone in the family is my patient," he said shortly.

"You prescribed the sleeping pills?"

"I did."

"Did Mrs. Elevel regularly renew her prescription?"

He rolled his eyes in irritation at the ceiling. "No, she did not. I've come to see Mr. Elevel, and I have a busy day ahead of me."

"What else did you prescribe to Mrs. Elevel?" I insisted.

"I'm a busy man and I don't have time to—"

"Mr. Elevel guaranteed me the support and cooperation of all the relevant parties, doctor. I have carte blanche to take my inquiry where I see fit. Do you have any objection to answering my questions? They seem pretty harmless."

"Don't threaten me, young man. I've been the Elevel physician for five years."

"I think that's why you could be helpful to me. I've known them for less than an hour."

Either the threat worked, or he found my humble approach gratifying. He walked to the window seat, put down his bag, and stared out over the garden. He kept his back to me as he spoke, I suppose as a way of putting me in my place. It didn't bother me much. I preferred the back of his head to his face anyway. To my surprise, without any prompting, he then told me almost everything I would have asked him.

"Mrs. Elevel didn't use sleeping pills," he began. "I prescribe them for Joe. He's an insomniac. Has been ever since I've known him. If he's lucky he gets three hours of bad sleep a night. The pills Mrs. Elevel took were from Joe's bathroom. She was not a woman who relied on medication of any kind. If it was socially called for she'd have a glass of sherry and make it last through an evening. Joe drinks, but in moderation."

I lit a cigarette and at once Dr. Lester pointedly cranked open the window.

"A year ago," he continued, "Mrs. Elevel had herself fitted for an intrauterine device but there were complications. Following that she went on the Pill. Joe was aware of all this. Generally speaking, they both have . . . had good health. If they had a vice, it was overwork. Mrs. Elevel has always used me strictly as a physician and so has Joe. They have never confided any problems of an emotional nature to me. I once suggested that Joe see a psychiatrist about his insomnia and he rejected the idea. He has the old-fashioned idea that going to a psychiatrist means you're fatally insane. For the same reason he discouraged Charlotte from seeing a therapist. Charlotte is a neurasthenic. She has a weak, overly sensitive nervous system, a fear of people, and a tendency to gastric ulcer. Neurasthenia is a blanket term. The world is full of neurasthenics who don't even know that's what they are. I prescribe mild tranquilizers to Charlotte. I haven't got the faintest idea why her mother took an overdose." The way he said it suggested Mrs. Elevel's suicide was a personal insult to him.

"Right now I have Joe on Stelazine. For the past two nights I've given him injections of Nembutal to make him sleep. They haven't worked. He hasn't slept for two days. If he doesn't sleep this evening I'm going to knock him out with something stronger. Lastly, I have no idea why Mrs. Elevel killed herself." It was the only time he'd repeated himself in a speech that had the studied roundness of testimony prepared for a jury. "Nor why Charlotte's run away, nor where she is now. Does that satisfy you, Mr. Kyd?" He turned and faced me.

"You've been very helpful, doctor. May I ask you one last thing?"

He looked at me with distaste. I took his silence for an affirmative.

"Is Calvin Moonhurst also your patient?"

He still didn't say anything.

"What do you prescribe for him?"

"Calvin is an epileptic," he said, pointedly picking up his bag. "He's on a regular dose of phenobarbital. Under normal conditions the medication keeps him well below the danger zone. I don't care to go beyond that. I've already abused my patient's right to confidence."

"You say 'under normal conditions.' I take it you've witnessed Calvin under abnormal conditions."

"I don't consider that Calvin's health has any bearing

on what you're being paid to do." He started to walk past me.

"In that case, you should have no objection to telling me about it."

He wheeled around, holding the bag up to his stomach as if I'd threatened to snatch it away from him. It was a curiously prim gesture for such a large man.

"Are you implying that I *might* have an objection to telling you something *with* a bearing on the case? Is that what you're trying to say?" His waxy yellow skin had become mottled.

"I'm trying to have a civilized conversation. I'm trying to get a picture of people who are strangers to me from someone who knows them, and I'm running into a lot of resistance."

"If I were you, Mr. Kyd," he drawled coldly, "I'd spend less time pursuing fruitless avenues of inquiry, and more time out of this house looking for Charlotte Elevel. I rather think that's what you've been employed to do."

"Unfortunately, it's no longer quite that simple." I noticed that, despite his flurry of movement, he wasn't going anywhere. "There's a small matter of blackmail involved."

"Blackmail?" he said. "That's the first mention I've heard of it. Is this a private theory of yours?"

"In the two weeks prior to her suicide Mrs. Elevel withdrew eighteen thousand dollars in cash from her private checking account. The money isn't accounted for. Yes, I'd say there were grounds for suspecting blackmail."

"I see." He breathed in and held onto the breath.

"I'm interested in Calvin's epilepsy. Isn't it true that in certain kinds of epilepsy a seizure can be followed by a state of maniacal excitement in which the epileptic doesn't, strictly speaking, know what he's doing? That in that state he sometimes commits a dangerous or violent act of which he later has no memory?"

"Quite the armchair doctor, aren't you, Mr. Kyd?"

"My wife was an epileptic, doctor. I once had an interest in the subject."

"There is nothing in Calvin's medical history to suggest he's prone to that form of automatic behavior. Last January there was some unpleasantness between Calvin and Tyrone Elevel. Calvin got upset about it. He had a seizure by the swimming pool. I was called, of course. Nothing much one can do except prevent the person from harming himself during the convulsions."

"Who's Tyrone Elevel?"

"Joe's son. He's paralyzed. People don't talk about him much. He was the victim of a hit-and-run accident five years ago."

"At about the time you became the Elevels' doctor?"

"Yes, that's right."

"Are you a specialist in that field of medicine?"

"No, I'm a general practitioner." He was getting angry again.

"Who treated the Elevels before you?" I asked.

"I'm sure I don't know."

"Thanks, doctor. I have some more questions but they can wait."

Chapter THREE

I watched him waddle down the corridor and wondered what kind of practice the doctor had. As soon as the subject switched to Joe Elevel's paralyzed son, he'd looked as if he needed a doctor himself. There was something too messy and malodorous about Lester for a straight Beverly Hills practice. Rich people like their doctors clean, and Dr. Lester looked as if he'd leave a stain on the floor if he stood in the same spot too long.

I was sore that no one had bothered to fill me in on Tyrone Elevel. Or was I? Maybe I was sore at being treated like a chauffeur with no references applying for a job.

I started opening doors until I got to a game room with a billiard table and a bar. I opened a tall jar of Spanish olives, ate about three dozen of them, and put the empty bottle back on the shelf. The sound of the racing engine being fired up again came through the open windows. It screamed, coughed, and settled into a smooth, steady roar. Then it stopped. I poured a few fingers of gin into a tumbler and tossed it off, then refilled it and poured the second shot down. All that carbohydrate set me up again almost immediately, and I stopped feeling irritated.

My next stop was Charlotte's room in the north wing of the house. It was a decidedly feminine room tricked out in the same soft baby tones and textures as her mother's. She collected sea shells, puppets, and antique dolls. There was a big Joan Baez poster over her bed and several gothic romance novels on the bedside table. It was the room of someone who lived in her imagination and liked sentimental, pretty things.

In her bathroom I found a purse resting beside the

sink and next to it a bottle of ten-milligram Valium and
an open vial of perfume. I emptied out her purse and
pocketed her wallet, address book, and checks. Whatever Charlotte's problem was, money, tranquilizers, and
the phone numbers of her friends hadn't seemed worth
taking along with her. She'd run out the way you desert
a building in an earthquake.

I wondered if she had a secret stash somewhere in
the room. If she was like most women, she would hide
her private valuables on the upper shelf of her clothes
closet. Because they have trouble reaching it, yet it's
still close to where they sleep, this strikes them as the
ideal place. It's where every burglar looks first. People
ought to keep their valuables in cornflakes boxes in the
kitchen, with the old paint cans in the garage, in the
thousands of mundane spots where a thief has no time
to look.

My fingers groped blindly along the shelf and en-
countered a stack of magazines, a fur coat wrapped in
plastic, and a shoebox. I took the box down and emptied its contents on the bed. There was a gray felt bag
filled with expensive jewelry and a red leather–bound
diary with a brass lock, which I broke open with a nail
file from the bathroom. After all the buildup, I was expecting to discover some darker side to Charlotte, but if
it existed, it found no expression in her diary.

Her last two entries told me nothing: "Nice day at
school. Leonardo said I was doing much better in the
tap dancing class. Bought a real cute pair of shoes at I.
Magnin's. Tomorrow have to do Ophelia's scene with
her father." And then: "Bummer at school! Forgot all
my lines but Leonardo thought my shoes were 'exqui-
site.' Would like to go to the movies tonight but I've
seen everything."

I fanned quickly through the other pages, spot-
checking the entries, but they never deviated much from
the breathless adolescent tone of the last two. I went
quickly through her drawers and found nothing but

clothes, a lot of them brand-new and still not worn. As I was about to stand up from searching the lower drawer, I noticed the lower pane of her balcony window was broken. A few fragments of glass littered the carpet and sill. I opened the window and stepped out onto the small stone balcony; it was constructed like a castle battlement, with indented parapet and vertical arrow slits in case of attack from the unwashed hordes surrounding Bel Air. On the balcony floor there was more broken glass and a key. It was a round metal shaft with two spiky cylinders around it—a key to a safe. Someone had hurled it from across the room, and it had smashed through the glass. I picked it up with a handkerchief and dropped it into an envelope from Charlotte's desk.

"There you are." Calvin ushered a man into the bedroom. "This is Charley LaSalle, Joe's attorney."

We shook hands. LaSalle couldn't have been more than a few years out of law school. He was dressed expensively but he obviously didn't think about his appearance; his shirt front was partially out and his tie looked as if he'd tied it in his sleep. Behind his glasses his soft brown eyes had a moist gleam of intelligence.

"Anything I can do for you, Mr. Kyd." His voice had a lazy twang. "I'm at your disposal." He plunged his hands into his pockets, pulling his trousers down even lower until he revealed a thin strip of white belly and jockey shorts.

"A couple of things," I said, wondering if he could smell the gin on my breath. "First, how's the Elevel nest egg going to split when it finally gets pushed off the shelf? Who has what? Who gets what? Second, do you know why Mrs. Elevel took out eighteen thousand in cash in the last two weeks? Third, is there any trouble with Joe's business—any unusual expansion, or conflict with a competitor?"

LaSalle whistled through his teeth, smiling ruefully. "I'll tell you," he said, "I don't know if I understand the money myself. Joe's got a holding company for nearly every dollar he owns. A lot of it's on vacation, in tax shelters, and a helluva lot of it's been sunk into land development in the Marina. If you cooked it all down and cashed it in, you'd have upward of twenty million in cash. After the revenue boys took their bite out of that, I don't know what you'd have. Mrs. Elevel was nominal head of some of the holding companies. Everything she had has reverted to Joe. Tyrone had some but they took it away from him. Charlotte's played quite a role, at least on paper. If it came to the bottom line, and this is according to Joe's last will, everything would go to Tyrone and Charlotte except for small legacies to other relatives and some money to orphanages. If Joe *and* his children were to die, the will would be contested among his closest relations. You've got to understand that it doesn't mean much. Joe's taken care of everyone in his family so lavishly, there wouldn't be grounds for any relative to pull a fast one." LaSalle sat down on the bed and polished his glasses with his shirttail.

"The last two questions don't ring any bells. Joe doesn't do business with anyone even marginally close to organized crime."

I thanked Charley LaSalle and told him I'd probably be getting in touch. Calvin was holding up Charlotte's address book.

"I called every number in it," he said. "Almost all the numbers were friends of the family, older people. No one can figure out where she'd go. She never went anywhere except to school and the movies and stores. She was a very orderly person. You would always know exactly where she was at any time of day. If she was going to go to a movie after school, she'd phone Joe."

"You don't think she was seeing some guy?" I fanned through the address book. "Or hanging out at a girlfriend's place?"

"Who?" Calvin shrugged. "I know her schedule like the back of my hand. There wasn't anyone. She just didn't have—"

"Much of a life." I smiled. "I mean outside her family."

"If you want to put it that way, no, she didn't."

"Then it's hard. It's like trying to catch someone who's never committed a crime before. There isn't a hell of a lot to go on."

"I prepared this list." He handed me a typed sheet of paper. It's everything I could think of."

Memo from Calvin Moonhurst to Thomas Kyd, Private Investigator:
Charlotte Elevel

Age: 23
Height: 5′ 5″
Weight: 128 lbs.
License No.: E128268
Vehicle: White MG, 1975 Convertible, License No. 654 Peace.

On the other side of the paper was a list of addresses, including her acting school, bank, health club, department stores where she had credit, cinemas and restaurants she frequented, hairdresser, garage, and health food store. In the bottom corner, Calvin had written a note: "She left behind all credit cards, and checks. Doubtful if she had more than fifty dollars in cash on her, probably nothing. She was wearing a blue denim skirt, a pink T-shirt, and white canvas espadrilles."

"Anytime you get tired of working for Elevel," I said, "come see me. A lot of this could help."

He nodded gruffly, patting his pockets in search of his pipe. I took out the envelope and showed him the key, and he nodded again, in recognition.

"That's to Mrs. Elevel's safe. It was open when we found her. Nothing in it but an insurance policy and some unused checks."

"Why would the key be on Charlotte's balcony?"

"Charlotte kept a spare key for her mother. I think

sometimes she kept some of her jewelry in the safe too."

Whatever Charlotte had found in the safe had upset her enough to hurl the key through the window.

"Who else was in the house that night?" I asked.

"Let's see." He got his pipe going. "There was Anna Maria, the cook; Pedro, the gardener; Joe; Charlotte; Tyrone; and me. Tyrone and I live in the bungalows. I was in and out, working with Joe on inventories for next season."

We found Anna Maria in the kitchen. She looked like a humble, harmless old Mexican woman until you looked into her eyes, and then it was clear she probably had an IQ of 190. They were heavy-lidded, slumbering Indian eyes that took in everything and gave back nothing. Her type always talked in a small, low voice, kept her eyes downcast, and gave everyone the impression she was busy memorizing recipes and thinking about her grandchildren. By the time she was fifty she had her gringo employers convinced she was deaf and just about blind. In fact, she had 20/20 vision and could hear the grass growing.

As we stepped into the kitchen, she was serving a bowl of soup to the young gardener. When he saw me, he dipped his face into his bowl and started making very serious eating noises. Anna Maria said something to him in Spanish, and he rose unwillingly to his feet. I waited for Calvin to tell the Mexican kid to sit down but he didn't. I think he liked people to stand up when he walked into a room.

"How's it going?" I nodded at the gardener.

"He doesn't speak English," Anna Maria said.

"Tell him to sit down." I took a chair at the table and gestured for Anna Maria to join me.

I didn't bother to explain that I was a private dick. Anna Maria had all that figured out before I opened my mouth. Questioning her was a slow, maddening game that she played like a master. She wouldn't volunteer anything. If you asked her a direct question she

would give you a straight answer but she wouldn't en-
large on anything. If there'd been a strange man in the
house the night of the suicide she wouldn't mention him
unless you asked. And even then she wouldn't bother to
tell you he was carrying a bloody ax and holding someone's severed head under his arm.

It took twenty minutes to piece together what she'd
seen that night. At nine o'clock she'd taken tea up to
Mrs. Elevel's bedroom. Mrs. Elevel had been in the
bathroom. Anna Maria had returned to the kitchen.

"Then I make Miss Charlotte's Ovaltine. Hot milk,
two tablespoons of Ovaltine, and three sugars. And six
cookies. Chocolate chip cookies."

"No napkin?" I asked suspiciously.

"Sí, señor. Also a napkin." She frowned and looked
swiftly at me from under those heavy lids. A ghost of
sly mockery swept quickly across her face. "Also a
spoon," she added gravely.

Pulling her leg was a mistake. She became even more
maddeningly conscientious in her description, filling her
story with irrelevant details. Embedded in all the scru-
pulously remembered junk were several facts. Anna
Maria had seen Charlotte enter her mother's bedroom
carrying some papers. A moment later she'd heard her
run down the corridor to her own room and slam the
door. Then Charlotte had hurried down the stairs and
rushed out of the house.

"Was she still carrying papers?" I asked.

"Yes." Anna Maria nodded.

"Was she carrying the *same* papers as when she went
into her mother's bedroom?"

"Oh no, señor! Different papers."

I leaned back in my chair and breathed deeply. "Describe what kind of papers."

"A big yellow envelope," Anna Maria said unhappily.

"What was special about the envelope?" I smiled.

"Nothing special," she said.

"What did you notice about the envelope?" I rephrased it.

"There was a very big photograph. Some of it sticking out of the envelope. But I don't see good."

"You say a very big photograph. Was it one big picture or lots of small pictures?"

"Small pictures," Anna Maria acknowledged.

There was a momentary silence. I smiled over at the gardener. I said casually, "There's a fly in your soup, Pedro."

He looked immediately down at the bowl, then back up, with confusion on his face. I winked at Anna Maria.

"Maybe Pedro's been studying nights."

She returned my gaze without flinching but a heavy flush was climbing up her throat to her cheeks.

"Hey!" Calvin suddenly picked up on it. "I thought he couldn't speak English."

"Is Pedro your son?" I asked Anna Maria.

"The son of my sister," she said gloomily.

"And he has no papers?"

"That does it," Calvin said. "You told me he was squared away with Immigration." He pointed accusingly at Anna Maria. "You said he had a green card, and a residence permit."

She didn't say anything. She just sat there with a faint look of contempt on her face, contempt for his callowness. Did he expect her to feel guilty because she'd lied to get her nephew out of Mexico and into a job where he could eat?

"I'm really disappointed in you, Anna Maria," Calvin said sternly. "That was very perceptive of you, Mr. Kyd. We could get into a lot of trouble over a thing like this."

"*You* could get into a lot of trouble?" I said. "You get cheap labor from these people. There's an illegal alien in half the kitchens in Bel Air. They're the ones who get in trouble. People like you just ring up an employment agency and have someone new sent over."

"It's illegal. No matter what you say, it *is* illegal to employ someone who's snuck into the country."

"In my book it's illegal to pay people chickenfeed for doing your dirty work. Especially when you know they've got to take the job because they have no choice."

"We're not talking about that," he said defensively.

"I'm talking about that." I said it slowly and softly and with enough menace to silence him. The Mexican had stopped eating. He was just sitting there, waiting for someone to drop the hook on him. His face was resigned, without bitterness, as if he'd always known the good breaks all ended with a kick in the teeth.

"Tell him, Pedro!" Anna Maria barked at him.

They exchanged a few rapid-fire remarks in Spanish. Then Anna Maria turned to me.

"Two weeks ago Pedro drive Mrs. Elevel to the Ralph's Supermarket. He wait in the car for her to buy food. But Mrs. Elevel no go into store. She go sit in the car of another man. Is a Mexican. Very bad man from Guadalajara. Pedro know him. He afraid to tell police because he have not his documentos."

"I'm thirsty," I said.

"Señor would like some coffee?" She got to her feet.

"Bad for my stomach."

"Milk?"

"Too much fat in it."

She stared at me. "Señor would like a glass of wine?"

"Hey, that's an idea!" I winked at Calvin but he obviously didn't approve. Maria set a bottle of already opened St. Emilion on the table along with a glass. A moment later she set down a plate of sliced cheese, salami, and olives. I wolfed down half of it and drank two glasses of wine in as many minutes. I felt a change for the better almost instantly.

"Who is this character Pedro saw, Anna Maria?" I finally asked.

"His name is Luis Coronado."

"Any idea where I could find him?"

She and Pedro shrugged simultaneously. I questioned them further but they didn't seem to know anything about his whereabouts. Pedro hadn't seen Luis Coronado since Guadalajara, where he'd been a wheel in the local vice trade. Luis Coronado was a pimp and murderer. He was tall, dark-haired, a ladies' man. On the day Pedro had seen him talking to Mrs. Elevel he'd been at the wheel of a lemon-yellow Porsche. He was wearing a white suit and had an Afghan dog in the back seat. That's what Pedro said anyway. From the description, Coronado sounded like a pimp. Was that supermarket parking-lot meeting the first of the payoffs? The date fit the first large cash withdrawal Mrs. Elevel had made. It was either that, or Pedro had seen her getting some Hollywood star's autograph. I decided to go for Pedro's story. He didn't look as if he had the imagination to invent the story, or the description, nor could he have known how well it tied in with the other things I'd learned that morning. The way I saw it, someone had been twisting Mrs. Elevel's arm about something—papers, photographs—which she'd paid for and stashed in her safe. But the squeeze hadn't stopped there. More installments had followed, as they always do. Charlotte had blundered onto the secret and left the house distraught. "Soon you will all know." By now someone should have heard something. I wanted to talk to Joe's crippled son, but based on what I'd learned so far, I knew that locating Charlotte had to be my top priority.

I couldn't tell Calvin what to do about Pedro but I got him to agree to keep the gardener on until I'd checked out the Luis Coronado angle. After that, if Calvin wanted to play God, he could turn the kid over to the Immigration people. I felt sorry for the Mexican. My grandfather was a British seaman who jumped ship off Long Beach and swam to shore. An English wetback, he hadn't had any documentos either.

Chapter FOUR

As I drove down the hill I could see the city obscurely suspended in wavering blankets of yellow and brown smog. A hot furnace-like wind was rising up, blasting down the canyons, blowing hard enough to litter the streets with broken palm fronds. It was the kind of day arsonists dream about.

On my way down, the prowl car I'd seen earlier passed me, going in the opposite direction. They took a long look at my 1965 Mustang with the shattered back window and missing hubcaps and pulled around to escort me out of Bel Air. On foot or in your own car, you don't stand a chance in that neighborhood; they'll still try and give you the bum's rush.

But the timing was bad. I ended up watching them in my rear-view mirror and didn't pay much attention to the old beige Continental behind them.

They were young Bel Air fuzz, more like security guards than big-city cops. Off duty, they probably turned on and read *Rolling Stone* magazine. It didn't make a hell of a lot of difference, though; they already had that look around the eyes and mouth that told you they were waiting for you to ask permission to breathe. In a few more years their faces would have about as much expressiveness as a can of mace.

They had zoomed up very fast to within a few feet of my rear bumper, and they kept that distance, around every curve, until I passed out of the Bel Air gate. It was one more exciting car chase to tell their girlfriends about.

I don't remember much about the drive back to my office. I know I took Sunset and jammed a Ray Charles cassette into the tape deck but the music and traffic hardly registered. I was thinking about money and how ugly it could make some people. I could still see that authoritarian look on Calvin's face when he realized the Mexican kid didn't have any papers, and on Dr. Lester's mug when he'd tried to intimidate his way out of answering my questions. How had I ever ended up working for that kind of people? After the doctor, the lawyer, the Mexicans, the armed prowl-car boys, I was just one more figure on the Elevel payroll. For a hundred a day and expenses they wanted me to find Charlotte and bring her home. But maybe Charlotte had a damned good reason for leaving. Maybe I was about to screw up her life by finding her. What was I doing in a dumb racket like this anyway? Ten years ago I'd been the most extreme kind of political radical. I'd thought that any system that let one man sit on twenty million bucks while in the same city people went hungry in rat-infested slums was obscene. It still looked obscene but now I was part of it.

When I got back to my office I put a call through to Ian White of White and Rinehart Investigative Services. I asked him for two operatives, one to check out Dr. Lester's record and another to see what he could come up with on Luis Coronado. Then I called Harry Bowkley at Pacific Telephone. He hadn't come in to work yet, which was a good sign; it meant he'd be there most of the night running programs through their computers. I was going to need Harry for running down the Elevel phone bills. It was a laborious way of discovering leads and connections but it had sprung results in the past. Sometime in the past few months I was sure calls had been made between Luis Coronado and someone at the Elevel house.

I looked at the photo of Charlotte Elevel and compared it to the one of her mother. Had both women been blackmail victims, or was one protecting the other, or had they been in it together? Neither of them looked the type, which didn't mean much. Prisons are filled with female felons who look as if they'd faint at the sight of blood.

The Rhona Flannery Academy of Dramatic Arts took up the top floor of a seedy 1930s office block on Hollywood near Cahuenga. The lower two floors were honeycombed with import-export firms, small-time theatrical agencies, cut-rate dentists, and some dubious-looking Arab charter flight companies. Rhona Flannery had surfaced briefly in the early forties as an M-G-M musical comedy star. She'd made three pictures that weren't much more than high-budget screen tests for the deadwood on the M-G-M lot and then the studio brass had turned her into a Mexican for the lead in *Just Over the Border*. The picture went into the toilet at the box office. It was the fourth movie of hers that had failed to grow legs and walk, as the money boys put it. Rhona Flannery, or Rosita Fandango, as she'd been renamed, didn't have her contract renewed. However, having failed at something, she decided, like so many people, to go into teaching it professionally. It had been several years since I'd even seen one of her old movies on the *Late Late Show*.

The hallways of the Academy reeked of disinfectant and stale cigarette smoke. The aura of The Method hung like a dull pall over the place. A dozen students waiting for a class to start loitered by a soft-drink machine. It was the hour for striking introspective poses. Most of the younger guys were into an early Brando look. They'd all taken a streetcar named desire to school and were debating whether or not to rebel without a cause. I felt sorry for some of the older students. Working nights in taco stands and twenty-four-hour supermarkets to come up with tap-dancing tuition is tough at twenty; by the time you're forty, it must be hard not to panic.

On the bulletin board there was a publicity still of a guy who looked like a Himalayan gorilla who'd played too much pro football. I'd seen him in a cop show on

TV several nights ago. A policeman had chased him down a deserted alley out into a vacant lot. He'd had one line in the show—*"Please don't do it!"*—and then a fruit truck had run him over. He was student of the month.

I glanced into some of the classrooms. A scene from *Hamlet* was being prepared in one; the actors looked wooden, so self-conscious in their roles that each one seemed alone on the small stage. Polonius had a Mexican accent and you could hear The Bronx rasping in every one of Gertrude's vowels. Hamlet was playing it like a streetwise punk who'd just been caught stealing the welfare check from his mother's purse.

Hamlet, another low-life scenario from the typewriter of Willy the Shake.

Next door a dance class was in progress. A guy in a leotard with a whistle around his neck was teaching a dozen middle-aged housewives to do interesting Afro-Mexican things to their pelvic consciousness. He kept talking about emoting with the buttocks, speaking with the hips, singing with the solar plexus. None of them looked as if they were going to set Vegas on fire; it was all strictly from therapy.

At the end of the corridor was a half-opened door marked OFFICE. A dream was standing behind the desk inside. Pale oval face, cool gray eyes, lots of tousled auburn hair, and a sensual red mouth that curled satirically the second she saw me. She wore a long green wrap-around skirt and a flimsy green silk halter that was a miracle of engineering. By all the known laws of stress it should never have been able to contain the thrust of her breasts. Her bare shoulders and stomach had a pale luminous glow. Her skin was beautiful. She didn't barbecue herself in the sun like so many women in Southern California. Her hands were delicate, tapered, with dark red polish on the nails. A girl who took care of herself. I made her out to be about twenty-five, maybe younger.

"Hello. I'm Thomas Kyd." I laid my wallet, open to the photostat of my license, on her desk. "I'm a private investigator. I think maybe you could help me."

She picked up my photostat and studied it, checking my face against the picture. Then she let out a soft sardonic whistle.

"My first live detective. You don't look seedy, or tragic, or even very tough. You even shave. I'm *very* disappointed."

"You're Rhona Flannery's daughter, aren't you?"

"Is that a guess, or did you know?"

"The mouth. When you said, 'My first live detective,' you stuck your tongue out a little and it suddenly came together, where I'd seen you."

"I'm dying of suspense."

"You reminded me of your mother in a movie."

She inspected me with a cool, grave stare as if I were some odd little person whom she might or might not decide to like.

"Close your eyes," she said, coming around from behind the desk. "Go on, close them. I want to try something."

I closed my eyes. I could smell her perfume near me and feel an excitement rising in my throat. I didn't have an idea in hell what she was up to; I just hoped it was going to take a long time.

"All right, Mr. Private Detective," she said, "let's see how good you are. Pretend I'm wanted for murder and you're giving my description to the police."

"Five foot eight. A hundred twenty pounds. Eyes gray. Hair auburn. Small gap between front teeth. Possible cap job. Pale complexion. Small mole on left cheekbone. Deeply recessed navel. Do you want me to go on?" My eyes were still closed but I couldn't smell her perfume any more.

"Be my guest." Her voice was coming from across the room now.

"Suspect talks with East Coast accent. Snotty private

school vowels. Smokes Pall Mall. High-breasted. Wears no bra. You know, I'd really have to verify some of these details before I could give an accurate picture. It still has a certain academic ring to it."

I opened my eyes. She was back in her chair, looking at me through a haze of cigarette smoke. My wallet was open in her hands.

"I'm impressed," she said. "I've hung out with guys who'd have a hard time remembering if I had five fingers on each hand. You're not a computer, are you?"

"I have a good memory for what I like."

"I was afraid you were another actor. We're enrolling this week for the fall semester. But a brief snoop through your wallet,"—she shoved it back across the desktop, with a kind of languid disdain—"tells me you are not an actor but a former army officer. An officer in Vietnam. That must have been weird."

"I hardly remember, it was so long ago."

"The strong, silent type." Her mouth twisted with subtle hostility. "Better not to discuss the gory details in front of women and children. I get it." Her eyes watched me closely for a reaction. "So, first you protected your country from the yellow menace. And now you're a cop."

"The cops might not agree," I said.

"Is that scar on your forehead from where a gook shot you? That is what they're called, isn't it, *gooks?*"

"Don't you think you're jumping to some melodramatic conclusions?" I tried to keep my voice casually amused. "For all you know I spent the whole war servicing typewriters in San Diego."

"But you didn't," she said with certainty. "I can just look at you and tell." She paused. "And you still haven't told me how you got that scar on your forehead. Don't you know women just love scars?"

"A cop in Berkeley did it a long time ago. It was an accident. He wanted to hit me in the teeth but my teeth were buried in his arm. Do you have any more questions?"

"My hero has a flaw," she said wistfully. "He doesn't like my questions."

"You haven't asked me any questions I haven't already asked myself." I leaned over and reclaimed my wallet from the desk. "You on the lookout for war criminals or just livening up a slow day?"

"I haven't decided yet. What exactly was it that you wanted?"

"Your phone number," I said.

"And then what?" She stubbed out her cigarette.

"Your address."

Smiling to herself, she fiddled with some papers on the desk. "I'm married." She looked up.

"So was Helen of Troy."

"I'm not actually married but I do have the clap."

"That's cool. So do I."

"You come on very strong, don't you."

"You're not exactly fresh from the nunnery yourself."

Stalemate. She gave me a pained look and wrapped her mouth around another Pall Mall. She was right. Everything I said was coming out glib and hard-boiled and without much grace. Grace was something I hadn't connected with women since my wife died. Keeping it cynical and remote had maybe been my way of staying faithful to the memory of what I'd had with my wife. Afterward I thought of plenty of things I could have said to this girl that might have softened her up. But maybe not. She'd laid down the sarcastic vibes from the second I walked through the door. She didn't let anyone near her without first shooting him full of little holes.

"Why was the cop in Berkeley trying to hit you in the teeth?" she insisted.

"I'd sold his mother some acid." I smiled. "After one trip she was hooked good. Couldn't get enough of the stuff. Used to follow me around on the street—typical junkie, runny nose, the shakes—begging me for a taste. A cop's mother addicted to LSD. The cop couldn't hold his head up any more. Everyone in the precinct was putting him down."

"Sure," she said.

"I guess you don't believe me. The truth isn't really very exciting. I like to drink beer and when I get tanked up on beer I like to take my bazooka and shoot rabbits in the Los Padres National Forest. Rabbits, hippies, Jews, you name it—I like to drink beer and shoot them. I've wiped out more defenseless women and children with that little ole bazooka than you've had hot dinners. But this one time in the woods I'd had one beer too many and the thing recoiled and hit me in the forehead."

"I think you need help."

She took a memo pad, scrawled something on it, and handed it to me. It was her phone number, a Beechwood Drive address, and her name, Lucy Jean Flannery. I filed it in my wallet and in return gave her the Polaroid shot of Charlotte.

"Know her?"

"You could say that." She rolled her eyes. "I play nursemaid to her. She needs a daily pep talk before she'll attend a class."

"She disappeared from home two days ago. Her father wants her found."

"God, it's about time. I hope she's eloped. No, that's too respectable. I hope she's having a wild secret affair."

"Is that possible?"

"Not really. Charlotte's terrified of men. I think the word people used to use is 'retiring.' I was wondering where she'd got to."

"Didn't someone phone here looking for her?" I asked.

"My mother's in Reno getting divorced. I'm just

helping out while she's gone. I wasn't around yesterday."

"Was Charlotte close to any of the students?"

"Not to my knowledge. She's been here four years. Most of the other students last a semester or two and figure they're ready for something else. Not Charlotte. She's been around longer than most of the teachers."

"Do you like her?"

"I must be sounding catty." She sighed. "Sure, Charlotte's a sweet kid. She's always giving people things. She always remembers everyone's birthday and sends cutesy little cards and key rings with astrological signs on them. She always tells me I'm strong because I'm an Aries. Now where's that at? If I'm strong, it's because I had to be. Charlotte never had to be. I guess maybe that's her problem. That and her old man."

"You know Joe Elevel."

"I don't need to know him. I hear about him from Charlotte all the time—what a swell guy he is, how he's always taking her out and buying her presents. Maybe I'm jealous. I've had three fathers. Two were lushes and the third one never wanted to take me anywhere except to bed. I don't know. I have a feeling her old man pays too much attention to her. I don't mean sexually. It's an emotional thing. He's kept her a little girl so long, she's afraid to try being a woman."

"Does she talk about her mother?"

"Not so much. I think she's in awe of her mother. Charlotte's terrified of sex, and I get the impression her mom considers that a pretty healthy attitude for her. Mrs. Elevel is very big in charity work. Charlotte's always moaning that she's never going to be as good and unselfish as her mother."

I glanced around the office walls at the eight-by-ten glossies of stars who had all wished Rhona Flannery luck and who were now mostly retired or dead.

"What do you think Charlotte would do if she found out her mother wasn't a saint?"

"Look, I'm not an expert on this girl. The truth is, the Elevels have endowed this school. This school is all my mother has. So when Charlotte calls me up I'm nice to her. Personally I think Mrs. Elevel's wrecked Charlotte's life with her puritanical bullshit. She's turned her into a mouse. I don't know what Charlotte would do if she found out her mother wasn't a straight arrow. Why, has Mrs. Elevel gone and done something outrageous?"

"She killed herself."

I watched her face closely, saw the muscles slacken, the blood imperceptibly retreat from the surface of the skin. It wasn't a dramatic reaction but for a second the news had jolted her like a stiff jab. Then she surprised me. She folded her hands on the desk and gave me a poisonous, saccharin smile.

"Aren't you cute," she said. "You get me to shoot my mouth off about this woman I've met maybe three or four times in my life. You let me put her down, and then you tell me she's killed herself. You're cute, but not very funny."

"Sorry. But check out a cemetery sometime. About the only thing they get right is the dates. I wanted your real opinion of the woman, that's all."

"Okay," she said matter-of-factly. "I didn't realize this was serious. You come on with this sexy, smartass line. I didn't realize why you were doing it. Charlotte's not the type to explode. If she found out something unsavory about her mother she'd crawl off into a corner and fall to pieces."

"Any idea where she'd go to find this corner?"

"Probably the movies."

"Have you ever heard Charlotte mention a Mexican guy called Luis Coronado, or heard her talk about Mexicans?"

"No." She stared coldly at a point about two feet to the left of my face. "Leonardo, the dance instructor, is Mexican. He's probably closer to Charlotte than anyone else. I've never understood their relationship. Leonardo's gay. Charlotte probably feels safe with him. I'd talk to Leonardo." She leaned back in her chair, smiled, played with a cigarette, and then fixed me with her languid gray eyes. They were liquid, glazed with mock desire, and unfriendly.

"Leonardo will like you," she said. "He's wild about soldiers."

"I didn't ask you for your phone number in order to get information out of you," I said.

She wiped the sarcastically seductive look off her face, examined me coolly, and shrugged.

"You'd better hurry up if you want to catch Leonardo. His class finished five minutes ago."

Suddenly a lot of Mexicans were entering the picture, and I wondered if that fact was a real lead, or simply coincidence. My gut feeling told me that Pedro, the gardener, had been telling the truth but maybe that was because his story tied in so neatly with the check stubs and the envelope from the safe. The mind has a yen for orderly patterns, it wants to tidy up information and store it away as fast as possible. Sometimes the trick is to presume nothing, to avoid putting the pieces together. Something that starts out as pure speculation, just an idle hunch, has a way of turning solid in your mind and closing out future possibilities.

Leonardo's classroom was empty except for a woman fastening a skirt around her leotard. She told me the dance instructor had gone home.

Back in the office, Lucy gave me Leonardo's home address. She'd freshened her makeup and had that flippant, sassy stuff going for her again.

"Mexican ballet dancers don't make it out of the barrio by waving limp wrists." She leaned forward over her desk and crushed a cigarette in the ashtray. "Leonardo's very butch, *muy* macho for a gay." She rolled a fresh sheet of paper into her typewriter. "I'm sure you're invincible but I just thought I'd warn you."

Chapter **FIVE**

Leonardo lived on a tree-lined residential street off Fairfax Avenue near Olympic Boulevard. It was a quiet, predominantly Jewish neighborhood, full of hospitals and retirement homes, with mainly elderly people on the streets. In a lot of the shops along Fairfax the men behind the counters were survivors of Nazi death camps. You could see the blue serial marks on their arms when they handed you your change. I had lived in the neighborhood briefly after returning from overseas and I used to observe these men, wondering what they had seen, and how they had managed to come out alive where millions had failed. I never came up with any answers. They were all reserved, silently watchful men, graduates of the worst institute in the world's history. When I found the faces on Fairfax bringing to mind Vietnamese faces in our POW camps, I moved to another part of town.

Leonardo's place was a ramshackle little stucco house stuck between an empty lot and the King David Retirement Hotel. Rusty gardening tools and tin cans littered the overgrown yard. I walked through them and rang the bell. There was a long wait. I heard a Johnny Mathis record, "Warm and Tender," being rejected, vague scuffling sounds, and a door closing. I rang the bell again. Leonardo answered it. He was dark-skinned, with a narrow face and liquid black eyes that studied me without blinking. He had changed from his leotard into white silk pajama bottoms and a black tank top with STRANGERS WELCOME printed across the front. Lucy had been right: the guy was built strong, and could give you a hammering. The only thing was, his chest was rising and falling as if he'd just run up a flight of stairs.

"Lucy from the Academy gave me your address," I said. "Charlotte Elevel disappeared two days ago and her family's worried. Can I come in?"

The question was academic. I'd stepped into the foyer by then. Up close Leonardo gave off a smell of moldy sweatsocks. A silver cylinder on a chain hung from his neck, which he held onto with his left hand while I shook the other one. Inside the cylinder I was sure I'd find a twist of cotton wool soaked in Amyl Nitrite, a stimulant administered to heart patients, and popped by thrill-seekers for kicks. Some gay bars and dance palaces in Los Angeles smell like locker rooms, there are so many people sniffing amyl. At the time you could buy the chemical in head shops for a couple of bucks; it went under the name of Locker Room, and was supposed to be one of a dozen different exotic scents that would add atmosphere to your home. How it ever slipped past the Food and Drug boys, I don't know, but there it was; for the price of a six-pack you could buy enough over the counter to burn your heart out.

"Nice place you've got here." I looked around. "Lucy said it was nice."

"Lucy has never been here." His voice was a stagy baritone and he had one of those show business drawls that sound English to anyone who's never met an Englishman.

"Charlotte Elevel must have described your place to Lucy," I countered. "I understand you were a close friend of Charlotte's."

He walked into the living room and took a chair across the room from the one he pointed out for me. The curtains were drawn and the only light came from candles set in alcoves. There were enough plants in the place to start a small cemetery. As my eyes got used to the gloom I made out a pair of women's shoes shoved under Leonardo's chair.

"You got comapny." I smiled. "Did I scare someone away?"

"No company." His voice left the English accent behind that time.

"Have it your way." I lit a cigarette and tossed the match into the ashtray on the table in front of me. Two of the cigarette butts in it were lipstick-stained. "Like I said, Charlotte took off two nights ago. I thought maybe you'd seen her."

"No, I haven't seen her."

"Any idea where she might be?"

"Nope. No idea."

"Ever been to her house?" I watched him closely and saw that his breathing was returning to normal.

"Oh, I went sometimes to give her extra tuition and . . . you know, they got a pool. Maybe I'd hang out, maybe I wouldn't."

I was having trouble figuring Leonardo for a friend of Charlotte's. If she felt safe with fags, she would have gone for the sensitive, effeminate type, someone more like a girlfriend. Leonardo was sharp enough to con her into believing he was something he wasn't, but what was in it for him? He looked like a steam-bath heavy, strictly from bondage and discipline. I couldn't believe he would have any genuine rapport with a sheltered, deeply conventional girl like Charlotte.

"I think you're lying." I picked up the lipstick-stained cigarette and tossed it in my hand. "You're lying about Charlotte, and you're lying about not having company."

"You better go now, mister." He rose to his feet. "I let you in as a favor and you give me shit. I like you to go now."

"When was the last time you saw Luis Coronado?" I watched his face but it stayed remote and shut tight.

"I don't know anyone by that name. Goodby, mister."

I walked toward the door leading back to the foyer and then veered left, through an archway hung with a beaded curtain. I pulled a chair from against the wall, and sent it crashing behind me. Leonardo tried to jump over it, but his foot caught, and he went down, cursing. I pulled open the bedroom door and froze. There was a girl lying spread-eagled on the bed, her hands and feet tied with rope. Only it wasn't Charlotte Elevel and it wasn't a girl. It was a teenage boy dressed in cocktail-waitress drag and a black wig. His face was garishly made up, a pointy, ravaged face with a mouth you might have used for straightening nails. Bruised needle marks discolored his arms and throat; the ones around his carotid and jugular were abscessed. The ropes were for show, strictly atmospheric aids, because he wriggled clear of them the second he saw me.

I grabbed Leonardo as he burst through the door and slammed him so hard against the wall the windows rattled in their frames.

"Shut up," I said. "Not a fucking peep out of you!"

He started to struggle and I leaned on his windpipe with my thumb.

"You got big troubles." I held him pinned. "By the time they let you go, you're going to look like something that crawled out of an enchilada." I ripped the inhaler off the chain on his neck. "They're going to nail you for narcotics and stick a morals charge so far up your ass you'll be sitting on it for the rest of your life."

He didn't disagree. His face had gone yellow and sticky with fear. The skin looked like something you could catch flies on.

"If any of your dope's in *him*,"—I jerked my thumb at the kid—"that's a couple more years. And your play-mate looks like he'd tell the cops any kind of story. A couple of hours without a shot and he'll start remembering all kinds of things that hurt him."

The kid was sitting on the edge of the bed. He had jumpy, hollowed-out eyes and under the makeup his skin was gray and filmy.

"You know this guy?" I asked him.

"Fuck you," he said.

"The next guy who asks you a question may just open your mouth with a shoe. If he doesn't want to get his shoe dirty he may use a can opener."

"I don't know him," he snarled. "He cruised me on Hollywood. Said he'd give me twenty bucks and all the reds I wanted for a private party. Then he made me put on these clothes and tied me up. I got to go to the john."

"Sit awhile." I turned back to Leonardo and said, "You can go two ways. One way you tell me something about Charlotte Elevel and maybe, just maybe, I don't make a phone call. Another way, you tell me nothing and I feed you to a couple of cannibals I know in the Vice Squad. One way or the other I'll get what I want. You can tell me now, or wait until your face looks like hamburger."

I didn't know anyone in the Vice Squad. If I ran him in, chances were no one would lay a finger on him and he'd be out on bail within twelve hours. I was doing what the cops call "jerking off a suspect," terrifying him into believing only his cooperation can save him from being brutalized.

"Are you listening to me?" I slammed him against the wall again. "You know what happens to child molesters inside? You shot a minor full of dope and tried to rape him. A lot of hard cases are going to see red when they meet you. Guys who'll stick a screwdriver in your heart because you've outraged their morals—"

I took the brunt of the first blow on my shoulder, and got knocked sideways. I ducked as the kid swung the marble bookend at my face. A sharp corner skimmed the skin on my scalp. I was halfway down, with one leg bent under me and my back against the wall. Leonardo was yelling at the kid to stop but the kid wasn't stopping. He had about as much self-control as a barracuda in a well-stocked goldfish bowl. I took another glancing blow on my forearm, which I'd raised to protect my face. He tried to pull my other hand away to get a clear shot at my head, which was his big mistake. I got a lock on his fingers, broke them, and hung on. He tried one last time with the marble bookend but his aim was gone. It smashed into the wall over my head. My left arm was dead and his left hand was broken but he wasn't through yet. He fell on me and bit at my face while his good hand went for my groin. I let go of his dead fingers and groped wildly for his other hand. He never got hold of my balls and his teeth never got a good bite at my face because I bent his fingers back then, four of them, until they snapped like chopsticks. We lay there for a while. Then he started sobbing and cursing. Then I vomited a little on him and the floor.

The crazy son of a bitch started groaning louder but I couldn't speak. It had happened too fast. I was still fighting to clear my vision. Someone had knocked the top of my head off and adrenalin was crashing through my body in sickening waves. Leonardo was plastered against the opposite wall. He looked as if the crack of the boy's fingers breaking had petrified him for life. I dragged myself to my feet and lurched over to the bed and pulled up the sleeve of my jacket. The underside of my forearm was bleeding but it was the growing discoloration that worried me more. A bruise that looked like a tropical sunset over a black sea was swelling under the skin, and my hand had gone numb. I didn't know if he'd shattered the bone or smashed the nerves that run like conduit wires from the elbow through the wrist.

At least the kid was finished for the day. He'd burned himself out in one crazy, vicious explosion and his hands were going to be in plaster for months. He lay there slumped, with his cheek flat on the parquet floor. His thin lips were drawn up in a smarl of pain and his eyes had gone glassy with the shock. At a glance he looked like a black-haired cocktail waitress passed out on the floor.

After a while he rolled over and sat up.

"I'm gonna sue you, cocksucker. My father's a law-yer. I'm gonna sue your ass." Then he fainted.

"Who is this animal?" I jerked my thumb at the kid.

"Just a hustler, like he said. He was cruising. I gave him a ride. I didn't know he was a maniac."

"Yeah."

"He wasn't dressed like that." Leonardo shrugged.

Feeling was coming back into my arm but I almost wished it would stay numb. I went into the bathroom and washed the blood out of my scalp wound. Then I poured some of Leonardo's after-shave lotion on it and tried to be brave. There was nothing to do about the laceration over my eyebrow where he'd bitten me; it was just there, an ugly cluster of puncture marks with a blue bruise growing around it. I didn't care about my looks. I just thought the son of a bitch might have ra-bies.

When I got back to the bedroom Leonardo was bent over the kid with a razor blade, carefully cutting him free of his clothes. His hands were horribly swollen and the fingers stuck out at the wrong angles. Leonardo helped him back into his jeans and shirt.

"I want to take my makeup off." The kid's voice was broken and adolescent and all his bravado was gone. "I don't want to sit in that fucking hospital with a bunch of people staring at me." He started to cry, rocking on the ground. "Look at my hands! Whatcha do to my fucking hands?"

I told the kid he could go to an emergency clinic and get his hands set and plastered. I told him a hustler with two busted hands wasn't going to do wild business on the street. I told him he could check into a public clinic run by a doctor I knew in Venice. It was a place that siphoned junkies off the street and into methadone pro-grams.

"If you screw up there," I told him, "they'll throw you out on your ass. Keep shooting downers into your throat and you'll be dead in a couple of months anyway. No one cares. Take your choice."

He reluctantly agreed to try the clinic, as if it were some big favor he was doing me. If things had panned out differently I would have been lying where he was, with my skull caved in by repeated blows from a blunt instrument.

I got through to the clinic on the phone.

"What's he like?" my doctor friend asked.

"He's like a six-foot cockroach with a couple of broken legs. He's mean, the way they get on barbiturates. I'm going to give him something to down him out. Otherwise he might bite you when he gets there."

Leonardo dissolved some Seconals in hot water, loaded up the kid's works, and spiked him in the leg. After a while he stopped twisting and turning.

"You want something for yourself?" Leonardo asked me. "A pain pill maybe? Some Demerol? He really hurt you."

"Tell it to the cops." I walked out of the bedroom, into the living room, and sat for a moment in silence. I didn't care what Leonardo did in his spare time. He could do it in the middle of Dodger Stadium on prime-time TV and I wouldn't even write a letter to my senator. But he was holding out on me and I felt ready to bust ass until he came up with something.

First I put through a call to my friend Harry Bowkley at Pacific Telephone. He already had printouts of the dozens of bills I'd asked Joe Elevel to request. The computer showed regular calls between Leonardo's house and numbers listed under Charlotte's and Tyrone's names. No calls had been made since the evening of Mrs. Elevel's suicide.

Then I phoned Lucy at the Academy. When she heard my voice, she asked me how the dog was.

"What dog?" I asked.

"What's the vet going to charge to have her fixed?" she asked.

"Is someone in the office with you?"

"That sounds about right."

"I get you. Someone looking for Charlotte?"

"Yeah," she said. "Excuse me a moment, Mr. Gervano. I won't be a moment."

"Someone called Gervano? A Mexican trying to locate Charlotte?" I felt a cold shiver in my neck.

"Yeah, that sounds reasonable."

"Give him Leonardo's address. Tell him Leonardo would know where Charlotte is. Call me when he leaves."

I put the phone down and waited impatiently. Who was Gervano? Someone who worked for Luis Coronado, or Coronado himself? I was getting edgy as hell at the thought of Lucy alone in her office with this character.

The phone rang. Leonardo stepped in and I told him to wait in the bedroom.

"He's gone," Lucy said. "He told me he was with an ad agency and they wanted to use Charlotte for a commercial. He looked like a pimp. Very chic. But he also looked like an ad exec. Ever since I met you *everyone* is starting to look crooked."

"Sure," I said.

"You sound funny."

"Listen, don't touch anything this Gervano touched in your office. In case he doesn't come here, I want his prints. Call you later." I hung up.

For a girl with no friends, who didn't go out, Joe's daughter was suddenly in big demand. Someone had to want her pretty bad to walk right into the Academy and ask for her like that.

My next call, to Ian White of White and Rinehart, did nothing to calm me down. His operative investigating Luis Coronado had contacted a gambling source in Guadalajara who had known Coronado back in the sixties. Coronado had started out as an enforcer for a ring of local extortionists and gradually muscled his way into the action himself. His underworld name was Fly Catcher. Coronado, alias Fly Catcher, carried around a matchbox full of live flies and let them out in bars, then caught them with his hands and put them back in the box; this was a trick that went down big in some whorehouses in Guadalajara. The gambling source hadn't seen him in Mexico for over five years, and word was Coronado was making big bucks in the Hollywood skin trade. The operative was trying to tap a source in the LAPD to see if they had a rap sheet on Coronado, who apparently had also branched out into the dirty-movie business.

"I can't wait to meet him," I said.

"We also have a little dirt on your Dr. Lester," Ian said. "Five years ago he got in trouble with some insurance companies. He'd stuck it to them one too many times on personal injury cases. The insurance boys figured he was taking too big a bite out of their apple so they ran a phony accident case through his office. Nothing wrong with the patient at all. Dr. Lester treated him for three months, handed in fake X-rays and EEG's, and a five-and-a-half-grand bill."

"He's still practicing," I said.

"Yeah," Ian grunted in disgust, "they pulled his narcotics prescription book in fifty-nine and someone sat on that investigation, too. He's got friends. Since the insurance investigation he's been clean. For 'clean' read 'careful.' He treats a lot of rich drunks and hopheads. A lot of people with obscure but excruciatingly painful diseases, like a big yen for morphine. I can't verify this, but word is he's been known to taste the medicine himself to make sure he's prescribing the right thing. Also, and this just may fit in somewhere, I hear he sweats a lot."

"If nothing else holds up we'll charge him on that."

"This is costing plenty, Kyd. Your client better be good for it."

"He's good for it."

"We got his furniture in our offices, you know," Ian said. "It's very crappy-looking stuff. You make sure you collect from this character." The phone went dead.

I pulled Leonardo's Amyl Nitrite inhaler from my pocket and called him in from the bedroom.

"Who's Tyrone Elevel to you?" I asked him bluntly.

"The guy's crippled. When I see Charlotte, I see him at the pool."

"Is he bent?"

"From the waist down he's silly putty. I hardly know the guy."

I picked up the phone and dialed a number at random. An elderly woman answered. "Is that you, Miltie?" she asked.

"I want Captain Marco. Vice Squad," I said.

"Who *is* this?" she demanded.

I never got to explain to her because Leonardo took the phone out of my hand and put it back down.

"Leonardo," I said. "My arm hurts and I'm in a bad mood. Stall me one more time and I'm going to send you down the tubes."

Leonardo sighed. "Once in a while I give Tyrone a little grass. Enough for a couple of joints. Charlotte doesn't know anything about that."

"How much?"

"Nothing. A taste." He held out his hands to show me they were empty. "I just lay it on him as a favor."

"You slay me," I said. "A little grass as a favor, huh?" I stood up and walked over to the shelves on the far wall. They were stacked with glazed ceramic pots and a wealth of fine stereo equipment. I yanked the shelves out of their wall plugs and the whole mess hit the floor.

"Whatta you want, man?" he screeched.

I didn't answer him. He had two matching glass-fronted antique cabinets by the door to the foyer, each filled with china and glassware. I kicked them both in and then threw an onyx ashtray at the mirror over the mantelpiece.

"These are just your things, Leonardo. Wait until I start in on you."

"Okay!" he shouted. "I give him coke. And speed. I make a hundred, maybe a hundred and a half, a week. And that's it!"

"What about the mother?"

"The mother?" He frowned. "I don't even know the mother."

"She's in my car. I'll go get her."

"What is this?" He seemed genuinely confused. "What do I got to say to Charlotte's mother?"

I didn't think Leonardo was lying. He didn't even know Mrs. Elevel had killed herself. "You're holding out on me." I looked around the room for something else to smash and fixed on an antique grandfather clock by the window.

"Charlotte was here," Leonardo gasped. "Okay. Two nights ago. She showed up around ten o'clock. I had someone with me. I didn't have any time for her. She only stayed a minute. She looked kinda nervous, shaky, you know, but she always looks nervous. That's all. I ain't seen her, heard from her, nothing. That's the truth."

"If that was the truth, you would have told me the minute I came in here."

"Look, man, how do I know I can trust you?" He collapsed in a chair and buried his face in his hands.

"You can't," I said. "You might tell me everything I want to know and I'd still run you in just for kicks. The longer I got to wait in this fucking dump the more likely I'm going to do just that." I bent over him and said, "Who's Luis Coronado? Who's Gervano?"

"I don't know these names," he said hysterically. "You're setting me up for something I don't know nothing about."

"I don't like you." I grabbed him by the hair and

pulled his head back until he was looking into my eyes.
"I don't like your boyfriend, but worst of all"—I banged
his head against the wall—"I don't like"—I banged it
again—"how you ain't got no"—and again—
"r-e-s-p-e-c-t for me!"

"I got respect!" he cried, tears forming in his eyes. "I
got plenty of respect. I'm gonna tell you everything. Just
let go of my fucking hair!" He took some deep breaths
then and rubbed his scalp. "The night Charlotte came
over she wanted pills." He glanced quickly at me to see
how I was taking it, then continued, "Sleeping pills. She
was real spaced-out, I mean weird. I never knew her to
pop anything but these mild tranquilizers but I had
someone here, dig? I wanted to get rid of her. I gave
her some reds and she blew."

"How many reds?"

"Wait a minute." He held up his hand. "Last night,
around two in the morning she calls me. She's way
down. Her voice is so goofy I don't even know who it is
at first. I ain't never heard her like this. She says people
are dirty and then she giggles and asks me if I'm dirty
too. She asks me about ten times if I'm a motherfucker.
She don't use language like that. I ask her where she is
but she just giggles. She says she's in her sleeping place.
Then she hangs up." Leonardo's olive skin was damp.

"How many reds?" I repeated.

"Eight, maybe ten."

"Or fifteen maybe twenty," I said.

"Look, I gave her a handful," he whined. "I didn't
count them."

"You better hope real hard she's alive."

"It was just a favor," he pleaded.

"Your kind of favors kill people." I got up and
walked to the door, with him following behind.

"I'm going to drive the kid to the clinic," he said,
"but I'm not going in with him."

"That's big of you."

"Look, you want me to call you if Charlotte calls here again?"

I handed him my card. "You positive you don't know Coronado or Gervano?"

"Never heard of them." He said it almost proudly.

"Well, they know you and they're looking for Charlotte too. They're hard-ons, Leonardo. They'll stick a shooter in your pants and when you've told them everything they want to know, they'll pull the trigger. If you're lying to me, you aren't worth a hill of refried beans. They'll kill you and an hour later they won't even remember what you looked like."

"What do I do?" He grabbed hold of my arm as I walked down the steps.

"Go stay with a friend. Call in sick to the Academy. But get your phone transferred to wherever you are in case Charlotte calls again." I shrugged him loose, crossed the overgrown yard, and moved off down the pavement. The street was dead. I walked to the corner, turned left, and hung against a wall, smoking. After a few minutes, Leonardo and the rubber-legged kid came out. Leonardo kept looking up and down the street for the hoods I'd warned him about, which strongly suggested he didn't know them.

Chapter SIX

After they drove away I walked back to my car. I opened the trunk, reached down into the jumble of skin-diving gear, and pulled out an oilskin bag. It contained a 7.65 Mauser semiautomatic and a dozen clips. I wrapped the bag and a screwdriver in an old copy of the L.A. *Times,* and walked back to Leonardo's.

His back door was easy. It had a single bolt on the door frame with the attaching section screwed into the plaster. With the screwdriver it took about four seconds to pop the door.

I sat in the gloomy living room and snapped a clip into the Mauser. I hate guns. I hate their look and their cold oily smell and their weight. I hate the sick thrill of power they give to weaklings. I hate the high-caliber pieces with the walnut grips that open up gaps you can put your hand through, and I hate the shiny little purse jobs that make a nickel-sized red and black hole. I hate guns because they remind me of things that should never have happened. But mainly I hate them because they scare the shit out of me.

A gun is just a bad idea waiting for its time.

I waited an hour for Gervano to show. I watched the street through a small curtained window in the bathroom. I heard an argument going on in the house behind Leonardo's, a woman tongue-lashing a man, a man bellowing at a woman. Apparently he had a drinking problem and she couldn't stay away from his friends. They were threatening to kill each other. But it sounded more like marriage than murder.

After an hour went by, I found some tequila in the kitchen and drank several glasses. It began to dawn on me that Gervano wasn't going to turn up, that maybe he was following some other lead to Charlotte, while I was waiting for him. Nothing made much sense to me any more. I was starting to suspect Charlotte might already be dead from an overdose. At that moment she might be sinking into a coma behind a locked bedroom door somewhere in the city, and there seemed no way to find her. When people run away, they leave traces of their movements: they're seen, they spend money, they do the hundreds of things that go into staying alive. But what if the runaway isn't interested in living?

On the way back to the Academy my uneasiness grew. Ever since leaving the Elevel place I'd had a vague apprehension I was being watched. At first I'd thought my tail was an old beige Continental, and then, going from the Academy to Leonardo's, a dark green microbus. On my way back to the Academy I went at an even speed, taking Highland north through moderately heavy traffic, and then turning off into residential streets, doubling back, and doing all the random moves that will usually flush a tail into the open. I decided I was being paranoid. The only beige Continental I saw was six cars ahead of me, and there was no law against going north on Highland and turning east on Hollywood, which is what we both did.

As soon as I got to Lucy's office, I called Ian White and had him send over a fingerprint man. According to Lucy, Gervano had touched the inside and outside doorknobs, a cigar in the ashtray, and several publicity shots of Charlotte. It would be almost impossible to lift his prints off the koorknob, which was touched hundreds of times a day. The round cigar might retain partial prints. The publicity shots, however, had come straight from the photographer to the school, and Lucy knew which corners Gervano had grasped. She had also had the presence of mind to take careful note of his appearance.

While waiting for the fingerprint man, I questioned some of the students who had come into the office. I didn't give them much information, just that Charlotte was missing and her parents were concerned. From their answers it was pretty clear that Charlotte was something of a school joke. One of them swore he'd seen her dancing in a topless joint in the Valley and another claimed to have received a massage from her in a Reseda Health Spa.

The only thing that gave me any confidence was that not a single one of her fellow students had the faintest idea where she might have gone. Anyone else looking for her was probably up against the same problem.

By then the fingerprint man had arrived and I told him to dust the publicity shots first. Lucy pointed out a spot where she knew Gervano had touched the glossy photo.

He went to work, dusted the first print, frowned, tried another, and stopped. He shook his head.

"This character doesn't have prints. All he's got are blanks."

"You're sure?" It was a very bad sign.

"Look for yourself." He shrugged, "You don't come across them much any more. But this character definitely had his hands ghosted. In Mexico probably, and not that long ago. See, the acid eats the print off and for a while it leaves big cracks. His cracks haven't come together yet."

I could feel time slipping by. A man with no prints, almost beyond doubt a professional killer, was loose in the city on Charlotte's track, and I was stalled with no ideas. Lucy asked if she could return the photos to Charlotte's file, which was lying open on the desk. I nodded and then changed my mind, picking up the file to look at it myself. There were a dozen looseleaf pages with records of courses taken and billing accounts. On the title page was a questionnaire with her name, address, and license and social security numbers. A second page was stapled to it, a change-of-address form dated three years ago, with a Void stamped on it.

"What's this?"

Lucy glanced at it for a moment and then said:

"Charlotte was going to share a house with one of the other students, a girl called Candace Laine. She arranged the whole thing and then could never get the courage to tell her parents. It was sort of an embarrassment to her. She put it off and put it off and finally she just chickened out. It was really a long time ago. Candy Laine still has the house, I think, but she's away in New York on location."

I called information and got the phone number for Candace Laine's Mojave Drive address. I was thinking how smart Lucy had been to get Gervano to touch Charlotte's photos, which should have given us perfect prints on him, when I felt it, like ice water trickling down my spine.

I understood why Gervano had never bothered to try and trace Charlotte through her dance teacher. There was no need to. Gervano had seen Charlotte's Mojave Drive address on her file while he was pretending to look at her publicity stills. He'd had that address over two hours ago when he left the Academy.

Chapter SEVEN

I didn't explain anything to anyone. I just tore out of the office and jumped into my car. When I turned the key there was a flat click. I opened the hood, took one look, and slammed it down.

My engine no longer had a distributor cap.

Cruising taxis in Los Angeles are as rare as hailstorms.

I ran back up to Lucy's office, explained what had happened, and demanded her car keys. The fingerprint guy and the students clearly thought I was acting like a hysterical nut, rushing in and out like that, but Lucy didn't ask questions. She grabbed her purse and hurried downstairs with me to her car.

"Give me the keys," I said.

"On one condition."

"For Christ's sake, give me the keys!"

"I'm coming," she said.

"But I'm driving," I snarled, and snatched the keys.

Lucy got the worse deal.

It was a spanking new Fiat sports car fresh from the dealer. What I did to the transmission and suspension in fifteen minutes must have put five years on it. I passed in the wrong lane, ran red lights, and when traffic stalled me, I put half the car on the pavement and kept cooking. We screamed down Sunset doing eighty, with the horn on, and nearly bought it from a truck pulling out from Crestline Drive. I swerved, lost it, got it back, and left smoking rubber all over the intersection. Lucy didn't say anything. I don't think she could unclench her teeth to talk.

"Who were those people in your office?" I demanded. "Who stole my goddamn distributor cap?"

She shook her head, her hands balled into fists.

I couldn't figure it. Gervano had left the Academy long before I arrived. Whoever had taken my distributor cap was coming from another direction.

"Are you sure Charlotte's there?" Lucy finally said as the car went into a screaming drift off Sunset into Benedict Canyon.

"I don't know." I jammed my foot to the floor. My whole body was soaked with sweat and my jaws ached from biting down. Charlotte—this rather insipid, sheltered rich girl had become painfully real to me in the last few minutes. Visions of a well-dressed Mexican with blunt, faintly deformed fingertips, stalking her down, flooded my mind. In my picture, he seemed to move forward with a mechanical inevitability, getting closer and closer, while I struggled impotently, as helpless as a man in a bad dream. How do you know which hour, which minute, which second will make the difference between life and death? It may be that by stopping at a red light you will give a killer long enough to snuff out a life. It may be that by driving like a madman you'll end up eating the windshield. I didn't think about that possibility. I pressed.

There was a beige Continental parked in front of 2200 Mojave Drive and a white MG with Charlotte's plates in the driveway.

I told Lucy to keep the engine running. If I didn't come out in five minutes she was to drive down the street and call the police.

The house was a one-story redwood ski-lodge affair. The curtains were drawn and there was no sound from inside. The front door was locked. I moved quietly around the back, where a sundeck was buttressed out on stilts. Below it the hillside dropped away to a ravine gorged with scrub oak and manzanilla. I had the Mauser out, with a shell in the chamber, and the safety off. The back of the house was covered in high sliding glass doors, behind which the curtains were drawn. A bit of curtain moved desultorily, tugged by the breeze passing in and out of a half-opened door.

I had a feeling going in there would be as much fun as walking through a plate-glass window.

I stepped back to the edge of the sundeck and then sprinted forward, coming through the open door low and flattened out like a swimmer making a racing dive. I hit the carpet, rolled over, and came up with both hands on the Mauser.

The living room was dead silent and though there were two people in it neither of them reacted to my entrance.

A smell of cordite hung in the air. There was a man lying face down on the carpet, his hand still clutching the stem of a banana plant that he'd pulled over as he fell. The back of his head showed a small charred hole, hardly bleeding, but still smelling of scorched hair. The back of Charlotte Elevel's head looked the same, only she was lying on a suede couch and the blood in her blond hair was already crusted. Everything had stopped for her a little earlier than for the man on the floor but their deaths had been identical, each shot in the back of the head with a low-caliber weapon.

I ran quickly through the other rooms in the house and then opened the front door. After the gloom of the house and the still horror of what it contained, the pale blue sky looked unreal. I shouted to Lucy to stay where she was and went back inside.

In a few minutes the whole place would be swarming with detectives and special police squads. I wanted five minutes to take in the scene just as it was, as the killer had seen it. It was a cool piece of work, executed, I thought, by someone whose profession was killing people. He could not leave prints because he had none. He would not drop cufflinks, keys, or any personal belongings because he knew better than to carry them on a job.

I walked over to the guy on the floor and went

through his pockets. He was a thin, balding man in his early fifties, his clothes cheap, nondescript. Half an hour before, he'd been standing next to me in Lucy's office while I studied Charlotte's file. I'd taken him for a much older student, one of the diehards who never give up on the dream of becoming an actor. His shirt collar was slightly frayed and the seat of his suit pants was shiny. He had about twenty dollars in cash on him, no credit cards, and a bill from a gas station in Pasadena for work on his old Continental. His address was a flea-pit boarding house in East Hollywood. He looked as if he lived on cheap liquor and takeout food.

I felt a stab of dull anguish when I found the private investigator's license in his wallet. It had expired four days ago. His name was Harlan Stackman and I wondered if I'd be like him in twenty years, with all the marks of a lonely, unprofitable occupation stamped into my skin and clothes.

It was his shoes that got to me. They were elegant city shoes from another decade, with as many hairline cracks in the leather as there were in an old person's face. The heels were worn down on the outside to within an inch of the soles. But the shoes were polished to a high sheen and he'd even blackened the heels underneath to hide their broken-down condition.

The poor bastard had been following me all day and at one point in Lucy's office he'd got close enough to touch me and I'd hardly noticed him. He'd coasted in my slipstream and when he saw his chance he took it. My distributor cap was in his suit jacket pocket. Someone had wasted him for winning the race.

I didn't know who'd hired him. I didn't know what he'd been doing to get wasted. I was beginning to wonder why anyone had ever hired me.

Charlotte Elevel's corpse suggested someone who'd temporarily let herself go to hell. Her face and hands were soiled, her fine blond hair oily, and her blouse caked with vomit. It looked as if she'd spent the last forty-eight hours trying to hold down an overdose. She was an innocent-looking, childishly pretty girl, a little overweight, with small, delicate hands and feet. A bridge of freckles ran across her sunburned nose and cheeks. What could this girl have found in her mother's safe to plunge her into such a suicidal frame of mind? Was it something so atrocious that it literally crushed the will to live?

Someone had systematically searched the bedroom but not the living room, which made me think he had found what he was looking for. Sticking out from under the bed was a yellow lined pad. Half a dozen sheets had been roughly torn off but the remaining top sheet bore the imprint of writing. It matched the writing in Charlotte's diary. I removed the page and stuck it in my pocket.

As I walked out of the bedroom my foot crunched down on some Seconals. They made a faint cracking noise, like cockroaches, which they might as well have been for all the good they'd done Charlotte Elevel. They were the same size as .22 slugs and they had powder inside them too—and I could tell I was getting screwy in the head from having seen those two dead people and touched their cold skin, or I wouldn't be having that kind of fragmented thoughts.

For a second I thought the floor was going to come up and let me have it. All the blood drained out of my head and my stomach churned with nausea. I leaned against a wall and gulped air until the disturbance subsided. "You've seen dead people before," I told myself, "what's so special about these two stiffs?" I looked over at them and decided I was right. There wasn't anything special about them. In comparison to most they looked relatively neat and untouched, as if any second they were going to sit up and carry on doing whatever they'd been doing when Mr. X pulled the trigger. It looked wrong. There should have been more difference between life and death, not this sick mockery of being alive.

They don't care what they look like, I reminded myself; what you're thinking is irrelevant.

I had to dial three times before I got the Elevel number right. Calvin answered. I told him what I'd found and how to get there. Lucy had been right: no one in the Elevel household had known of Charlotte's failed attempt to move into the Mojave Drive place. I wondered if she'd be alive today if she'd had the nerve to break away three years ago. Joe came on the line then and gasped a lot of hysterical things at me. I told him I was under no legal compulsion to tell the police anything he didn't want me to tell them, but since I still didn't know anything, that wasn't really a problem. I don't think he understood a word I said except that his daughter was dead.

I called Hollywood substation next and told the desk patrolman there'd been a murder, and gave him the address. Before I hung up I could already hear him sending it out to the radio cars. In another few seconds news of it would reach the detectives' squad room and all kinds of organized hell would be set in motion.

I walked quickly out to Lucy.

"I don't think you want to come in," I said. "It's a murder. Charlotte and some guy. The cops'll want to talk to you. Tell them what you want."

"What do you mean?" She was shaking.

"Tell them the truth," I said. "If you can figure it out, tell it to them."

"I don't want to go inside," she said. "But I don't want to stay here by myself."

We walked back around the deck to the sun terrace and looked out over Beverly Hills swimming in the yellowish brown smog. I could hear the steady tap-tap of some kids playing basketball in the driveway next door, and distant radio music floating down from higher in the canyon. The sun terrace looked down on a fire trail cut in the sloping chaparral. It was lined with motor-cycle tracks. I used to ride dirt bikes on them when I was a kid, when my family still had the house in Beverly Hills, before my father got blacklisted by the studios and drank himself to an early death. Twenty years ago I'd been down on that same fire trail, tearing hell out of the dirt without the faintest idea what a corpse looked like.

"Do you need that?" Lucy gently squeezed my arm.

I realized I was still holding the Mauser. I must have been in a state of shock to walk around with a loaded weapon in my hand and not even realize it. I pulled the clip out and shoved it with the gun into my pocket.

"Thanks," I said. "You probably saved me getting shot. By the cops."

It was probably the wrong moment. I was sweating and my stomach was jumping with adrenalin but I kissed her then. Her face was a blur under mine; her lips curved open and her tongue softly met mine. Her body felt warm and luxuriously alive against me.

We could hear the sirens from the bottom of the canyon now, distant, then suddenly all too close.

I kept that moment, the firm heat of her breasts and the smell of her perfume, in my head after the cops arrived. It got me through some bad hours.

Chapter **EIGHT**

A swarm of patrol cars, unmarked cars, Photo Unit and Medical Examiner's cars, and press media wagons choked Mojave Drive. Up and down the street the neighbors of Number 2200 were being canvassed. A group of irate journalists milled in the driveway, rushing toward the front door every time a detective came out, and murmuring in protest when he refused to make a statement. Someone had nailed down the lid on the murder of Charlotte Elevel.

Inside the living room the forensic chemist had finished taking blood samples and was packing up his equipment. The boys from the Latent Prints Section were lifting the last of the prints from the bathroom. There were so many detectives and members of special units in the room that the average person would not have noticed the bodies of Charlotte Elevel and Harlan Stackman. They lay in the positions in which I'd found them hours ago. The coroner's man had placed plastic bags over the corpses' hands in order to preserve any traces of hair, skin, or material that might have got stuck under their fingernails if there had been a struggle. Two ejected shell casings had been recovered and tentatively identified as probably coming from a .22 automatic pistol.

I felt a surge of relief when someone finally threw sheets over the corpses, tied them onto stretchers, and got them out of the room.

In the bedroom I could hear Captain Cray barking into the telephone.

From the moment he arrived on the scene Captain Cray had shown he knew how to do the right thing in the wrong way. Everyone in Cray's book got the same treatment: the tough, nasty, thorough one. When his own detectives reported that none of the neighbors had seen an unfamiliar car parked on the street, or heard gunshots, he publicly cursed them out and sent them back to question the neighbors again. The only bit of his public relations I appreciated was when he told Calvin he'd throw him off the sun deck if he made one more allusion to Mr. Elevel's important friends down at the Hall of Justice.

After a perfunctory offer of sympathy to Joe, Cray had gone to town on the old man for not having reported Charlotte's disappearance.

"You got a whole police force at your dispoal, Mr. Elevel, and you go with one man. A nobody with a piece of paper says he's some kind of official bill collector. We got the best-equipped police force in the country. If we'd been informed we'd have checked your daughter's school file first thing. Every patrolman would've had her license plate. We would have picked up that MG in a few hours. Cops drive by this house all day long. Who hired this Stackman character?"

"I don't know." Joe sat stony-faced. He was hardly listening. Someone from the Medical Examiner's Unit had given him a sedative so powerful that his voice sounded like a slowed-down record.

"Stackman was even dumber than your fella." Cray jabbed a thumb in my direction. "Stackman did nothing but follow your fellah around all day. If it hadn't been for the lady at the Academy your fellah would still be trying to hitch a ride up to the scene of the crime." Cray paused to light a cigarette and blew smoke over Joe. "Anything like this ever happens again, Mr. Elevel—God forbid—you make sure you call us."

Cray gripped my arm and led me into the bedroom.

"Okay, meatball," he said, "I got everyone's statements and it don't add up. Who do you think hired Stackman? Was Elevel double-checking you?"

"I don't know. I don't think so."

"You don't think, so we'll forget that. I got two names, Luis Coronado and Gervano. I got eighteen thousand cash missing. I got a bonafide suicide and a daughter who runs off with something and is so involved trying to kill herself she probably don't ever see the guy come in. The something ain't here. It don't make a lot of sense. If these greasers were putting the squeeze on Mrs. Elevel, what's the big rush to get the something back? She's dead."

I didn't say anything.

"So this little something still involves someone else. It's still a hot piece of merchandise and the squeeze's got to continue."

"Not necessarily," I said. "If it was incriminating photos, for instance, Coronado might have wanted them back. The blackmail might be over but he might have been afraid the photos would be traced back to him."

Cray grunted unhappily. He wasn't the type to acknowledge an intelligent remark. He was just willing to refrain from insulting you.

"Me, I'd like to take the whole fucking family down to the station, sit 'em down, and turn on the lamp."

"What's left of the family, you mean," I said.

He started to say something but was interrupted by the phone's ringing.

"Yeah, Captain Cray speaking." Held in his meaty hand, the receiver looked like something he was about to take a bite out of. His thin mouth curled impatiently as he listened. He had the kind of hard, wary face with cold, unflickering eyes you find on so many detectives, a face stamped with a savage stoicism. His job had taken him down some real shit holes and the anger and revulsion was almost palpable in all his gestures.

He was mad when he put the phone down.

"We got a sheet on Coronado. He runs some porn theaters in Hollywood and a few dirty bookstores. We ain't got enough of that scum in this city, we got to import more from Mexico."

"Are you going to pick him up?"

"No, we're going to give him a two-week vacation in Tahiti. Of course we're picking him up." He fixed me with eyes the color of ice-gray sludge. "Will the Mexican gardener identify him?"

"I think so."

"Big deal." He shrugged contemptuously. "A wet-back gardener thinks he saw Coronado talking to Mrs. Elevel in a parking lot two weeks ago. It isn't enough for an indictment. What I want is this guy Gervano but he don't make mistakes."

Two detectives came into the bedroom and reported that they had checked all the sewers and garbage cans in the vicinity but had found no sign of the murder weapon.

"Your hands looked awfully clean," Cray said, "and neither of you stink."

"I just washed, chief," one of the detectives protested. "Honest. We went through them with a fine-tooth comb."

"Yeah, well, just check it all again. And don't just *look* in the garbage, stick your fucking hands in and feel around. You haven't got a single stain on your suit sleeves. Now get out of here."

"They'll never find it," Cray snorted. "I've seen hits like this before. Gervano used a stolen car and an untraceable weapon. He's a pro. He don't go around dropping off presents for us in garbage cans." He looked at me, daring me to say it. "That's right, Mr. Wise Guy." He smiled. "I know it, and they know it, but I still got to send 'em back out there. You want to know why?"

"Sure." I smiled. "Why?"

"Because once, years ago, I was wrong. It was a professional hit like this one, only the victim was shot with a high-powered rifle. We didn't bother to look very hard for the murder weapon. The next day a kid found it lying in the street right in front of the house. It had been lying under my squad car. I lost a promotion on account of that. The other reason I make those lazy fucks go out there is because a hard-nosed fuckhead of a captain made *me* do it. But mainly it's because I like giving people a hard time."

"If Coronado is Gervano," I said, "the girl from the Academy can identify him. His fingertips are still healing. They leave special marks."

"I told you from Coronado's rap sheet—we already know he ain't the same guy." He looked at me and smiled ferociously. "Don't play too dumb with me, pal. I know you're dumb but you ain't that dumb."

I shrugged. "I haven't slept for thirty-six hours."

"I ain't slept for twenty-two years," he scoffed.

"You afraid of nightmares or something?"

"The only nightmares I got, I give to guys like you." He pushed his face into mine. "Tonight I'm going to the Elevel dump and getting statements from everyone. If I find out you're withholding anything from me I'm going to shit on your license."

The phone rang again. He picked it up and listened with his eyes nearly shut, concentrating. Then without saying a word he gently replaced the receiver.

"I'm off the case," he said. "Your Mr. Elevel has had me yanked. I got a living room full of his crappy furniture and none of it's paid for yet. They must have thought it would influence my investigation."

Lucy was serving coffee to Joe and Calvin in the kitchen when we came out. Perhaps a dozen police officers were still at work in the living room. Captain Cray's manner now showed a frigid restraint as he informed Joe that Deputy Chief Granville would be conducting any further investigations into his daughter's homicide.

"I said some rough things about your fellah." Cray gestured toward me. "He found your daughter in six hours. That ain't bad. If he'd found her earlier he'd probably be dead. He's also been getting some help from another detective service, White and Rinehart.

They don't come any better. Right now, frankly speaking, we ain't got no leads. If Kyd here has any, and I think he has, he ain't talking. Deputy Chief Granville, my replacement, ain't going to have any leads ever unless you mail them to him with a notarized letter saying your feelings won't be hurt if he follows them up." He took them all in with his eyes, turned sharply on his heel, and walked out.

I followed Cray to the door and thanked him for the plug.

"I don't like you." He jammed his notebook into his pocket. "I like that cocksucker Granville even less. That's all it was, Kyd. I'm just one more guy using you."

"You calling me a whore, captain?" I said it as friendly as possible because Cray looked as if he were made out of steel plate.

"You peepers are worse than whores." He lit a cigarette and let the smoke slant across his hooded eyes. "People don't pay you to do things *for* them. They pay you to do things *to* other people." He shook his head in disgust. "The only good thing about a peeper is that he works alone. If he fucks up, it's all his fault. Like you." He grinned, "You fucked up. You ain't got no assistant sales manager or sergeant to lay it off on. Now you got to go back in there and kiss ass and hope Elevel keeps you on at a hundred a day. Shit, you're worse than a whore. You're dumb."

"It's known as sour grapes, captain. A Joe Elevel doesn't like the sound of your voice and you're lifted like a chess piece and dropped down somewhere else. You're probably a good cop but you don't know how to talk to people."

"I could break you," he said. "I could run you in and there'd be animals playing chopsticks on your kidneys all night, and in the morning we'd let you go. You wouldn't have a mark on you. But you'd piss blood for years."

"It wouldn't put you back on the case."

"What case?" he sneered. "Gervano's a ghost. You'll never collar Gervano. And Coronado is clean. He has Beverly Hills Jew lawyers to do his laundry. It's straight blackmail. Coronado got something on the Elevels. When this girl ran off and it looked like it was going to pop, Coronado hires a Mexican mechanic to hit her."

"Maybe," I said.

"Tomorrow Deputy Chief Granville will give you a call." Cray contemptuously stubbed out his cigarette against the door jamb. "Granville's a career cop. He plays golf with the right people. Granville will want to know if Elevel still wants you on the case. If he does, by the time Granville is through with you, you're going to feel like you got licked all over by a dinosaur with a warm tongue. Granville's going to pick up Coronado and question him but there's no charge. And by then there'll be Jew boy lawyers coming out of the walls and they'll have to let him go."

"You got something against Jews?" I said.

"I got something against everyone, asshole." Cray seemed to draw a faded pleasure from the idea of his own fierceness. "And for bugs like Coronado I only got one message. But it don't matter because the way things are rigged I can't touch him."

"I could touch him."

"What's on your mind, meatball?"

"How'd you like to solve the case under Granville's nose?"

He looked at me very slowly with his cold gray eyes, and then his eyebrows arched in a very artful way. "Sure." He started moving toward his car. "Call me when you got it all tied up. All the evidence air-tight, money-tight, legal-tight. Call me then and I'll be glad to make the collar. But don't ask me to stick my neck out."

I wanted to tell him that strictly speaking, he didn't even have a neck but I left it. It was too bad he'd been pulled. He was an ugly, tenacious cop who must have had quite a service record to make captain; he hadn't done it through cultivating political and social connections, that was for sure.

Chapter NINE

I'd been retained to find a missing person, and that part of the case was over. Now was probably the moment to call it a day and leave the rest to the police. Most of my business centered around civil actions, and I didn't have the kind of authority and muscle you need to punch a hole in Coronado's type of organization.

I stayed out on the street for a moment, thinking about it. A jasmine plant in a nearby garden was pumping the hot night air full of an almost alcoholic sweetness. A killing is always lousy but this one had left a very bad taste in my mouth. If I'd checked Charlotte's school file first thing instead of flirting with Lucy I would have arrived before Gervano. Also there was something particularly repulsive about the way the victims had been murdered. This kind of rubout was reserved for criminals. A hit man executing a girl like Charlotte was like a professional boxer punching a small child to death.

Maybe the killer was a cool technician, flawless at his work, but I didn't believe you could stomach that kind of work without also being a cheap sadist with a lot of screws missing. And that kind of person makes mistakes.

In the end I didn't know what my real motive was for sticking to the Elevel case. Maybe I'd lost my self-respect doing so much divorce work, work in which it didn't seem to matter which party you represented. Maybe I'd located too many missing people who should have been allowed a chance to get away, tracked down too many debtors for businesses and landlords whose profits were already too high. Maybe there wasn't a hell of a lot to my life anyway, and I felt I had nothing to lose. A psychopath had put himself out for hire, a guy who snuck up behind people and blew their heads open. I didn't like him. It was reason enough.

Back inside the house I took one look at Joe and realized he wasn't in any condition to make decisions. I motioned Calvin aside and fed him a line to keep myself on the case, intimating that I'd discovered some leads which the police weren't ever going to be able to follow up.

He bared his crooked teeth in a thin smile.

"Like what?" he said.

"When I tell Mr. Elevel I guess he'll tell you."

"Sure," he said. "What do you make a day, Kyd?"

"Oh, a hundred a day and expenses. I cheat a little on mileage toward the end of the month."

"You probably do," he said with friendly contempt. "You go ahead and follow up your secret leads. Right now you're the least of our worries."

With Joe knocked out of action Calvin was starting to flex his muscles. The sanctimonious act had been put on the shelf and some of the concealed toughness was coming through. It had been Calvin who'd put in the fix and had Captain Cray dropped from the case. There weren't going to be any cops asking any questions at the Elevel place tonight. It had been Calvin who'd arranged for someone from the medical unit to sedate Joe. The old man had chosen well. He'd found a fixer from the gutter and put him in Gucci shoes, and the fixer was playing the Elevel influence like an organ pipe.

Lucy drove me back to the Academy parking lot to pick up my car. She didn't think detective work was so exciting any more. Once we got on Sunset she started to tremble and then she pulled off the road and burst into tears. All I could do was hold her until the storm of emotion played itself out. Everyone's reaction to death is different. At the time I couldn't feel anything but this frozen numbness familiar from the war. There wasn't a word or a gesture that could relieve it. Like a man lying down in a blizzard to die, I just didn't care. When she stopped sobbing I snapped on the dashboard light and studied the blank sheet of paper from Charlotte's pad. Most of the imprints were illegible without a magnifying glass but I could see the letter had been written to a Mrs. Kramer.

"Who's Mrs. Kramer?" I asked.

Her face was puffed and wet with tears, and from its expression I could see she thought I was an insensitive bastard.

"I guess you see that kind of thing all the time." She pulled herself together.

"You only have to see it once."

"There is something about you"— she chose her words carefully—"a little too mechanical, a little too cold. I watched you in there. I think they left something out when they made you." She put the car into gear and accelerated back onto the road.

After a moment I put my hand on her knee but she firmly removed it.

"I'm fine now. With me a little hysteria goes a long way." She gave me a brittle smile and then pointedly ignored me. Great.

"If it wasn't your car," I said, "I'd tell you to get out and find a taxi."

"I believe it."

"I've been insulted, beat up. I broke a kid's hands today, and I found two dead people. A hundred bucks doesn't really cover that kind of action. I don't need you telling me I'm a heartless son of a bitch on top of it."

I let her chew on that awhile and then I said, "Do I have to cry when you cry? Do I have to cry exactly the same way?"

"How do you cry, Kyd? Just out of curiosity."

"With my teeth when I'm asleep. I gnash my teeth and groan. I'll send you a chewed-up pillowcase to prove it."

"Okay, you've made your point," she said. "You just scared me. You seemed very remote back there."

"Let's forget it." I put my hand back on her knee. "The reason I scared you was because whoever hit Charlotte and Stackman scared me. I'm thinking, for instance, that you're the only material witness who can identify Gervano."

"Now you are scaring me!" She shot me a glance.

"Do you live by yourself?" I asked.

"I'm staying at my mother's until I can find an apartment but Mother's in Reno."

When we got to the Academy I gave her my front door key and told her it might be safer for her to spend the night at my place. I was living that year in a bungalow behind an unrented main house at the very end of Bundy Drive. I told her there was a studio couch and sheets in the cupboard and a bottle of gin, half full under the bed, and if she spoke kindly to it, the TV might work. It disturbed me that the police hadn't bothered to provide protection for their only real witness. It also seemed a little strange how readily she agreed to hide out at my place. She must have had other friends.

We said goodby in the dark parking lot behind the Academy. I wasn't planning on kissing her but suddenly she nestled against my chest and the beautiful tone and scent of her body hit me like a wave. I didn't understand her. We hardly knew each other, and a moment before she'd been revolted by my cold-blooded attitude. Now she was grinding herself against me. I didn't know whether to be happy or suspicious, whether she was beautiful or dangerous.

For a moment or so I didn't care if she was Lucretia Borgia. She was long-legged and pale and lovely and I wanted her, in the back of my car, in her empty office, or right there on the ground of the parking lot. Finally she gripped my wrists, gave me a long lingering kiss, and pushed herself free.

Before I could do anything she was in her car again,

blowing me a kiss as she drove out of the parking lot.

I straightened my clothes and walked slowly back to my car. The smell of her perfume clung to me, and I felt as dazed as a sixteen-year-old. I couldn't believe my own reactions. At this rate I'd be sending her flowers next and tap-dancing in the gutter like Gene Kelly in *Singin' in the Rain*.

I put the distributor cap back on and started up my car. And then a little voice whispered that things like that kiss just didn't happen, and I ought to look elsewhere for an explanation of Lucy's behavior. Probably the shock of the murder had triggered her reaction; she was unconsciously trying to reaffirm something that had been threatened by the sight of Charlotte Elevel. She'd needed someone and I happened to be right there. Or, I reminded myself, maybe I'd been in the wrong business too long, had become so complex in my cynicism that I could no longer recognize a genuine gesture of desire.

Chapter TEN

Harry was behind his desk in the basement of the phone company offices on Wilshire. He was stoned on grass, as usual, and was beginning to hit his normal stride now that the sun had gone down. His desk was covered with a messy assortment of Chinese takeout food, empty beer bottles, and computer printouts. The phone company made Harry wear a suit to work but he could make a suit look like a stained tablecloth from a sleazy restaurant in about ten minutes. He was one of the few people I knew who could function accurately on half a lid of grass a day. He worked in eighteen-hour stretches and went through a six-pack of beer every four hours. The phone company paid him a lot of money as a data processing consultant, and did its best to overlook his straggly beard, his ponytail, and the smell of dope and incense clouding his office.

The preliminary work on the Elevels' phone bills had already been done, and Harry provided a list of names and addresses to fit the toll call numbers dialed from the house. Without being asked to, he had also made a list of the numbers which overlapped. There were seven separate phones in the house, four private and three business numbers. I took out Charlotte's and Mrs. Elevel's address books and checked them against the phone bills. It took about an hour to sort the numbers into three groups. There were calls to friends; to business premises like restaurants, dry cleaners, and garages; and to people who didn't appear in either address book. This last group interested me. Twice Mrs. Elevel had called the All Rite All Nite Book Store on Hollywood near Vermont, a sex-shop marital-aid joint which I guessed belonged to Luis Coronado. Also, Mrs. Elevel had called Dr. Lester's office and then his home on the evening she killed herself. I wondered what they had had to talk about. If she had intended to be dead in a few hours the subject wasn't likely to have been her health.

Computers have to be asked the right questions. We asked the phone company computer a lot of questions but the answers didn't mean much. There were too many numbers, too many potential cross-references to investigate even a fraction of them. The most important lead might be any one of a hundred couples listed in Mrs. Elevel's address book. Or perhaps the most revealing calls had been local ones, which didn't appear on the bills.

After a while I asked Harry to pull Luis Coronado's bills for his home in Brentwood and his Hollywood bookstore. No calls had been placed from either of them to any of the Elevel numbers.

It was the kind of slow, uninspiring work that most detection jobs come down to. Finally I asked Harry to run all the Elevel and Coronado numbers through the computer and see if any overlapped. This time the computer paid off like a fruit machine: in the last hour a call had been placed from Coronado's store to Dr. Lester's home number.

"People use pay phones, too, you know," Harry said.

"They get careless, too, like this one." I looked at the strip of white tickertape with Dr. Lester's number on it. What was a woman of Mrs. Elevel's position doing phoning a porn bookstore? And what was a hood like Coronado doing phoning Dr. Lester an hour after Charlotte's murder? There was a web gradually taking shape in my mind; it held two victims but as yet no spider.

"You know—" Harry guzzled from his beer bottle— "this is all strictly queer. You can't use it as evidence. The only thing it's good for is getting me fired, and making people miserable. By that I mean I got a friend who thought his old lady was cheating on him but he doesn't know who. He can't afford to hire a guy like you, so instead he comes down here with a list of all his friends and finds out that two of them call her every day while he's at work. Now he's unhappy. His friends are unhappy. His old lady's unhappy."

"That gives me an idea," I said. "Run a check on this girl Lucy Flannery." I waited impatiently while Harry tested out Lucy's home number against those of the Elevels, Dr. Lester, and Coronado. In the past three months a dozen calls had been made between Lucy Flannery and Charlotte Elevel, which pretty much fit Lucy's interpretation of their relationship. However, there was nothing on the phone company records to indicate any connection between Lucy and Dr. Lester or Coronado, which was a relief.

"How soon after a call is made does it show up in the computer?" I asked Harry.

"The second you put the phone down."

"Try my number. I've got a girl staying there and I want to know if she's talking to anyone."

"It's your funeral." He typed out the question on the keyboard and then handed me the piece of tickertape. An hour ago Lucy had made a collect call to Reno, Nevada, to someone at the Desert Inn. She had also phoned Calvin Moonhurst's bungalow and then the main house.

"This girl a suspect?" Harry asked.

"More like an object of my paranoia."

"So why are you keeping me up half the night running checks on her?"

"I don't know. When very good things happen it makes me nervous. This girl seems to like me."

"I see what you mean." Harry ran his fingers through his beard. "There must be something wrong with her."

"She's at my place now."

"Wow, a real live girl in your place. I didn't even know you lived somewhere. I thought you slept in all-night movies and laundries, Thomas."

"She's waiting for me."

"And you're in a basement miles away checking up on her. Tell me, Thomas, do you take their fingerprints before you let them touch you?"

"She's nice, Harry."

Harry stuffed a forkful of pork chow mein into his mouth, chased it with a gulp of Carta Blanca, and smiled through the resulting mess. "What's she look like, Thomas?" He eyed me craftily.

"You're wrong," I said. "She doesn't look like her at all." He was referring to my late wife.

"Get out of here, why don't you." He waved his beer bottle. "You got a house, a girl waiting. Next thing you'll tell me you're a human being with needs and feelings."

Chapter ELEVEN

Overhead the sky was a low, radiant blur, mirroring the lights of the city. No moon or stars were visible. There was only this blank but illuminated screen of smog, like a TV channel that had gone off the air. It looked as if dawn were about to break. It would look like that all night long.

As I drove up Bundy Drive the sky got slightly darker and the hum of the city receded. It was quiet at the end of the street, where my house was. The slopes of the hills gave off a dry breath of sage and dust faintly touched by the cool, medicinal scent of eucalyptus.

I parked and got out and listened until I could detect the dim but massive hum coming from the dark hills. People say the city never sleeps but neither do the hills.

Out of the corner of my eye I saw a shadow moving, and I stood still. An instant later there was a warm furry presence twining itself around my foot, and making insistent pleading noises that reminded me guiltily that he had not been fed since yesterday. He was a strange cat and only mine in a limited sense. Periodically he disappeared for weeks at a time, to return looking surprisingly fat and well-groomed. I suspected he was like one of those men who has different wives and families on opposite sides of a city. His other owner obviously fed and groomed him well, gave him his shots, and supplied him with flea collars. Still, the cat insisted on slumming with me for at least two weeks out of every month, proudly depositing his daily catch of lizards, mice, and birds at the foot of my bed every morning, and waking me by sitting on my face so that I couldn't breathe.

His name was Two Timer and he escorted me to the

door, rubbing his head against my ankle. I knew this was a cat's way of signing his name to people and things. A little gland between the eye and ear secretes a private scent which they like to spread around as widely as possible. By the time I reached the front door any other cat would have known who I belonged to.

I let myself in quietly with the spare key buried in the flower pot. There was a small light on in the living room but the studio couch was empty. I could see Lucy lying fully clothed on my bed in the recessed alcove. She was sound asleep.

I fed Two Timer, then went into the bathroom and showered. The hot spray was so soothing on my neck that I nearly fell asleep on my feet. I had that limp, tranquil feeling that sometimes comes with deep fatigue. I got into a bathrobe and went back into the living room and made up the studio couch for myself. I didn't really know what to do about Miss Lucy Jean Flannery lying on my bed with her skirt up around her thighs. She was a material witness in an important murder case. She was there because she needed protective custody. On the other hand, she had very pretty legs, and in repose, her face had a flawless, haunting innocence that hurt me in the chest to look at. I was like a man trying to walk simultaneously in opposite directions. I'd quite earnestly made up the studio couch with a firm intention of sleeping on it alone, but in the bathroom I'd carefully shaved, something I don't do before crashing out.

I lay back on the studio couch and thought about the case. Was Joe Elevel holding out on me? Had he hired Stackman? Had Charlotte taken something from her mother's safe that somehow implicated Joe? Was Lucy Flannery involved somewhere? Was she a great lay? Would she find my slight paunch and the mat of black hair on my chest offensive? In bed did she come on like a tigress, or a clubbed fish? Was there as much eroticism inside her as there was floating seductively on the surface? Most of all, what in hell was she doing phoning Calvin?

Lucy stirred drowsily and then pulled herself up, straightening her skirt.

"What are you doing?" she asked.

"Watching you."

"Oh." She nodded as if that made everything clear. "It's nice here. Quiet." She reached for her purse. "I snooped a bit. Do you mind? I thought I ought to tell you in case you dusted the place for prints."

"Very funny. Did you find anything interesting?"

"Oh, there's not much I don't know about you." She lit her Pall Mall and gave me a deadpan look that was more Humphrey Bogart than Lauren Bacall. "I washed the dishes as penance for being so nosy. I'd say, and this is just a rough guess, that about two weeks ago you had pot roast. We'll have to wait for the lab boys to run a check on it. The library was revealing too. An extensive survey of the suspect's books revealed four copies of *Crime and Punishment,* all stolen from different libraries. And you haven't bought a record in at least four years. And you steal towels from hotels. And you keep a box with hash and pills in it under your bed."

"Go on," I said.

"You don't mind dirt but only in certain places. Like the kitchen is awful but the bathroom's spotless. The curtains are filthy but the sheets and towels are clean. You seem to drink a lot of gin. Mainly alone, I'd say. There are some women's clothes hanging in the closet but since there aren't any other signs of a woman in the place, I presume they belong to someone who no longer lives here, or else you wear them, in which case I've been, as they say, sorely abused." She smiled.

"And?" I said.

"It would seem you are either a dipsomaniac transvestite or else a divorced man with a preference for gin and your own company."

Her last remark hung in the air with the finality of a challenge, or at least something that demanded an answer.

"You have the makings of a real detective," I said.

"Or a bitch." She laughed. "Isn't that what you were thinking?"

"No, I was thinking, why would a girl like you call Calvin Moonhurst?"

She flushed angrily. Then said coldly, "Have you been hiding outside the window or something?"

"I just got back. But I'm right though, aren't I? You did phone Calvin."

"Of all the preposterous . . . ! What if I did? And how do you know I did?"

"And your mother too, in Reno, collect to the Desert Inn."

"My God!" She wriggled her shoulders in disdain. "I can't stand this. How do you know that?"

"I was at the phone company. The calls were toll calls so they registered on the computer."

"Am I a suspect?" She was blinking her eyelashes in a rather defensive imitation of a vamp. "I must be or you wouldn't have checked up on me. Well, I'm very flattered. Are you going to slap me around? Do I get the third degree?"

"You get a glass of gin if you like it. Otherwise there's milk." I stood up. "Probably pretty old milk."

"Gin please." She frowned. "With ice."

When I came back from the kitchen with the drinks, I noticed she'd freshened her lipstick and the smell of her eau de cologne hung lightly on the air. She put down the book which I had a feeling she'd picked up about two seconds before I entered the room. I liked her.

"I'm not sure," she said, "whether this is very exciting or damned insulting. I called Calvin because I wanted to know how Mr. Elevel was. I was probably the closest thing to a girlfriend Charlotte had. I wanted to tell them that if I could do anything to help, they should call on me. I hope that satisfies you."

"I was never dissatisifed. Only curious. I thought it was possible you had eyes for Calvin. No, I *didn't* think it was possible. That's probably why I asked. The phone call puzzled me. I should have guessed it was a formal call."

She sipped experimentally at her drink and said, "This detective business isn't just a job with you. It's a permanent state of mind."

"I've always been suspicious. I was suspicious as a kid."

"You were a kid?" She pretended amazement. "Are you sure?"

"Look, maybe it amuses you to pretend I'm some kind of robot. But you're way off base. I'm thirty-three years old. My wife is dead and I have a private business that brings in enough to keep me in clean underwear. I live alone. I'm not tough but I'll kill a man if he tries to act like an animal to me, which is to say, if he tries to kill me. If I'm suspicious, I'm not suspicious enough, because people are always susprising me. I've seen little kids in Vietnam, seven- and eight-year-olds, attack and kill old people for their clothes, so they could sell them. I've worked on a case where a man who'd lived fifty-three years with the same woman blew her brains out because he was tired of the way she fried eggs. I live alone because I want to and I drink because I'm weak and because I like to feel good even though I'm not very good. And one way I make up for that is by being careful about my work, by forcing myself to question things that seem fine, or respectable, or lovely, like you. But the main thing is that I don't make speeches. Ever."

"You should try it more often." She set her drink down on the bedside table and said, "You weren't listening in on those calls, were you? I mean, you didn't hear what was said."

"No."

"That's good." She laughed uproariously with a kind of spontaneous bawdiness that reminded me of a schoolgirl telling a dirty joke.

I couldn't think of an answer to her laughter but I assumed she'd discussed me with her mother in some private female way. After a while she asked me if I could do something about the light because it was shining in her eyes. So I turned it off. We sat in silence in the dark, she on the bed, me on the studio couch, sensing each other across the ten feet of black smoky air. It seemed an exciting, promising silence, a tense, mysterious darkness. It also seemed childish and obvious and maybe for that reason appealing.

I got up and walked into the alcove and sat down beside her on the bed. She drew herself up and rested her hands around my neck. I reached around her back and loosened the knot of her halter and her breasts came free. I touched them slowly and softly and her body shivered like something delicate in the wind. We sat for a moment trying to read each other's faces in the dark. Her breasts were taut and heavy in my hands and the nipples stood out with desire. She opened my robe and slipped it off my shoulders and then ran her hand down my chest. I found the snap on her skirt, unwrapped it, and rolled off her underpants. She was naked under me, and there was nothing delicate left about her.

It was very violent for both of us the first time, like a long-delayed explosion. There was no thought or technique, just a crazy, frenzied friction of two nervous systems going for broke.

It was protracted and tender the second time and righter than it had been for a long while. It went on through tenderness into something hotter and more consciously carnal. She whispered some barely coherent things in my ear, and we took time to explore some luxurious forbidden deeps. It was a sweet savage ride all the way, and when we got there a lot of lights went on and off, and a wave crashed through my body that left me stunned and gasping. I'd forgotten what it felt like to be thrown that way, and after a while I wanted to find out again.

I didn't sleep a whole lot that night. I wasn't as tired or cold-blooded as I had thought I was. I fell asleep liking her, and I still liked her in the morning.

Chapter TWELVE

There was a nervous neatness about her that reminded me of a cat constantly grooming itself. She was already up and had showered, washed her hair, and made up by the time I got out of bed. A pot of hot coffee was waiting on the coffee table with some toast and marmalade, and my clothes were on a hanger over the kitchen door.

The call from Deputy Chief Granville came midway through my second cup of coffee. He had a suave headwaiter's voice that you felt could develop a cutting edge without much provocation. But he was reasonably polite to me, which meant I still rated some special consideration for having a client worth twenty million dollars.

Granville had done more or less exactly what Captain Cray had predicted last night. Coronado had been picked up for questioning but his alibi couldn't have been better; at the time of Charlotte's murder he'd been in a judge's chambers working out a lawsuit against one of his book distributors. Pedro, the Elevel gardener, had made a positive identification which was practically useless without corroborating evidence.

Granville then informed me I had to hand over the personal effects I'd taken from Charlotte's and Mrs. Elevel's purses.

I didn't know how long Granville intended to play nice with me so I pumped him for all I could get. He didn't have a lot to say about Harlan Stackman, and what he did say depressed me.

"The guy was an old hack," Granville said, "a loser who scratched small change from finding missing parakeets for old ladies. We got his IRS file. He made so little the last few years he was eligible for welfare. He didn't even have an office. He worked out of the cafeteria across the street from his boarding house. He's got an ex-wife in Utah and we'll try and contact her. The guy was a lush, a deadbeat who probably spent his whole life looking for people who'd moved." There was a pause on the line. Then he continued, "Right now we're hauling in everyone with an MO like Gervano's and making inquiries."

I liked that phrase "making inquiries." There were probably a dozen underworld contacts having inquiries made of them at that very moment—small-fry grafters, fringe boys, runners, anyone the police felt they could lean on for information. If enough ribs were bruised, enough teeth loosened, if someone wanted to sing to beat a rap of his own, a lead might get beaten into the open. It was going to be a long day for some people.

"By the way," Granville said, "I looked you up. It looks like you do clean work."

"Thank you."

"You've also got an outstanding citation on a faulty muffler from the Highway Patrol."

"I'll take care of it right away, chief."

"It's already been taken care of," he said smoothly. "You play ball with us, Kyd, and we'll see you're treated right. I understand there was some difficulty with Captain Cray."

"Not to my knowledge."

"Oh." He sounded disappointed.

I felt I'd come a long way in the wrong direction when people like Granville thought they could make me a member of their club. I could see him on the golf course, promising important men he'd get their drunk-driving charges dropped.

"Incidentally," I said, "that girl from the Academy was afraid to go home last night so she stayed here. So far she's the only person who can link Gervano to the murders. What about putting her into protective custody?"

"Who is she?" He sounded annoyed.

"She's Rhona Flannery's daughter. Her father is something big in textiles. He throws a lot of donations into Republican campaigns. There's a lot of weight there which ought to be handled carefully. I just thought you ought to know that, chief. No offense, you understand."

"Right, yes. I was under the misapprehension that Captain Cray had taken the necessary precautions. Please convey my apologies to her."

"The chief says he's sorry," I mouthed deadpan to Lucy.

"I'll have an officer at the Academy in an hour."

"Thank you, chief. Have a good day." When I put the phone down, Lucy was looking at me strangely.

"You really know how to turn on the slime, don't you? My father's a stunt man at Paramount, not a textile mogul."

"You wouldn't have got the protection otherwise. This guy Gervano doesn't kid around and he knows you could finger him."

She looked dubious.

I said, "The back of your head isn't any harder than Charlotte Elevel's was."

"You're revolting." She shuddered.

"I want you to stick close to that cop."

"Well, I hope he's good-looking." She gathered up her things. "If I'm going to be sitting in his lap all day and having him hold my hand while I tinkle."

"Come here." I caught her hand and pulled her into my lap and kissed her. "You're nice," I said, "very nice." I kissed her some more. "I want to see you again. Alive."

She stood up, smoothed her skirt, and walked to the door. "I don't think that'll be a problem. You stay alive yourself." She blew me a kiss and was out the door.

From the instant I'd met her she'd shown a curious blend of forwardness and hostility. The kiss she'd blown me suggested affection but her words had come out as a taunt. I seemed to know more about her, and less, than I had last night.

I tried to put her out of my mind. I brewed some more coffee and took out the imprint of Charlotte's note. Using a magnifying glass and a very sharp pencil, I was able to fill in some of the words, but the pressure of Charlotte's pen had fluctuated as she wrote, and many words were missing.

> Dear Mrs. Kramer,
>   Why are you doing ——— or ——— to gain ——— misery from ——— a horrible thing. Do you ——— idea what ——— will do to them? How ——— ever think ——— . . .

It went on like that for fifteen lines, with no names mentioned except her parents' and no direct mention of what Mrs. Kramer was supposedly doing. Nor did I have an address for Mrs. Kramer. Her name wasn't in either Mrs. Elevel's address book or Charlotte's. The Western Section Los Angeles directory listed more than 150 Kramers.

The one person who seemed likely to know who Mrs. Kramer was, was Luis Coronado. I didn't really know what I was looking for when I left the house but I figured someone would warn me if I got too close.

Chapter **THIRTEEN**

The All Rite All Nite Book Store was a small place on Hollywood Boulevard squeezed between a pawn shop and a joint that called itself the Scandinavian Spa and Health Club. A photographer's studio called All Rite Photo took up the second story of the bookstore. I presumed you could do it in the health spa, read about it in the bookstore, and get pictures taken of it at the photographer's.

Across the street two guys in a sedan were parked in a LOADING ONLY zone. One was reading the funny papers and the other was drinking coffee out of a thermos. You could have dressed them both up in kangaroo outfits and stuck them on a Rose Bowl Parade float and they'd still have looked like undercover cops.

The saleswoman behind the cash register in the bookstore wore a red wig. She had monumental breasts that hung down like balloons filled with water, and a face like a Pekingese who has just lost the blue ribbon at the dog show. She was reading a movie magazine and picking the skin off her sunburned chest. Her lips moved as she read and possibly even moved when she looked at the pictures. In the rear of the store a heavily built man was poised halfway up a ladder, rearranging books.

"I think they're going to get back together again," the saleswoman said. "It's one of those fatal attractions. They can't escape no matter how hard they try."

"I don't know what you're talking about," the guy said.

"Taylor and Burton. I think she was crazy to leave him."

"Who cares?" the guy said. "Taylor and Burton can drop dead."

"What's eating you?" The saleswoman shrugged.

"Help you, mister?" The guy climbed down and sidled up to me. He didn't look me in the eyes and his voice was pitched very soft. "Browse." He gestured expansively. "Look around. We got everything here."

I think he figured me for a shy customer afraid to ask for the particular book that would turn me into a frothing sex maniac. I beckoned him to the end of the store and asked him in an undertone if he had any books with young children in them.

"Sure, mister. We got a whole children's section."

"I mean real young," I said.

"You mean like *babies?*"

I swallowed a lump in my throat and lowered my voice to a haughty whine. "Yes, that's it. It's for a friend, you see. Isn't it peculiar what people like?"

"You want with pictures, or drawings, or both, or just like a book you read?" He might have been asking me what I wanted on my pastrami sandwich.

"The latter," I said. "I think."

"Which?"

"The book. Just the book. My friend likes stories."

"Sure he does." He climbed up the ladder and took down a white-jacketed volume in a cellophane wrapper. "It's very well written." He tapped it. "Translated from the French. One of our best-selling items."

I took the book and examined it hungrily.

"Sorry, you can't open it. But we guarantee the contents. You friend hasn't got any problem there. It's all guaranteed. It's twenty dollars, mister. We take Master Charge, BankAmericard, American Express, and plain old cash."

The back door opened and a slim, beautifully dressed Latin man emerged. He wore a pale gray English-cut suit, a pin-striped blue shirt, and a blue silk tie. His skin, faintly pitted with smallpox scars, was the color of

pale milk chocolate. He was good-looking in an unhealthy way. He was the kind of guy I disliked on sight
but I knew from experience that women would always fall
for him. He glanced sharply at me, once, then walked
over to the cash register and took out a handful of bills.

"Count them," he said to the saleswoman.

"A hundred and eleven, Mr. Coronado."

He slipped the money into his outside pocket and
looked coldly at the saleswoman's peeling chest.

"I got sunburned something awful from falling asleep
on the beach. You oughta see my legs."

"Go upstairs and tell Art I want four hundred cash
now," Coronado said quietly.

"What'd ya say, mister?" The salesman resumed his
pitch. "Is this the kind of thing your friend's looking
for?"

"Can't I just glance at the inside?"

"Sorry. Store policy. Otherwise we've got members of
the public living in the store and they mess up the
books. You know, they got dirty hands and the pages
get soiled. I'm not saying you've got dirty hands. It's
just a lot of guys want a free read, and that ain't the
business we're in."

"I think I'll take it," I said. "But show me some of
the other stuff, too." I kept him busy climbing up and
down his ladder until the saleswoman came back. She
handed Coronado an envelope. I wondered what he
wanted that much cash for. Wouldn't someone like him
use credit cards for most purchases, or did he like to
flash a big roll? He looked spruce and unworried;
Granville's detectives hadn't laid a hand on him, as far
as I could see.

"I'll be at the track," Coronado said. "If those bulls
across the street give you any trouble, call my lawyer."

He walked out of the store and stepped into a yellow
Porsche Carrera coupe waiting at the curb.

"Gee," I said, "is that guy a movie star or something?"

"You kidding?" The salesman sniffed. "He owns the place. Five hundred clams is nothing to him. He'll put a grand on a horse. And if he loses, he laughs. That's class. We're a chain, see. There's six stores like this one, same books, same color scheme, same everything."

I wondered if Coronado's five other bookstores each had a replica of this guy serving the customers.

"For two fifty more," the saleswoman said as I paid her for the book, "I can throw in a discount card for our chain of cinema theaters."

"I like to read."

"Oh yeah? I know what you mean. Movies, I can take 'em or leave 'em."

"Give the man his change, Arlene." The salesman watched her count out the change into my hand, then he handed me the book. As I left the store, he called after me, "You know where we are now, mister. Don't be a stranger."

I returned to my car and sat in it. I hadn't learned anything new except that Coronado gambled heavily and Granville had put two apprentice morons on his tail.

I slit open the book I'd bought, read the first paragraph, and threw it out the window. I opened my notebook and listed it under expenses—Dog Vomit: $21.69—with the receipt.

I glanced again at Mrs. Elevel's suicide note and compared it to Charlotte's letter. What the hell had they both been so upset about? Since Coronado owned a photo studio, perhaps he'd got hold of some compromising pictures of the mother or daughter. But was that worth taking an overdose? I just couldn't see either Charlotte or her mother steaming up a camera lens. But then, I had never felt happy with the sexual angle on either of them. For all I knew, Coronado might have eight-by-ten glossies of mother and daughter taking on the Los Angeles Rams and half the occupants of the San Diego zoo. Who could tell? If the whole thing came down to a sexual escapade that mother and daughter wanted to suppress, then it had to be one so awful that they both reached for the pill bottle. But why did someone else want Charlotte dead?

I was getting nowhere sitting in my baking car. In fact, I knew considerably less than I'd imagined I knew last night. For instance, Gervano. I'd assumed Gervano was working for Coronado but there wasn't any evidence of that. They were both Mexicans, but as far as I could see, Coronado wouldn't want to kill Charlotte so why would he hire Gervano?

The only person who'd even seen Gervano was Lucy. There was no proof that it had been Gervano who went from the Academy to Benedict Canyon. Did Gervano, or whoever the killer was, even know Harlan Stackman? It was possible that three strangers had converged in that Benedict Canyon living room.

The only certain thing was the actual murders. Everything pointed to their being a contract job by a professional, an anonymous killer who was no more than a tool wielded by someone else. Similarly, Harlan Stackman, as a private investigator, was a tool employed by an unknown client. So that suggested there were two separate and conflicting parties, both using representatives, with an interest in Charlotte Elevel. And I was the third representative, with Joe as the interested party.

What in hell was everyone so interested in? What could make an outside party want to get rid of Charlotte and simultaneously make Charlotte want to kill herself?

You can't win a game of chess by just sitting there thinking about it; at some point you have to pick up a piece and play. I didn't have the kind of intellect necessary to make headway on a case by reflecting on it. I got leads by threatening and baiting and generally making a nuisance of myself. It was just that I had a sneaking suspicion my hard-guy act wouldn't set very many knees knocking in Coronado's mob.

I unstrapped my gun, wrapped it in a windshield rag, and locked it in the trunk. On the way back down the street I looked at myself in the shop windows and tried to rearrange the expression on my face. I wanted to look sly but essentially moronic. It was easy. By the time I got back to the bookstore I looked like the son of the couple inside.

There was a tiled staircase, hung with ferns and ivy, leading from the street up to the floor over the bookstore. Along the outside walls ran glass-paneled cases filled with publicity photos of minor nightclub acts: Priscilla and Her Python, Geza Droginov—the Hungarian Hypnotist, Felix Mangovani and the Jumping Beans, and fifty others.

At the top of the stairs there was a landing and two doors. One said Studio, the other Lounge. I went for the lounge. It was a small room tricked out with lots of mirrored tile to make it seem larger. There were a couple of pieces of suede and tubular steel furniture, a shag rug, and a large white ceramic ashtray filled with sand. A spread of girlie magazines lay fanned out on a steel-and-glass coffee table.

After a moment's wait, a brawny Italian came in and introduced himself as Art Grande (pronounced as in Randy). He was dressed in tight French jeans and high-heeled yellow sandals. A salad green silk shirt was open over his hairy chest and tied in a knot at the waist. His grip was crushing. He had thick, bristly hair and a liverish complexion. His eyebrows were black and tufted like horns over nearly yellow eyes. He had a big, agent's grin that had never been hooked up to the rest of his face, and his nostrils looked huge, as if he could blow out candles without even trying.

"So." He exhaled profoundly. "What can I do for you?"

"My name is Leo," I said, "Leo Kronenberger." It was the name of the author of the book I'd just bought downstairs. "My girlfriend sent me over to see if you could take some pictures of me. Sort of special pictures." I looked into his face. The hundred-watt agent's smile was burning brightly but his eyes were pitiless and flat, watching me.

"It's her idea," I continued hastily. "She's rich. She'll pay plenty for them."

"Why don't we go next door into the studio?" He held the door open for me and showed me into a large, very white room. The windows had been permanently sealed shut and the atmosphere was overly bright and airless. We sat down in canvas director's chairs that were placed a little too close for my liking.

"Special pictures," he said. "Nude shots?"

I laughed stupidly and nodded.

"That's no problem." He studied me carefully.

"The thing is—" I fumbled around for a cigarette. "She doesn't really want them of me. She wants pictures of us."

He frowned, and his eyes narrowed almost imperceptibly.

"Of her and me," I said, "together. Don't ask me why, but she does. And this is one little lady who's used to getting her way. And how!"

"Real rich, huh?" He nodded approvingly.

"Hey, listen, if you're worried about the bread, forget it. You ever hear of Lodi Star Petroleum Industries? That's her husband. He owns it."

"That's beautiful, man," he said. "When do you want the pictures taken?"

"Well, see, that's the problem, Art." I got my cigarette lit. "My girl would really go for these pictures of us but it would have to be discreet. Like I wouldn't even tell her we were being photographed." I looked at him closely. "D'you get what I mean?"

"Sure." He smiled blandly. "You want to surprise her."

"Yeah." I giggled nervously. "That's it. I want to surprise the bitch."

"How many pictures would you want?"

"A couple of rolls in color. But they've got to be clear. You've got to be able to tell it's her and me and see exactly what we're doing."

"Sure."

"I mean, we won't have any clothes on. You realize that. And we'll be . . . you know . . . we'll be moving around."

"You're talking about at least a thousand bucks." He shrugged. "At least that."

"Gee, that's more than I thought," I said, crestfallen. "Couldn't I pay you half of it after I get the pictures?"

"Hey, pal, a minute ago you said she was loaded."

"Oh, she's loaded all right," I said bitterly. "She's got so much money she doesn't know how to waste it fast enough. This broad buys houses the way I buy socks. But see, the pictures have got to be a surprise. I can't ask her for the thousand dollars until she's been surprised."

"I get you now." He looked pleased. "That makes sense."

"Now the other problem is taking the pictures," I said. "She's my girlfriend, right, but I work for her too. I'm the chauffeur. So a couple of times a week I take her out in the car and we go over to this motel on the beach. That's the only place you could get the pictures."

"Listen,"—he patted my arm—"it's a piece of cake. You come up with the five hundred dollars and we'll take care of the rest."

"Oh, I'll come up with it." I nodded sagely. "No sweat about that. Tomorrow I'll go to the bank, and the day after that we can do it." I got to my feet and then said casually, "By the way, I'll want copies made. Say three sets, plus the negatives."

He walked me to the door. "Call me when you're ready." He turned on the smile and this time his eyes joined in, glowing with interest and pleasure. He could have been looking at a stack of banknotes someone had dropped on the street.

"You bet I will." I walked out into the hallway and started descending the stairs. At the bottom I turned and looked back up at him.

"I'm looking forward to seeing the pictures, Art." I waved. "I hear from the Elevels you do very fine work."

Chapter **FOURTEEN**

Art Grande knew what I was talking about. I didn't. I was just guessing.

"Hey, where you going?" he called. "Come here. I wanna talk to you."

"Just tell Coronado that I dropped by and that his boy left something behind in Benedict Canyon. A very interesting something."

"Come here, pal. Hey!" He started coming down the stairs very slowly. "What's the rush? Come here—"

I ran down the street to my car, jumped in, and closed the windows and locked the doors. Grande was outside, trying the handles, and swearing a blue streak. I started the engine and then slid over to the passenger side and pointed down at the gutter.

As I pulled out, I could see him in the rear-view mirror, bending down to pick up the book. I would have paid $21.69 anytime to see the expression on his face.

The Elevel driveway was choked with cars, including an unmarked police car, and Charlotte's white MG. I parked near the front steps, started to go in, and then changed my mind and strolled over to the pool. A gnarled-looking older man in white tennis shorts was cleaning the pool tiles with a vacuum hose. He had the short base and thick trunk of a fighter. He looked tough.

"Hello there. Can I help you?" His voice had a smooth, educated cordiality to it. He turned off the vacuum pump and smiled warmly. Beneath the white hair on his chest I could make out a faded tattoo of a camel, and there was a knife scar on his stomach that had been made by someone who didn't make a living from practicing surgery. I told him who I was, and he got us some deck chairs and set them under an umbrella. Then he told me his life story.

His name was Stanley Roth. He'd been born fifty-five years ago in Brooklyn, made it halfway through college, and then enlisted in the navy. They'd made a fighter pilot of him and sent him to the Pacific Theater for the closing naval engagements of the war. He'd stayed on in Japan after the surrender, married a Japanese girl, and opened a restaurant in Tokyo. He'd lost his wife in a plane accident five years after they were married. He returned to New York, married again, and for a time ran a restaurant in Manhattan. When the '67 Israeli-Arab war broke out he was forty-nine; he'd immediately flown to Tel Aviv to enlist. He was a Jew. They hadn't needed him, and the war was over in six days, but he'd stayed on anyway. He sold everything and divorced his wife. After that he floated through Europe. In London he took a paramedic course for a year and gave karate lessons at various private schools. He studied art history in Paris and finally lost the remainder of his savings in an unsuccessful restaurant venture in Amsterdam. Down to his last six hundred dollars, he'd hit on the idea of coming west to California. He'd worked here in gas stations, bars, taco stands, and as a waiter at Chasen's, and had finally landed a job as the Elevel pool man.

Los Angeles is a city filled with people who are wildly out of context. Sometimes the mark of the true native is that Los Angeles is the last place you'd expect to find him.

For a man who'd come down in the world he seemed unfazed. He didn't appear to miss what he'd lost, but he didn't put down his past accomplishments either. Outer circumstances didn't seem to touch him at all. Listening to him talk in his polished, self-assured way, I kept having to remind myself that he wasn't the owner of his grandiose surroundings. Even dressed in nothing but

tennis shorts he had a physical composure and aristo-
cratic manner that belied his job. Joe Elevel, by comparison, would have looked well-suited to the job.

"I say I'm the pool man." Roth smiled. "Actually I'm
more the lionkeeper. In another age I'd be known as a
gentleman's gentleman, but Tyrone Elevel isn't a gentleman so I think of myself as his keeper, or his nurse, or
his companion. Companion isn't right either. Old
women have companions. Tyrone isn't an old woman."
He chuckled. "He's a young Attila the Hun."

"Minus the use of his legs?"

"Yes, from the waist down Tyrone's life is over. He
hasn't forgiven anyone for that. He was an athlete, a
high school star in half a dozen sports when it happened. All the big schools wanted him. If I were a religious man I'd say there was a curse on this family. Five
years ago a hit-and-run driver rammed Tyrone on his
motorcycle."

"You say 'rammed him.' Deliberately?"

"Tyrone says so."

"And that's when Dr. Lester started treating him?"

"No, Lester goes back a long way. Lester delivered
Tyrone. He was the family doctor when they lived in
Pasadena."

"How badly strung out is Tyrone?" I asked.

"You know about that." Roth looked troubled. "He
goes on binges, once, maybe twice a week. Cocaine and
speed. He's still an exceptional athlete and he takes his
body very seriously. He swims, he lifts weights, he prac-
tices karate."

"In a wheelchair?"

"He can get around on crutches alone. Not for long
distances, but he can get around. Also he has several
vehicles. A motorized wheelchair and dune-buggy go-
cart thing with special hand controls. He's in that
now." Roth gestured vaguely at the surrounding chaparral. "Somewhere up there. Proving something to himself. You ought to prepare yourself, by the way. He's

very aggressive with men, especially with men who look like they can handle themselves physically."

"Could Tyrone kill someone, say, in a rage?"

"I wouldn't like to say that. If he's wired up on speed, though, he could cause real damage. He's never in need of something to be sore about. One of the reasons the family hired me was because I could physically control him."

"Control him?" I said. "Do you mean he attacks you?"

"Regularly, Mr. Kyd." He laughed. "I told you I was the lionkeeper. Tyrone respects brute force. He can be as charming as you'd want and a second later literally at your throat. With me, fortunately, it's been refined down to a game. He roars but he rarely tries to bite. He'll intimidate anyone he can, and he's got the family and the rest of the staff pretty much terrorized. He believes everyone is plotting to have him committed, which isn't true at all. In fact, it's cost the family a small fortune to keep Tyrone *out* of an institution."

"Could you tell me something about that?"

"I think my predecessor sued the family for a broken collarbone received in the line of duty. But the major unpleasantness was nine months ago. Tyrone got very nerved up on speed and did something he's never done before or since. He drove his buggy into Beverly Hills and went into a bar on his crutches. It was a high-class leather bar. Tyrone took offense at the way someone was looking at him and fractured the man's cheekbone. People tried to restrain him and he broke other things too—teeth, fingers. Fingers and teeth and jaws are expensive items in Beverly Hills when it's the son of a multimillionaire who breaks them. There were a lot of damage suits settled out of court and a mess of assault charges, which I imagine cost something to get dropped."

"You've put together a pretty disturbing profile, Mr. Roth." I considered what he'd told me, and a lot of things made sense that hadn't before: Joe Elevel's anxiety to deal only with certain cops, for instance, and the family's silence about Tyrone's existence. It was only a guess, but I had a hunch Deputy Chief Granville had helped Joe get the assault charges against Tyrone dropped.

"Have the police questioned Tyrone or you?" I asked.

"Tyrone's place might as well be the house next door," he acknowledged. "We've had nothing."

"Where was Tyrone late yesterday afternoon?" I asked.

"Out there." Roth pointed to the hills.

"Would he be physically capable of taking a fire trail over the hills into Benedict Canyon and onto a paved road, then walking into a house and shooting two people with a twenty-two?"

"Emotionally he wouldn't."

"But it's physically possible."

"Physically Tyrone could climb a tree just using his arms." Roth smiled wearily. "If I thought it was possible I don't think I would have been so frank with you about Tyrone."

"What does that mean?"

"I'm not sure. I like Tyrone. He trusts me. I wouldn't like to be the one who—put it this way: I would never play a part in sending him to an institution or a prison."

"I appreciate that, Mr. Roth. I have no interest in harming Tyrone either. But two people are dead. I've barely scratched the surface of this case but it already looks like it goes very deep. There are all kinds of people involved. The way Tyrone's sister was killed was very slick, and it could happen again."

Roth looked thoughtful. His fingers played a light tattoo on his crossed arms.

"There's a Tao saying that fits what I've heard about that killing," Roth said. "When a virtuous task is perfectly performed, the one who performed it vanishes with its doing. It seems to apply to criminal tasks too."

Our conversation seemed to have taken a bizarre turn.

"The killer was very expert," I said. "He made one mistake though . . ."

"Yes?" Roth looked mildly interested.

"That's the thing about perfect crimes, especially murder. Some of the sickness that went into it is bound to rub off somewhere else. A killing makes a big echo."

"Are you trying to say that the act of murder hangs around the one who did it? Like an aura?" The idea seemed to amuse him.

"Put it this way. So-called perfect crimes depend for their success on the imperfections of the people investigating them. You can't make something perfect out of murder any more than you can make good wine out of sewer water."

"I see your point." Roth smiled. "A very moral way of looking at things. Well, I'd like to help you in any way I can."

"Can you tell me anything about Tyrone's relationship with his mother and sister?"

"It wasn't good with either of them. That doesn't mean very much, since Tyrone's relationships are uniformly lousy."

"Except with you."

"At a restricted level, yes. I play with Tyrone. I'm not afraid to play with him. I'm not afraid to strike him. We have a rather . . . hair-raising set of games, with unorthodox rules which would seem incomprehensible and probably frightening to an outsider. When I lived in Japan I became interested in the martial arts. I studied with a Master, in fact. He was my wife's father. It is that sort of thing I try to do with Tyrone."

"I don't know whether I understand you, Mr. Roth. What kind of games?"

He sighed, and a smile hovered on his lips, like a faint memory of pleasure. "Right now, for instance, you and I are sitting here facing each other. We are conversing in a civilized fashion. The sun is shining. The hills are still and peaceful. The water looks motionless and serene. But the tranquility is based on something which could vanish at any second. There are an infinite number of violent possibilities latent in this situation. I might, for example, suddenly hurl myself at you and aim a blow at your windpipe. I have no intention of doing any such thing. But it's a possibility. If you were Tyrone, I might do such a thing. If you were Tyrone, you might try to attack *me* when my guard was down."

"I can see that kind of behavior is possible," I said. "I don't really see why it's necessary."

"Tyrone has a violent vision of the world," Roth explained. "He imagines that death is waiting for him; therefore he busies himself preparing to fight against it. It's a way of passing the time, Mr. Kyd, a technique for making his life interesting. He prefers it to slowly and silently rotting in his wheelchair. Of course, he's a wildly erratic and self-indulgent samurai. He abuses his body with drugs, and he takes a vicious pleasure in humiliating people. Charlotte and his mother probably considered his obsession with self-defense a fantasy. But then,"—Roth gestured eloquently with his hands— "Tyrone is alive and they're not."

"Has Tyrone ever mentioned to you what he's specifically afraid of?"

"He claims that five years ago he was deliberately run over by someone. He was in a coma for a week and suffered amnesia. All that he could clearly remember, he says, is the instant before the car hit him."

"Did he get a look at the driver?"

"That's the problem." Roth shifted in his chair. "The only way he was ever able to describe the face was to say that it looked like himself. He had a moment of recognition."

"What do you think?" I asked. "Was Tyrone deliberately hit? By someone who looked so much like him that he thought it was himself?"

"The way Tyrone rode his motorcycle, chances are he would eventually have killed himself anyway. I can't give you a yes or no answer to your question. I think at a psychological level, at the moment of his accident, Tyrone saw his own death coming at him. In that fraction of an instant he understood that he'd conjured it up for himself. He was responsible for what was happening, so death wore his face."

The still air was broken by a distant buzzing that grew louder. A cloud of yellowish dust moved along one of the trails, vanished behind a ridge, and reappeared. Whoever it was, he was pushing his machine to its limits, accelerating so hard that the engine screamed to be put in higher gear. At last it became visible as it negotiated the trail that zigzagged along the slopes nearest the house. It was a black dune buggy with heavy balloon tires and red and silver flames painted across the hood. An antenna projected six feet into the air with a red flag flapping at its tip.

It approached the pool area and then veered around and headed for the garages to the side of the main house.

A moment later, Tyrone emerged in a motorized wheelchair. He drove directly toward us and then stopped at a distance of about twenty-five yards. The sound of his engine revving from a low growl to a high-pitched scream echoed into the hills. Slowly he lifted up two stainless steel crutches, laid one atop the other, and then held them out in front of him as if they were a warrior's lance.

"Just keep talking," Roth said.

There was a squeal of burning rubber and a snarl of acceleration and then Tyrone was heading on a collision course with our table, screaming like a bronco rider. I gripped the sides of my deck chair. He was almost on us, with the crutches extended, aimed at Roth's head. At the last second he jammed on the brakes and turned the wheelchair in a wild circular skid that took him backward to within a few inches of the pool. He killed the engine and smiled, pleased as punch with his neatly executed performance.

He was dressed in driver's white coveralls, racing shoes, and sunglasses. A white silk scarf around his neck gave him a dashing, fighter-pilot look. He was a very handsome boy, with wavy black hair and the strong Elevel chin. His face was deeply bronzed and radiantly healthy-looking, but there was a belligerent, sneering line to his lips. They seemed in constant motion. You felt the flickering smile was only an attempt to repress another expression that wanted to take over his face. An expression of rage, or profound grief. He took off his sunglasses and subjected me to a flat, challenging stare. He had his father's bright blue eyes but they gleamed with a malicious amusement that was absent from the parent's. He was too childishly self-conscious to be all that frightening. He narrowed his eyes and frowned with excessive menace in a style that went out when talking movies came in.

"This is Thomas Kyd," Roth said. "He's a private investigator."

"I'm thirsty." Tyrone unzipped the front of his suit and peeled it down to around his waist. His chest and arm muscles had the perfect, sculpted definition of a Greek statue. "I want some orange juice," he demanded. "Go fetch."

Roth rose to his feet and walked over to the pool house, vanishing through a sliding door.

Tyrone removed a tube of Ambre Solaire from his pocket and then rubbed himself briskly with the orange cream.

"Why don't you take your shirt off?" Tyrone remarked. "The sun has vitamins in it."

"No thanks."

"Afraid I'll kick sand in your face?" He barked with laughter. "I hear you busted up one of Leonardo's girl-friends. Beating up a fairy is really impressive."

"Why don't we cut this out," I said quietly. "Your mother killed herself and yesterday your sister was mur-dered. Your pal Leonardo was the one who gave your sister the pills for an overdose. Are you interested in any of this, or do you want to play cowboys and Indi-ans?"

"Don't get tough with me." He scowled. "I don't *have* to do anything."

"Maybe you just *can't* do anything."

He went pale with anger and began moving his wheelchair around the table.

"You try something with me," I said, "and I'll throw you in the pool and jump on your head."

He stopped, and the ferocious smile trembled on his lips.

"I like you, Kyd," he said. "You're okay."

"It doesn't take much to impress you."

"You want to arm-wrestle?" He wheeled himself up to me.

I thought his brains were scrambled, the way he switched subjects and changed moods.

"No, I don't want to arm-wrestle. I want to talk to you."

"Just once," he said. "Then I'll do the other thing."

We squared off on the table and gripped hands. His hand felt like a block of rough wood. He squeezed my knuckles as hard as he could but I kept my hand limp. It was going to be the wrist and arm that determined the contest, not the power of either of our grips. I hadn't arm-wrestled anyone since I was in college, and from the look of Tyrone's forearm and biceps he'd done nothing but practice for the last five years.

"All right." He snickered. "Begin *now!*"

I tensed my arm but he didn't go for a quick pin. He just sat there, letting me struggle against his immovable arm. I couldn't budge it an inch. I wasn't going to tire myself out so I slacked off and waited for him to make his big push. There was no way I could beat him but I might just have enough to stop him from beating me. Slowly, with a contemptuous smile curling his lips, he began to bend my hand down. My face was running with sweat and I wondered what the hell I was doing playing macho games with this crippled beach boy.

"Try harder." He chuckled.

Just as he was about to pin me, I jabbed him hard with the tips of my fingers on the inside of his biceps, where the nerves run across the bone. His arm loosened involuntarily. A grimace of pain swept his face, and I pinned him fast. Then I jumped back, out of range of his fists, and smiled insolently.

"You cheated!" he cried indignantly. "You hit me!"

"What did you expect?" I shrugged. "You should have been ready for that possibility. I pinned you. You lost."

"He hit me!" Tyrone protested to Roth, who laid a tray with a pitcher of orange juice on the table. "I had him beat and he poked me in the arm." He was still too astounded to be truly angry.

"A very wise move on Mr. Kyd's part." Roth smiled. "By your rules Mr. Kyd was bound to lose. Only a fool goes to certain defeat. Mr. Kyd just changed the rules."

Tyrone's eyes brimmed with hot, angry tears and his face was red with pent-up emotion. "But you can't just . . ." he blurted out. "That's not fair. What if I . . ."

"Then *you* would have won," I said. "Next time figure out who you're playing with. You don't like the outcome, write to Charles Atlas. Maybe he'll send you a chest expander for a booby prize."

Tyrone couldn't believe his ears. Roth gave me a faint smile of understanding as if in theory he approved of my needling Tyrone but wondered whether I knew what I was doing.

"Why did Dr. Lester lie to me, Tyrone?" I asked him. "He told me he'd been the family doctor for five years, and I've just found out he delivered you."

"Why don't you ask him?" he snarled.

"How come you've never tried to find out who ran you over?"

"Someone did run me over," he protested.

"Then why wasn't there an investigation?"

"Because no one listens to me in this family. Because Lester said I was cracked. Because something fishy is going on. They're all fishy. As far as I'm concerned, they can all drop dead. That little weasel Moonhurst, I hope he gets it next. If someone else doesn't get him, I will. He almost got it once from me, and next time I'll make sure of it." Tyrone was all bluster and bravado now. "Moonhurst is so scared of me he won't even use the pool. He even keeps his door locked."

"What's so fishy about your family?" I persisted.

"You know what my mother spent her whole life doing? Worrying about other people's kids. Not her kids. Other people's. She had such a lousy conscience she had to go out and adopt the whole world. And when I got run over she behaved like it was some act of God to punish *her*. Not me. *Her!* It wasn't any act of God. The bastard did it on purpose."

"Why would anyone run you over?"

"Just because I don't know why something happened doesn't mean it didn't happen. I knew there was someone after me. I had a feeling for weeks."

"How did you know?"

"I'd be tearing around on my bike and there'd be a car parked off the road in some place where there was no reason for it to be. Just parked. And then it would take off. That happened a lot of times. I was being watched."

"Have there been any subsequent attempts on your life?"

"Why bother?" He shrugged and glanced disdainfully

at his legs. "I guess they figured this was good enough."

"Have you ever heard of someone called Mrs. Kramer?"

He drained his orange juice and brought it down hard on the table. "No, I haven't heard of anyone called Mrs. Kramer."

"What did the guy who ran you over look like?"

Tyrone shot Roth a glance. "You told him," he said. "Why don't you keep your big mouth shut? I don't even like to think about that."

"Why not?" I asked.

"It just gives me a creepy feeling." Tyrone frowned. "The guy's eyes were just like my eyes."

"Or your father's," I said.

"Man, you really are sick." Tyrone laughed harshly. "My father wouldn't kill me. He feels guilty enough as it is."

"You keep harping on your parents' bad conscience. Why should they have a bad conscience?"

"Don't ask me. Even when I was a kid they were that way. Like something bad had happened and we were all meant to go around feeling guilty about it but no one ever said what it was. Well, I don't feel guilty. I don't feel guilty about things I *have* done. I'm damned if I'm going to feel guilty about things I haven't done."

"What would you do if I told you who killed your sister? If I gave you a piece of paper with an address where you could find the killer?"

"I'd kill him," he said. His eyes were bright and shiny. "It would be my privilege." He looked at Roth, as if for approval.

"Okay," I said. I was getting tired of his fanatical heroics. There was an intensity and an almost demented personal dignity about Tyrone that I found exhausting. I wondered how Roth stood it twenty-four hours a day.

"One last thing," I said. "And please don't yell, 'Banzai!' and throw a karate chop at my windpipe. Where were you yesterday afternoon?"

"I was here. In my room." He shrugged. "I was around. Ask Roth."

I looked at Roth. He said, "I told him, Tyrone, that you were in the hills."

"What did you tell him that for? I thought you said to keep my mouth shut."

"I thought our keeping quiet was necessary to protect you," Roth answered. "After talking to Mr. Kyd, I realized that was a mistake."

"I don't care." Tyrone looked challengingly at me. "I was out riding. You don't even have to check the trail near Mojave Drive. I go there a lot. Yesterday I was there around four thirty. I went up the trail to within about twenty yards of the house, and turned around. It's one of my regular runs. I do it every day."

"Were you there today?" I asked.

"Yeah." He reddened. "That's right. I was. So what?"

"Nothing. What's the matter?"

"Nothing's the matter." He clenched his fists. "I was curious. I wanted to look around. Charlotte was in that house for two days and I was up there on the trail below, both afternoons. I bet she heard my car. She could have called out to me. She knew it was me. I might have been within shouting distance when she was killed."

"How do you feel now?"

"I feel . . ." He suddenly looked like a cornered animal. "I feel like I'm going to be sick." He started to weep with horrible dry sobs that convulsed his chest. "I don't want to talk any more." He said to Roth, "I want to go to bed."

He looked pitiful with his face twisting on his beautifully muscled chest, and the tortured, eerie sobs coming from his mouth. His knuckles went white, gripping the wheels of his chair. I felt as if I'd opened a door and seen something no one was ever meant to look at.

I sat at the table and watched Roth push Tyrone in

his wheelchair toward one of the bungalows: the upright older man with his military bearing, and the Adonis-like cripple, trailing his white silk aviator's scarf from his clenched hand.

What was wrong with him, though? I wanted to know. It was more than paralysis. He had the petulance and the one-track mind of a very young child. Yet there didn't appear to be any physical impairment; he could speak clearly and coherently when he wanted to. I didn't know what to think of the relationship between Tyrone and Roth. The older man was simultaneously guru and flunky. One thing was sure, the kid had straitjacket written all over him. And if they ever institutionalized him, he was finished. He wouldn't give in without a fight; they'd fry his brains with electric shock treatments, and if he still had any spunk left after that, they'd open his skull and turn down the volume control. For the rest of his life he'd be a docile murmur in a wheelchair parked in front of a hospital TV set. Maybe Roth with his Zen-samurai pitch could control the kid, but what about those times he strayed off the property?

Chapter FIFTEEN

On my way over to Benedict Canyon I tried to figure out why Roth had lied to me about Tyrone's whereabouts on the afternoon of the murder. Roth was right. It was suspicious that Tyrone had been within shouting distance of the house. But if Roth had changed his mind and decided to tell the truth, why hadn't he informed Tyrone? The way it came out, Tyrone had been caught flat-footed in a lie. Of course, looked at another way, by admitting that Tryone was in the hills at the time of the murders, Roth had ruined a potential alibi of his own. It made no sense.

I had expected to see the Mojave Drive house crawling with police but the property was deserted. I went behind the house where the hillside fell sharply away and started poking around. There was a trail that forked off in opposite directions; one led up to the paved road and came out about forty yards above the house, the other looped around and ended in a cul-de-sac in the brush. Tyrone's tire tracks were everywhere. He'd explored both forks, turning around in the cul-de-sac, and taking the other to within a few yards of the paved road. He had said he'd taken the trail to within twenty yards of the house but I could see round depressions in the dirt where he'd gone farther on his crutches, right up to the road. What had he been looking for?

It was hot and the air shifted in rustling eddies over the dry hillside. An hour ago Tyrone had been standing in the same spot. Yesterday he had been there too. It was an awfully ponderous chunk of information, considering that my client wasn't paying me to link his son to his daughter's murder.

There should have been cops with metal detectors

combing the hillside for the murder weapon. A detective should have followed the tire tracks through the hills straight into the Elevel backyard, and questioned Tyrone. Why weren't the police pursuing the leads? If it was Elevel money and influence limiting the investigation, what was Joe trying to hide?

A patrol car was parked in front of the gate to the Elevel property when I got back. It was manned by the same two young cops who'd given me the business yesterday morning on my way out of Bel Air. They stopped me, and one leaned in the window while the other walked around my car.

"Haven't we met before?" he said, with studied coldness.

"Don't think so, officer."

"He doesn't remember us, Earl," he said to his partner.

"I'd love to shoot the breeze with you two guys but I've got a client waiting inside."

"You're the peeper, right?"

"Right." I waited a moment. "How about moving your wagon, officer, so I can get in there and look through some keyholes?"

"You sure you aren't a reporter? See, Earl and me are supposed to make sure nobody from the newspapers gets in."

I showed him the license in my wallet. He took it and then walked around to the other side of the car to consult with Earl. After a couple of minutes, I started to get out of the car.

"Nobody told you you could move," the one called Earl said. "Get back in that car."

I got back into the car and lit a cigarette. I could see them out of the corner of my eye. They were just standing there, talking. Every once in a while they'd throw me a searching look, as if daring me to move or say anything. Five minutes passed like that. Earl took a leak against a bush and then ambled over to the police car and checked its wheels. He pulled out his service revolver, broke it open, and checked the interior. Then he got into the police car and backed it away from the entrance.

The other one walked around my car several times, inspecting it from all sides. Then he leaned his head in the window and stared solidly into my eyes.

"Here's your wallet." He let it drop into my lap. "You can go in now."

And that was it. I passed through the gates, wondering what in hell that episode had been about, and how you got your kicks from pulling that kind of number.

Calvin answered the front door and stood leaning exhausted against the jamb. He appeared dejected, and there was a pronounced thickness to his speech.

"You must have had some talk with Tyrone." He made a face. "Dr. Lester had to shoot him full of sedatives. He was in hysterics." Calvin took off his tinted glasses and passed a hand over his eyes. They were glossy, compelling, almost black eyes with something shiny and fixed about their stare. They looked far too vivacious for that bleached deadpan mug.

"Joe's in the library with the police." He ushered me inside. "You know, Joe's heart isn't that strong. This is going to kill him if he's not careful."

"Have the police come up with anything?" I asked. He gave me a blank look and then shook his head as if to clear it.

"Sorry," he mumbled. "Dr. Lester gave me a tranquilizer and I'm a bit woozy. Yes, the police are trying to run down something on this man Stackman. And they have Coronado under surveillance. They seem very professional."

"Who? The police, or the killers?"

"Right now I guess I mean the killers. They didn't have to shoot Charlotte," he said bitterly. "Charlotte wouldn't hurt a fly. I still can't believe Mrs. Elevel would ever get involved with a degenerate like Coronado."

"Maybe it was Charlotte," I suggested. "We don't know who was involved with whom."

"But they were both so . . ." Calvin looked at me with pained determination. "I'm telling you they were both good, decent women. There was never anything sordid about them. Oh Christ!" he groaned. "I tell you I'd like to get that Coronado alone and beat the truth out of him."

"That would be against the law," I said mildly.

"Well what's the law good for if scum like that can blackmail and murder people like the Elevels?" he asked hotly.

"Don't give up hope," I said, not exactly with a lot of conviction. "Things take time."

"Well, have you got any ideas?" he demanded. "If you ask me, the police are never going to get anywhere."

"I have to make some calls. Is there a private phone I could use?"

He led me into the breakfast room off the kitchen and closed the door. All day long, starting even last night at the scene of the murder, I'd had a feeling of anxiety. Something was staring me in the face but I couldn't see it. I'd forgotten something, or failed to consider something, and it was right in front of me. It had nagged me on and off all day, and I knew that when I thought of it I'd want to kick myself. Maybe that's why I was so slow in coming up with it.

I dialed the telephone company and asked for Harry Bowkley in the accounts department.

"Harry," I said, "run a check on 650–2354. It's listed under a Candace Laine, 2200 Mojave Drive, Benedict Canyon. Give me all the toll calls made in the last three days up to five o'clock yesterday afternoon. Around five there should be a call to the police. Forget what comes after that."

I sat in the breakfast room, smoking cigarettes and looking out the window at the garden. The marble statues were still spitting water at each other, and Pedro the gardener was manuring the lawn. Every moment or so he'd flail his hand through the air to drive off the flies attracted by the fertilizer. Another gardener, this one Japanese, was polishing the brass statue of the cowboy in the tulip beds. He had to climb up on the back of the horse to get at the cowboy's face and hat.

"Only one toll call was made." Harry came back on the line. "It's a Pasadena number, 681–1166, listed under an Alma Kramer, 478 South Euclid."

I let out a long sigh of relief. "You just made my day, Harry. I needed a break. Run a check on her too."

"How was your ladyfriend last night?" he asked. "The one you were spying on?"

"None of your prurient business. I'll call you later for this Kramer woman's calls."

In two days Charlotte had called this Kramer woman in Pasadena and had written the woman a letter, which the killer had probably taken. The Elevels used to live in Pasadena. Dr. Lester used to practice there. And Harlan Stackman had his car fixed there. It was time I had a talk with Joe.

On my way to the library I met Deputy Chief Granville, who was coming out. He was a short, broadly built man in his late forties with a high coloring and short-cropped sandy hair. He was dressed in double-knit burgundy slacks and a paler burgundy blazer with white piping. A red tie with a pattern of crossed golf clubs was fixed to his shirt by a golf ball tie clasp. Heavy gold cufflinks in the form of golf balls repeated the theme. His shoes were white patent leather loafers with double brass chains. His shirt had broad pale red and white stripes that matched the slacks, the blazer, and the tie. He looked like something his wife had cut out of an interior decorating book, maybe one of those bright, chintzy bathrooms where the rug, the wallpaper, and the variously colored walls all fit together and give you a headache. Even his complexion matched his clothes.

"All the material evidence you requested is in the trunk of my car, chief."

"Let's get it." He fixed me with a look of mingled suspicion and displeasure. All the deference he'd tried to show me on the phone that morning was gone. "Now."

We walked out to my car. He looked at the shattered back window as if it were one more in a long line of marks against me. I opened the trunk and handed him the pillowcase filled with Mrs. Elevel's and Charlotte's effects.

"This should have been handed over last night," he said. "We found your prints on Stackman's wallet and the phone. You shouldn't have touched anything."

"Next time I find a homicide I'll walk to the nearest police station and report it verbally. Come on, chief. Those phones were used by a dozen different detectives."

"Don't act smart with me, Kyd."

"I wouldn't try."

"That's Strike Two." He glared. "One more wiseass remark and we do something to your license."

"I have some information," I said. "Would you like to hear it?"

Granville rubbed a fist across his jaw. "Start talking."

"Coronado's Hollywood store is connected to a photographer's studio run by a bimbo called Art Grande. There were calls made from the Elevel house to both the store and the studio. I sold Grande a line of goods this morning about wanting to have myself photographed with my girlfriend. I made it as clear as possible that my girlfriend was married to a very rich man, that she wouldn't know about the photographs, and that I wanted copies. Grande was ready to do it. He'd done it before. It was perfectly obvious I wanted the film to blackmail my girlfriend. It was also pretty clear that Grande intended to keep a copy himself and put the squeeze on my girlfriend himself."

"So?" Granville said.

"So maybe it might be worth watching Grande. It might not be such a dumb idea to get a search warrant and tear the place apart. Grande keeps cash up there. There's a safe. There just might be some of that missing eighteen thousand dollars in it. You could get the serial numbers from the bank."

"What else?" Granville said.

"The Elevels' physician, Dr. Lester, received a phone call from Coronado's bookstore about an hour after Charlotte was shot."

"How do you know that?"

"I know it."

"That's not an answer." He flushed.

"I think the call's more interesting than how I found out it was made."

"This is all shit. Phone calls. A Mexican gardener spotting Mrs. Elevel and Coronado. Hearsay that Grande makes blackmail films. No judge is going to give me a search warrant on that."

"You've got a suicide who called her doctor twice just before she died. Why did this doctor fail to mention that when I questioned him? He also told me he'd been the family doctor for five years when in fact he delivered their first child, twenty-five years ago. Sixteen years ago his narcotics prescription book was yanked. Five years ago he was charged with malpractice by an insurance company. Both investigations were put to sleep. Why? Right after Charlotte Elevel is shot to death your prime suspect, Coronado, phones Dr. Lester. Why? Was it a social call? Maybe Coronado had an upset tummy. Whatever Charlotte took out of her mother's safe was recovered by the killer. If you ask me, that little something involves Dr. Lester."

"I've known Sam Lester for ten years. It doesn't add up. He's a very wealthy doctor. He doesn't need this kind of trouble."

"Right now all you've got is a John Doe warrant, and a houseful of people you don't want to question. Last night the police let the only person who could identify Gervano wander off. There isn't even a police guard on the Benedict Canyon house. The surrounding area hasn't been searched for a murder weapon. There's a trail behind the house that leads straight back to this place but it looks like no one's bothered to check it out."

"You've got a bad mouth, Kyd. And you're wrong. But mainly you're a cheap nobody. I did a little checking on that girl from the Academy, and her father isn't in textiles." Granville handed the pillowcase to his driver, who was a stringy-looking character with a face like a killer rabbit. He stood a few feet behind me, with his hands looped in his belt, giving out bad vibrations.

"It's illegal to drive a car with a smashed back window, isn't that right, Frank?" Granville asked.

"It sure is, chief," Frank said.

"It's also illegal to drive without a spare tire. And with a loose muffler. Correct me if I'm wrong, Frank."

"You're absolutely correct, chief."

"All right, Kyd." Granville held out his hand. "Let's see your license for that pop gun in the trunk."

"At home."

"You've got two bald tires." He opened the car, got in and tried the emergency brake. "And a defective emergency brake." He returned to the trunk and rummaged through my belongings until he came up with a bag of skin-diving equipment. He looked inside it and then placed it on the driver's seat. He returned to the trunk and looked some more.

"Check the front seat, Frank," he said. "Might be something there."

Frank found the skin-diving bag on the driver's seat

and emptied it on the ground. "Look what I found!" he said.

"Just check it," Granville barked.

There were several lead weights, a snorkel, an abalone iron, a canteen with several inches of tequila in it, and a tin box with a two-year-old roach.

Granville shook his head in disgust.

"Possession of narcotics. Driving with an open container of alcohol found in the driver's section of the vehicle. Possession of a concealed weapon without a license. Half a dozen vehicle violations. That's just about three too many misdemeanors for the state licensing board."

"You'd make a lousy highway patrolman," I said. "You're talking about moving violations. This is a stationary vehicle on private property and I'm not even in it. Second, the gun wasn't concealed. I wasn't even wearing it. Third, if you search an empty car without a warrant, or reasonable suspicion, it's illegal search and seizure, and the whole rap is inadmissible. Any judge would throw you out for wasting the time of the court. Ask Bugs Bunny." I jerked my thumb at his driver. "You think you bother me with this pathetic jive? You think you can jerk me off like some nameless asshole? And tell Bugs Bunny to stop getting behind me or I'll send him to the dentist." I wheeled around and stepped away from the driver, who was itching to show me what a kidney punch was all about.

"You want me to take him, chief?" The driver's hand reached for the revolver holstered at the back of his waist.

"Is this an Italian western?" I asked. "Are you two for real? I give you the only information you've got and you let this hotdog pull a gun on me for vehicle violations. Get out of my way. I'm going to talk to Elevel."

"Freeze!" The driver steadied his service revolver with both hands.

"Freeze your mother, Bugs." I walked past him.

"You're off the case, Kyd," Granville shouted. "You're through. We're handling it."

"Not after Elevel hears what I've got. You blew it, Granville. I could have handed you the bust on a plate. Now you get nothing." I'd reached the front door. "You want to solve a crime, Granville? Why don't you go arrest your tailor."

Chapter SIXTEEN

Going down the dimly lit hallway, I turned a corner and nearly ran into a tall customer in green slacks and a gray suede jacket. He had longish black hair, a high pale forehead, and dark blue eyes that met mine with a frowning intensity. It wasn't a bad-looking face but at that moment it had an unhealthily determined expression. I moved to the side to let him pass and then stopped dead in my tracks.

I'd made way for my own reflection in the mirror backing a linen closet door.

I stood there for a moment and tried breathing deeply. Blowing off steam wasn't going to get me anywhere with Joe, and this case was too important to lose over a burst of temper. There wasn't any point in getting mad at Joe. Granville had probably bulldozed him into firing me. It was better to think about the two bodies I'd found. Better to think about how slick and effortless a thing it is, if you're a bastard with a thin smear of feeling and no imagination, to put a hole in the back of someone's head. That's what made the case worth solving.

There are ineffectual, vicious grafters like Granville, and pitiless, effeminate toughs like Coronado. It's their world, apparently. They breathe up too much oxygen and expect the rest of us to get by on the pollution they leave behind. Getting indignant wasn't going to change that. But getting myself put back on the case might.

Joe was alone in the library, sprawled motionless in a dark green leather armchair. His hands lay limp in his lap. His sunken eyes had a glazed, fixed look, and all the energy seemed to have deserted his limbs.

"It's no good," he said. "Granville's leveled with me.

They can't touch this man Coronado. If my wife did something and there are photos, I don't want to see them. It's over."

"You think your wife had an affair?" I took out a cigarette and snapped it into my mouth, faintly amused.

"What the hell does it look like?" There was a trace of rage in his voice now.

I shrugged. "It must have been a sensational affair."

He looked at me with hatred.

"A humdinger of an affair," I reflected. "And strange as hell."

"My accountant will mail you a check, Mr. Kyd."

I sat down on the edge of his desk and flicked some lint off my trousers.

"You know, what beats me, Mr. Elevel, is that this is not the Middle Ages. Women are in the habit of committing indiscretions without killing themselves in remorse. Daughters are known to discover their parents' infidelities without going into suicidal shock over them. An affair isn't *unspeakable*. In fact, I'd say it's one of the major topics of conversation in your social group. How many women do you know who'd kill themselves if their husbands found out they were unfaithful?"

"My wife wasn't like that," he growled, sitting up in his chair.

"I don't think she was either, Mr. Elevel. That's why I don't think she just had an affair."

"What are you trying to say to me?" he said coldly.

"That if the guy who hit your daughter in the head could see you now he'd rupture himself laughing. There's lots of money in this family but somewhere it got low on guts."

"If you don't get out of my house," he hissed, "I'll bend a fire poker over your skull. Get out!"

"Why don't you bend one over the guy who killed Charlotte?"

"Tell me where he lives, and I will."

"Tell me what Dr. Lester has on this family and maybe I could do just that."

"I don't know what you're talking about."

I told him how I'd used the phone company records to link Dr. Lester to Coronado and Coronado to his family. I also told him about Charlotte's letter and phone call to a Mrs. Kramer in Pasadena. "Nothing's over, Mr. Elevel, unless you decide to put a lid on it."

"I don't know any Mrs. Kramer."

"But you know Dr. Lester."

"There's nothing to tell there," he said miserably. "Many years ago there was a great sadness in my family and Dr. Lester did a service to us. It's no one's business what it was. He stuck his neck out very far for us. I know he's had his difficulties as a doctor and I've used my influence to straighten things out for him."

"That's it, huh?"

"That's it. I can give you my word that none of it has anything to do with my wife or daughter's death."

"I think you're very wrong," I said.

"I know I'm not." He said it quietly, with sad conviction. "If it helps any, I'm willing to offer a twenty-five-thousand-dollar reward to anyone, including you, who helps catch these people. Does that satisfy you?"

"I don't want your money, Mr. Elevel." I stood up to go. "But it might loosen a few tongues." I started for the door and reached it and then he said:

"What did you think of my son?"

"He's not as bad as he thinks he is. He's got plenty of guts. He's a little crazy."

"And Granville?" There was a hint of a smile on his face. It was the first one I'd ever seen.

"Granville is a man who's gotten small and musty and mean from living inside too many people's pockets. You can sometimes buy the Police Department, Mr. Elevel, but they usually sell you their damaged goods."

"I don't know. He's been useful in the past."

"Yeah, well, I know he specializes in getting charges dropped. That isn't the same as making convictions."

"And you think you can make a conviction? You seem to know a lot about my affairs."

"Not enough," I said. "But give me time, and keep Granville off my back, and I'll see what I can dig up."

"You're a very cocky young man for someone who can't afford a decent car."

"Lowers the tone of the place, having it parked out there, doesn't it? Well, what can you do? If I drove a Rolls I'd have to wear an expensive suit, and if I wore an expensive suit, I wouldn't want to get it messed up, and the next thing you know I'd start wondering whether anyone really liked me, or whether it was just the fancy package."

He smiled thinly and sat down at his desk. He opened the drawer, took out a check, and filled it out. "I think we have an understanding, Mr. Kyd. This is a check made out to you for ten thousand dollars. If you're successful there will be another fifteen thousand dollars forthcoming. These seem like large amounts of money. They are. But my family, what remains of my family,"—he grimaced bitterly—"means a lot to me. I would like to keep Tyrone out of this. I'm sure he's not in it, but to be on the safe side . . ." He cleared his throat. "I think I've made myself clear."

"No thanks," I said. "I'm not Granville."

"I would feel better if you took the money."

"I wouldn't." I smiled. "It cost you several hundred dollars to find your daughter. It cost someone probably between three and ten thousand dollars to have her murdered. I carry a gun sometimes, Mr. Elevel. A few times I've had to use it. People have died because of me. If I start working for you for twenty-five grand, in my eyes I'm not that different from one of Coronado's hired cockroaches." I paused and looked at him closely. "Someone has to do my work," I said, "but killing people shouldn't be good business."

It was not a bad line, if you care for that sort of thing. I told Joe that if he really wanted to help me out he could lend me Charlotte's MG. That brightened him up right away. He wasn't a bad guy. He just had a rich man's fear of facing someone at close quarters who didn't owe him. He only felt safe surrounded by people he could control. After the last few days, I thought he was about as safe as a liquor store in a Watts riot.

Chapter SEVENTEEN

Granville and his pet killer-rabbit were gone when I came out but I wasn't taking any chances. I cleaned my car of the tequila and roach and strapped on the Mauser. I don't like guns but when I think of other people's, mine starts to grow on me a little. I had made the wrong noises in the wrong quarters and it was not unlikely that soon someone would try, in some abrupt, unfriendly manner, to teach me some manners. Given a chance, Granville would no doubt have liked to beat me to a pulp with a golf club. It being a liberal age, he would have to be satisfied with lodging a complaint against me with the state licensing board and instructing his men to harass and obstruct me in every way possible.

In a way, it's always more fun playing with people who hate to lose.

There was a floppy straw hat and a pair of cracked sunglasses on the passenger seat of Charlotte's MG. I put them on, settled myself well down in the seat, and started it up. It was a neat, sturdy piece of automobile, with less than three thousand on the clock, and that fresh-leather-and-plastic smell that new cars have.

The world looked blue through the sunglasses but not as blue as the uniforms on the two cops waiting in a parked car outside the gate. They gave me a glance but they were looking for a cheap nobody in a battered Mustang.

On my way to Pasadena I decided to drop by the Academy to check on the police guard on Lucy. My visit to Grande had upped the risks for both of us.

I walked around to the parking lot and entered the building through an open back entrance. I took the service stairs to the third floor and stepped out into the deserted corridor. All the students were in the classrooms. The only person around was an elderly woman swabbing down the scuffed linoleum. I was pretty sure she wasn't an undercover cop.

"Where is he?" I said, bursting into Lucy's office.

She glanced up from her desk.

"You sound like a jealous husband. Where's who?"

"The police guard," I said.

"He got a call half an hour ago and left. He said everything was all right now. Isn't it?"

They were taking me up one side and down the other with their piss-ass tricks. Granville had real style pulling the guard on Lucy, real panache. I felt ready to make a crowd out of him and play four-wall handball with the pieces. That would be a treat but afterward it would be about as much fun as sitting on a broken bottle. I eased myself into Lucy's chair, closed my eyes, groaned, rubbed the back of my neck. It wasn't as much fun as doing the fandango on Granville's kisser but after a minute of it I thought I could talk without biting someone's head off. Lucy pressed a cup of coffee into my hand and turned the office fan in my direction. After a minute or so I thought I might be persuaded to try rejoining the human race. I called Ian White, told him what had happened, and asked him to send over an operative to guard Lucy.

"And don't send me some dingaling who goes out for coffee and danish and has to go to the john every ten minutes. I want the best man you've got. Someone *serious*. Perferably a psychopath. Armed. This is a very nice lady, Ian. Don't send me some juiced-out ex-cop with half his cylinders missing."

"Take it easy, Thomas," Ian said.

"The best guy you've got." I hung up and shook my head. This character Granville had to fall. I wanted him almost more than I wanted the man who'd wasted Charlotte. My clothes were soaked in sweat and my hands were trembling. "I'm going downstairs to check around the building," I said. "Lock yourself in the ladies' room until I get back."

"Is all this really necessary?" She made a face. "You're scaring the hell out of me."

"I'm sorry. But I'd feel a lot better if you were more scared. There are people out there making moves, and it would make a lot of sense for them to put you out of the picture."

I stood in the doorway of the building's back entrance and slowly looked over the parking lot. It was an unpaved stretch of ground shared by the various businesses on the other floors. On the far side of the lot there was a boarded-up taco stand and a row of weather-beaten wooden garages. Some of them were open and you could see trash, discarded tires, and old paint tins scattered in the back. The garages didn't have locks and most of them were missing slats. In the farthest garage on the row I could just make out the gleam of polished chrome, the front bumper of a new car, lurking in the darkness.

I turned left as if I were leaving the parking lot, crossed the street, walked a block, and then returned on the opposite side. I moved quietly along the row of garages and slipped into the garage next to the one where the car was hiding. The light was bad and in the gloom I stepped on some broken glass, which crunched loudly. I heard a car door slam, the roar of an engine, and then a Buick peeled out and took the alley leading to Hollywood Boulevard. There was too much dust from the squealing wheels for me to get the license plate, and all I saw of the driver was the back of his head.

On the cement floor next to where the car had been were several of those twisted South American cigars that look like old strands of telephone cable. Whoever it was had been waiting there long enough to smoke three cigars. The only man I knew who smoked those cigars was Gervano. Granville's spite and incompetence had almost got Lucy killed.

She tried not to panic when I told her what had happened but I could see that Gervano's return had knocked the wind out of her. She was streetwise and tough in a vivacious, mocking way. She'd probably done a few dope deals as a student and known a couple of people on the fringes of the underworld. But she wasn't ready to handle the threat of a real hood who wanted to kill her. Frankly, I wasn't either. That is, until the guy from White and Rinehart arrived.

He was a short, thick-necked Sicilian built like a tow truck. He looked like you could hit him anywhere with a pick-ax handle and all you would hear would be the splinter of wood. He was dressed in conservative Mafia style, a dark blue banker's suit with a lot of white cuff and collar showing.

"Tony Turino." He shook my hand with a grip as dry, solid, and cool as the handle of a gun. "Two entrances," he said. "Across the street plenty of apartments. And you got a walk from the entrance to the car."

He moved with a restrained quietness to the window, looked down, and drew the blinds shut. Wherever he happened to be standing the surrounding space belonged to him. He had the impassivity and controlled stillness of a man who has made a profession out of being dangerous.

"Your mother, she is a beautiful lady," Turino said to Lucy, and smiled with feline warmth. "And you have your mother's beauty. We will do everything right, eh? Everything like Tony says."

Lucy watched Turino with a kind of fascinated dread. The courteous Old World gallantry of his remarks, and his genially pursed lips bore no relation to his eyes, which had the fixed brilliance of a snake's.

"You're armed?" I said.

"Mmmm . . ." He nodded. "Always, since I am very young. In Palermo, even before my confirmation I have my gun."

Lucy sat back in her chair and groaned. She was pale.

"Not for killing people," Turino protested. "For shooting the birds."

I saw Lucy into her car and then had a private word with Turino.

"Chances are the guy's Mexican," I said. "The one who was here was driving a new purple Buick with white walls. There's a reward out on him. He knows how to do it, Turino."

"Yeah." He stroked his cheek meditatively with fingers that resembled thumbs. "Okay." He smiled remotely. "A very beautiful girl, eh? I used to see her mother in the movies in Palermo. They get all the old movies back there. Is a nice girl."

"I'd like to keep her that way. If you're so hot on the mother, Turino, I guess you'll take good care of the daughter."

His eyes scanned the area behind me. He said, "You are very lucky. Of all the guys at White and Rinehart, I like killing Mexicans the most."

"That's the first nice thing I've heard all day."

After twenty-four hours with Turino, I figured Lucy would think of me as a soft-hearted adolescent with his heart set on the ministry. I wondered where Ian White had found the Sicilian. The line dividing Private Investigator Tony Turino from a Mafia torpedo was as thin as the chrome on a Saturday night special, which was fine with me as long as Ian White didn't also use him to collect on outstanding debts to the White and Rinhart agency.

Chapter **EIGHTEEN**

There was heavy rush-hour traffic on the way to Pasadena. As far ahead as I could see, snake-like lines of chrome and glass fumed motionless in the sun. Was I being followed? Yes, I thought so, by at least ten thousand murderous commuters. Was Gervano somewhere behind me, close by in another lane, chewing on one of those twisted black cigars? I couldn't tell, and the heat was so demoralizing I didn't care. All I knew was that I was closer to the truth than I'd imagined; otherwise Gervano wouldn't have been waiting in that garage outside the Academy.

Above the cars a shimmering chemical haze diffused the sunlight. I inched forward, braked, and nervously studied the heat gauge. Every hundred yards or so an older car had pulled off the road with a boiling-over radiator. In every direction there was nothing to be seen but a dim yellow haze blanketing the hills, flatlands, and buildings of the city. The drivers around me had the spent, listless look of a patient inside an iron lung.

Each was isolated in his own slowly moving iron castle. The only way you could make human contact was to have a car accident.

It was like that all the way to Pasadena and then not much better until I got onto the residential streets. With the help of my map and wrong directions from a gas station attendant it took me another half hour to find 478 South Euclid.

I parked several numbers down and sat in the car for a while, scoping out the street. It was cool and quiet, shaded by rows of stately plane trees whose roots had buckled the pavements. The houses were old two-story wooden affairs with dilapidated porches and gabled roofs. Most of the cars in the driveways were from ten to twenty years old, gas-eating tanks with huge fins, owned, I imagined, by elderly people who never drove them much faster than thirty miles an hour. There were no kids around, no toys on the front lawns, no basketball hoops over the garages. Now and then an old man or woman would pass with a grocery cart from the supermarket on the main drag. Not stacked high with food to feed a family, but with a small collection of inexpensive items, just enough to keep a single person alive for a day or two. You got the feeling that between social security checks, things got very lean on South Euclid.

The Kramer residence looked even more rundown than its neighbors. The lawn was burned a yellowish brown and most of the house's coat of green paint had flaked off. Beneath it, the weathered gray shingles looked as if the backfire of a passing car could bring them down. There were a few pieces of rusty garden furniture on the porch and a large mat with the WELCOME worn off by too many years of wiping feet.

I pulled the bell chain and a weak tinkling sounded in the hall, followed by the sound of footsteps moving over warped floorboards.

"Who is it?" an elderly voice rasped.

I explained who I was and asked if I could talk to her. The door swung open and she scrutinized me suspiciously. She was at least sixty years old, a big-boned, stooped woman in a pair of black cotton slacks and an army fatigue jacket. The sparse, wispy hair above her colorless face was dyed orange. She had a thin, bleak mouth and unusually avid green eyes that met mine and held them. She had no hips, no bosom to speak of, and large, heavily veined hands speckled with liver spots. Even stooped over she was as tall as I was.

"Is Kramer your name?" I said.

"That's right. You've told me your name, and it doesn't mean anything to me. What do you want?"

"I'm a private investigator. I'd like to ask you some questions."

"Private investigator." She ran the back of her hand across her nose and sniffed. "My sister hired one of you fellows once. Squandered her inheritance and didn't get a dime's worth of anything in return. Just who do you think you're investigating?"

"I'm not sure." I reached for my wallet. "But you're probably the only person who could tell me."

"No, don't show me your identification. Any Tom, Dick, or Harry can have a card printed up saying he's the President of the United States. It doesn't mean a damn thing to me. Will you come in, sir?"

The hallway was a dim cavern of dark furniture and smelled of pets and their food, and dust. I followed her into a high-ceilinged back parlor that resembled a cluttered Hollywood antique store filled with overstuffed armchairs, beveled mirrors, and art deco bric-a-brac. The walls and ceiling were the color of very old newspapers. Alma Kramer's possessions were just old enough to have become fashionable again. I wondered if she realized she was living amid objects for which chic younger people would pay exorbitant prices.

"Sit over there." She pointed me to a bamboo sofa with faded brocade cushions while she perched on the edge of an armchair. From that position she looked down on me across the width of a mirror-topped coffee table. On the table rested a cut-glass decanter with a dozen small matching glasses.

"It's peach brandy. Make it myself." She fitted a Camel into a nicotine-stained ivory holder and gripped it between her long yellow teeth. The ivory holder and her teeth looked as if they'd come from the same elephant, which didn't surprise me as much as the fact that she smoked. I'd had her figured for a lady who chewed her tobacco. She set out two glasses and poured them full of the peach brandy, slid mine across the table, and let her own sit where it was.

154 KYD FOR HIRE

"All right, young man," she said. "Shoot."

"I'm working for a man called Joe Elevel."

"Makes ugly furniture, that the one? Don't know him. From the look of what he makes, don't want to." She sipped her brandy and glared pointedly at my untouched glass. I picked it up, held it to the light, breathed in its bouquet, and took a token sip. It was vile, sweet, raw, and had an aftertaste that only got worse.

"Delicious," I said.

"You think so. I think it tastes like a peach pit pickled in gasoline. You don't have to humor me, young man. I know the difference between a decent liqueur and fruit-flavored lighter fluid. What's this Joe Elevel want?"

"He wants to find out who killed his daughter. Yesterday afternoon she called this house. A couple of hours later someone shot her in the back of the head."

"Is that who that girl was? She wouldn't give her name but I remember the call. She was intoxicated or on drugs and babbled a lot of nonsense. I couldn't make head or tail of it."

"What exactly did she say?"

"She said I'd ruined her life and destroyed her family and she called me a ghoul and a monster. That's what she said. I just hung up. I'd do the same, too, if she called again."

"Do you have any idea why she called you?"

"I'm sure I don't." She swallowed off her peach brandy and grimaced sociably. "It's Rosemary, my sister, you want to talk to. This poor girl must have thought I was Rosemary."

"Rosemary is a *Mrs.* Kramer," I said. "Is that right?"

"When a woman marries a man as Rosemary did, she takes the man's name. When a woman *divorces* a man she takes back her maiden name. My sister has no right to call herself *Mrs.* Kramer. It's just an affectation. Now she's just as much *Miss* Kramer as I am."

"Why doesn't she call herself by her ex-husband's name?"

"Which one?" Alma Kramer sneered. "Goncalves, Koontz, Hagerbaum, or Pagrowski?"

"She married four times?"

"There are very few mistakes my sister hasn't made *at least* four times."

"She sounds like quite a character."

"A character, eh?" Her nose twitched disdainfully. "A weak-headed immoral child, sir, hardly a character."

"I'd like to talk to her."

"A character!" She snorted. "Rosemary'd like that. And you'll talk to her too. She's at the Lutheran church right now, at what she likes to call a party. I call it a sweltering church hall filled with a lot of old fogeys who ought to know better. People say you get wiser and more dignified when you get older. But if you were a wild vain little tramp when you were young, that's all you are when you're old, and that's all Rosemary is, and all she'll ever be. She says she goes to these grotesque affairs to play bingo and talk to her girlfriends but Rosemary's never had a girlfriend in her life. She goes, sir, because she has the deluded idea that some senile lonely widower is going to fall head over heels in love with her. Yes, fifty-eight years old, and looks every day of it, and so arthritic she can hardly stand up, much less dance. You'd think she'd have read the handwriting on the wall by now. But not Rosemary. It's mudpacks, and beauty treatments, and white frocks to the bitter end. Ugh!" She ground out her cigarette in the ashtray.

"If I sound harsh, believe me I have good cause. Rosemary's carrying on broke my father's heart." She screwed another Camel into the ivory holder. "My father was Barnaby Kramer. You're probably too young to have heard of him. He invented the first coin wrapping machine for the U.S. Treasury but someone stole the idea before he could patent it. He would have been in the encyclopedias."

"Has your sister ever mentioned a man called Luis Coronado?"

"Rosemary tries to hide everything from me. I wouldn't be surprised if this Luis Coronado was a boyfriend of hers."

"Excuse me, Miss Kramer, but is that gun on the bookshelf loaded?"

"It wouldn't be much use if it wasn't." She glanced proudly at the pearl-handled automatic lying between a jade figurine and a bowl of potpourri. "My father taught us both how to shoot when we were girls. I can take that gun apart and clean it and put it back together again with my eyes closed."

"Any special reason for keeping a loaded gun around?"

"I'd say at least a million good reasons. Black ones, Mexican ones, yellow ones, and white ones. I was robbed five years ago and they took everything precious to me. Letters, photos, albums. Don't ask me what they wanted with them. It was just spite." Her face flinched at the memory and her eyes reddened, although I couldn't tell if it was from emotion or the peach brandy. She had drunk two generous shots of it and was onto her third. I waited a moment for her to recover and then asked why her sister had hired a private investigator. Her eyes lit up with scornful pleasure.

"It was the brat," she said. "I don't call it a child because it was a brat and probably a bastard too. And I don't call it *her* brat because it wasn't hers. Rosemary liked to tell people it was hers but it was no more hers than it was mine. My sister always wanted to have a baby more than anything else in the world. What she wanted a child for, I'll never know. When she had one, she didn't know what to do with it. They took it away from her, which was exactly what they should have done."

"You mean she adopted a child?"

"Adopted my foot!" Alma Kramer shifted in her seat and leaned her head toward me as if she were going to whisper a secret. Then she slapped her knee and shouted, "She bought it! Bought it like a pound of cheese and a quart of milk thank you. And don't think I mind telling you about it. If you're a reporter in disguise and intend to splash this story all over the papers, it doesn't matter a hoot to me because I haven't been able to hold up my head in this neighborhood for a quarter of a century and it's no skin off my nose."

I assured Alma Kramer I wasn't a reporter and the news seemed to disappoint her. But her spirits quickly revived. I had a feeling she'd told this particular story many times before. It had a well-rehearsed ring to it, like a passage from a book that she never tired of reading aloud.

"I'll tell you," she said. "It was shortly after Koontz left Rosemary. Koontz was her second husband. Leaving Rosemary, by the way, was the only smart thing Koontz ever did in his life. After he left, Rosemary tried to get money out of Father but he wouldn't have anything to do with her so Rosemary went and worked in a bar. I call it a bar but there are less polite words for it. They had them in Egypt and they had them in Roman times and they probably had them in cave-man times. Today they call the girls 'hostesses.' Doesn't amount to a hill of beans, they're still *whoors*. So Rosemary went to work at this bar and got involved with this fellow, Hollis Brownlee, who was supposed to be a house painter. Brownlee even painted this house. You can see what a poor job he did. And Brownlee got Rosemary the brat."

"How did he do that?"

"He pulled it out of a hat," she snapped. "Don't ask me how he did it. I just know he got it for Rosemary. Came with papers and everything. Brand-new baby boy paid for with the money Rosemary'd saved from her immoral earnings. Then Rosemary went away and no one saw her for a couple of years, and by the time she got back she'd changed her story. Said it *was* her boy. Folks believed it too. Slicker'n grease when it comes to telling lies, my baby sister.

"Well, it's the same with all liars. They just can't keep track of who they've told what to. By the time she got back Rosemary was even telling *me* it was her baby." Alma Kramer's lips described an ornate sneer of amusement. *"Me.* When I knew for a fact she didn't have any more chance of having a baby than of having a litter of pigs. When I'd seen the boy's real father right here in this house. When she'd told me herself she'd paid an arm and a leg for the brat. And she has the gall to turn around and deny the whole thing. I ask you."

"The *real* father?" I let my mouth drop open in dumb, witless admiration of what she was telling me.

"Sure." She slowly rotated her foot, examining it with a smug, judicious look on her face. "He just turned up one day about a month after Rosemary got the kid. Said his name was Smith and he wanted to see if the baby was all right. All lies, of course. I'd bet my lungs Smith wasn't his real name. And he couldn't have given a damn about the baby or he wouldn't have sold it to Rosemary."

"What did this man look like?"

"Look like?" She paused, her lips pursed, her eyes wandering toward the ceiling. "Ordinary. Wouldn't have recognized him the next day. After twenty-five years he wouldn't look the same anyway, but I guess you didn't think of that."

"I may be the slow type, or maybe you're just damn swift. What did the baby look like?"

"A fat little thing with mousy hair and blue eyes. Rosemary stuffed him something awful and he was never anything but trouble. Wetting his bed and breaking everything and not an ounce of sweetness in him. Rosemary had him five years and then they arrested her for drunk driving and hitting a man. She was so drunk she never knew she'd hit anything, to hear her tell it, but the judge thought different. It wasn't her first offense with cars and drinking. They sent her away to the penitentiary but they might as well have sent her to hell for all the difference it made."

"What happened to the boy?" I asked. "What was his name, by the way?"

"Rosemary called him Bucky but she said his real name was Lawrence. Of course he didn't have any real name. Lawrence Koontz was just a name Rosemary made up for the birth certificate because she was still calling herself Koontz. Well, the authorities took the boy away and Rosemary decided to put him up for adoption. He must have gone into one of the state orphanages. Rosemary tried to get him back when she came out but they wouldn't hear of it. They've got rules about that kind of thing. You aren't allowed to know where your child went, and he isn't allowed to know where he came from. Rosemary tried to find out but she never got anywhere."

It was getting dark outside but Alma Kramer didn't turn on any lights. In the gloom her colorless face was dim except for the gleam of her eyes and the flash of her moistened lips. Her voice had thickened and there was a new coarseness of feeling in her manner. Somehow, no matter what she'd done, I thought I would like the sister better.

"When did a detective come into this business?" I asked.

"I'm getting to that," she growled. "A lot of folks would be happy with just what I've told you."

She made her sister's mistakes and sufferings sound like a box of chocolates she was doling out. So far I couldn't see where her story verged from truth into half lies. Perhaps what she'd told me was all true. Perhaps she was holding back something which would throw everything she'd said into an alignment that implicated her. Right now she was in a singing mood, so let her come out with it, I thought. When she'd had her say, I could use some of it to box her in. I noticed she was looking at me coldly, expecting me to say something.

I said, "How about a shot of that lighter fluid? This story could drive a person to drink."

"It's not that bad for home-made, is it?" she said, as if she'd put one over on me. "Help yourself. There's plenty more where that came from. I guess you could say it's a man's drink. I used to make it for my father. He'd have two shots before dinner, regular as clockwork."

I tossed off the full tumbler and shuddered, thinking if I had to take two shots of it every night I'd be dead too.

"You're not like that other private detective," she said, and then added, with a touch of what I realized was supposed to be feminine coyness, "if you are a private detective, that is."

"I've got a gun." I grinned. "And a license. You can't get much more private detective than that."

"Let's see." Her eyes narrowed.

"Aw, come on."

"Go on. Let's have a look at it." She was smirking at me in a way that made my flesh crawl. She seemed to be drawing me into some intimate, obscurely obscene complicity. I raised my pants leg, unbuttoned the holster snap, and hoisted out the Mauser. It gave off a dull bluish gleam in the nearly dark room. She took it in her heavily veined hands and snapped on the standard lamp by her chair.

"He didn't even have a gun," she sniffed, "the other fellow that Rosemary hired." She studied the Mauser with admiration, nodding to herself, very much the connoisseur. "Krauts know how to build a shoulder weapon." With a swift movement of her fingers, she released the catch and the clip dropped into her palm. "Automatic lock on it, right?" She held the gun to the light and peered into the breech. "Otherwise some fool'd maybe forget the cartridge in the chamber and blow his little finger off. Nice piece. You know how to take care of a weapon." She replaced the clip, checked the safety, and handed the Mauser back to me, butt first, with a jaunty, swaggering twitch of her shoulders. It was really turning into the boys' night out, and I no longer had any doubt I was in the company of a regular guy.

"I don't know about Rosemary," I said, "but you *are* a character."

She tried to look indifferent but her skin darkened into a sallow blush.

"This other detective . . ." She peered coolly into her glass. "The pipsqueak . . ."

"Stackman," I said, and watched her.

"That's the one. Runty little fellow married to a fat woman big enough to toss him across the room. Pint-sized men always go for the big women. Anyway, as I was saying, when Rosemary decided she wanted Bucky back, she hired Stackman to locate him. That was twenty years ago. Stackman took her money but he never found anything you couldn't stick under your fingernail. After that Rosemary just quit talking about the brat. She married Hagerbaum, who sold cosmetics door to door, but that didn't last long, and then he left her, and she married Pagrowski, a Polack who couldn't speak English worth a damn and beat her up when he was drunk, which was just about every night from the time they laid eyes on each other. Pagrowski left her after a year. Talk to Rosemary about Pagrowski and you'd think he was the sweetest man that ever lived. My sister always says she was married to the most *marvelous* men." Alma Kramer's falsetto imitation of her sister's voice set my teeth on edge.

"But Rosemary never did have anything but a passing acquaintance with reality. Anyway, by the time Pagrowski took off, Rosemary'd just about lost her looks and, being a soft-hearted old fool, I let her come live with me. She was almost all right there for a while. Oh, she'd go out with men once in a while and drink too much but mostly she stayed home and tried to act like the lady she wasn't . . . then this fool from the orphanage came to see her and started it all up again. He was just a troublemaker. Said he was acting on Bucky's behalf to trace the boy's real parents."

"You mean that fifteen years later this boy, Bucky, was trying to find out who his natural mother and father were?"

"That's what I said, didn't I?" she grunted proudly. "Of course Rosemary was dying to know all about Bucky but this orphanage fellow wasn't giving anything away. He said he wasn't authorized to tell her anything. He sat right on that sofa where you're sitting now, and Rosemary talked his ear off. All about what a pretty baby Bucky had been and how they'd tricked her into signing him away. And all kinds of lies about Koontz, who was supposed to be Bucky's father even though Koontz had never even seen the boy. Well, I tell you, I felt sorry for Bucky and figured if the boy wanted the truth he had a right to it. When Rosemary was out of the room, I told this fellow how Rosemary had never had a baby at all. I told him she bought the boy from Hollis Brownlee. And how its own father had visited it when it was little and wasn't any more interested in it than an old shoe. Didn't want it. Sold it the way you sell a puppy. That woke him up all right."

"Do you remember this official's name, or whom he worked for?"

"Don't recall his name. He had a red beard and long hair. Decent-sized fellow, a little shorter than you. After that we never saw him again, or heard anything from Bucky, which was for the best. Of course Rosemary got all excited again and hired Stackman but he didn't do any better than he had fifteen years before. Every once in a while he'd tell her he'd found some new clue but it

was just a way of getting money out of her. It was just a
fantasy for Rosemary. She's been living the last five
years as if any minute Bucky's going to walk through
the door, or call her on the phone."

"When was the last time she saw Stackman?"

"I think she talked to him a few days ago on the
phone. It wasn't anything but Stackman up to his old
tricks. He had some story about one of Bucky's foster
parents having an idea where Bucky was, but it was
going to cost money to hear about it. I know she isn't
ever going to find out anything. Hiring Stackman again
after all these years is just second childhood for Rosemary."

"May I use your phone, please?" I got to my feet.
"I'll charge the calls to my office."

She showed me into the kitchen and left me alone
there. I called Harry at the phone company. He'd run
the Kramer toll calls against those of everyone else involved in the case and had come up with one hot piece
of information. Someone in the Kramer house had
phoned Mrs. Elevel the evening she committed suicide.

I sat at the kitchen table and tried to force everything
I knew into some pattern that would include all the people involved in the case. It was a do-it-yourself headache. From looking like straightforward extortion, the
case had suddenly telescoped back a quarter of a century, and the number of suspects seemed to be swelling
every minute. How much of Alma Kramer's story could
I believe? Her picture of her sister was so obviously distorted by envy that I didn't know how much of it to
credit. The only consistent pattern I could detect was
the death of everyone who learned anything about the
case. Had Stackman been working for Rosemary Kramer's interests when he showed up in the Benedict Canyon house, or was he trying to put the bite on someone
himself? The state of his clothes, his lack of a gun,
seemed to point to his having been an honest, unsuc-

cessful investigator, not a sharper trying to gnaw a corner off someone else's pie.

I went back into the parlor and caught Alma Kramer
pouring herself another shot of her peachy rotgut. She
looked up resentfully, left the glass untouched, and then
busied herself drawing the curtains. She moved about
with an elaborate air of dignity, taking a little too long
over everything, the way a drunk will. She didn't have a
hell of a lot to recommend her. Her thin, pinched nose
and dry cheeks had turned red, open-pored, and oily.
There was something unwholesome and menacing about
her. She was just tall and big-boned enough that you
didn't feel safe turning your back on her. I'd never before met a sixty-year-old woman who could physically
intimidate me but those strong hands looked as if they
could take something by the neck and squeeze the life
out of it. I'm not saying I couldn't have flattened her
with a slap on the face. She was sixty years old, for
Christ's sake. But she was as big as I was, and with the
drinking and the loaded automatic on the bookshelf,
she made me uneasy. She had been mad about something all her life, and she was still in search of a satis-
factory outlet for the anger. You got the impression that
by this stage almost anything would do.

"Stackman's dead," I said by way of conversation.
"Shot to death along with Elevel's daughter. A twenty-
two automatic in the back of the head. Little hole, in
through the back, out through the front, and it's goodby
pipsqueak forever."

She sat down and stared back at me, blinking rapidly,
as if she couldn't quite get me into focus. Her expression of shock didn't last long. A few seconds later she
tossed her head and said, "I've told you all I know.
Stackman was no friend of mine, and I don't know this
Elevel girl."

"I know that. But the police don't. A phone call was
made from this house to the Elevel house several nights

ago. The same night the girl disappeared. The same night her mother killed herself."

"That is something you'll have to take up with my sister." She glanced at the decanter of peach brandy and her right hand tightened into a fist. "I'm tired of defending Rosemary. If she's got herself into trouble, she'll just have to take the consequences." She rose to her feet and put her hands on her hips. "I'd like to get this settled now. If you like, I'll walk you to the church hall. The meeting will be breaking up soon. If you don't catch Rosemary there, she might go off drinking with one of those old fogeys and not be back for hours."

"That would be very kind of you." I stood up.

"I take a walk about this hour anyway." She picked up the tray of drinks and the decanter and disappeared into the kitchen, where I guessed she probably polished off that shot she hadn't wanted to take in front of me. She came back with a crocheted shawl pulled over her army fatigue jacket. She had also slipped into a pair of old black shoes which looked like service issue and probably had belonged to her father. As she walked down the corridor to the front door, they made a metallic clicking from the steel taps in the heels and toes.

I waited on the unlit porch while she locked the door.

"A lot of women would be afraid to walk around these streets at night," I offered.

"A lot of women would." She shrugged. "I carry a gun. They haven't made the darkie yet who scared me. One of these nights one's going to try and snatch my purse, or interfere with me, and he'll get a little surprise. Right between the eyes."

She sounded slightly disappointed that it hadn't happened yet. We walked down the steps, and over the flagstone path to the pavement. The street was warm and quiet and smelled of flowers and freshly cut grass. Across the street I could see the rectangular blue glow of a TV set shining through the drawn draperies. As we walked down the street I saw a similar glow in each front window. Several streets away a car peeled off from a traffic light, leaving an angry roar in the night air, then silence again. Alma Kramer stumbled and grasped my arm and then held onto it. She didn't hold it gently like an old woman in need of support. She gripped my biceps firmly like a cop steering a defendant into the courtroom. We walked like that for several blocks, without speaking, accompanied by the biting clink of her steel taps on the concrete pavement.

I saw the shoe from half a block away, a shiny black leather pump lying on the edge of a pool of light cast by a street lamp. It didn't register at first. I just thought it looked interesting in a surreal kind of way, a high-heeled shoe all by itself on the deserted pavement. As we drew closer, I saw that its heel was wedged into a crack in the concrete and then I felt Alma Kramer's fingernails digging into my arm.

In the gutter a woman's head and shoulders protruded from underneath a parked car. At the sight of her, Alma Kramer howled, clutching at me.

"Rosemary," she said in a strangled voice. "Baby Rosemary . . ."

I slapped her once firmly on the cheek and she sat down abruptly on the curb, like an automaton.

Her sister Rosemary was as tall as Alma and considerably heavier, a lush, overripe woman with not much left of her hourglass figure. She was dead.

I pulled her out from under the car and dragged her onto someone's front lawn. She was still warm but there was no pulse and her eyes responded to nothing. Above the ear and at the base of the skull her blue-rinsed hair was matted with blood. It looked as if she'd been hit as hard as you can be hit with something like a lead pipe. Her heavily painted face was twisted into an exaggerated grimance of surprise. Her eyebrows looked pathetically puzzled, as if death had asked her an impossible question and punished her for not knowing the answer.

For a moment I just kneeled over her, with my

bloodied hands digging into the grass. She smelled of
lilac perfume, face powder, and wine. A great, plump,
painted woman in a flowery rayon dress. All dolled up
with too much costume jewelry and a stained white
feather boa around her neck. She could have been doz-
ing there on the grass, sleeping off a binge. But she
wasn't. She was as dead as Mrs. Elevel, as Charlotte, as
Stackman.

"And all that time I was talking about the poor baby,
she was lying here," Alma Kramer sobbed. "The poor
baby. She was the prettiest thing . . ."

"Don't touch anything," I said. "I'm calling the
cops."

The man whose front lawn we'd borrowed let me use
his phone. I called the Elevel house first and got Calvin.
I explained what had happened and told him to get
Joe's attorney over to Pasadena as fast as possible. I
was going to have to inform Granville of the murder.

"They could tie me up downtown all night," I said.
"And I've got more leads to follow up."

"Tyrone's disappeared," Calvin told me. "We've got
people combing the hills for him."

There was a long pause. I said, "He picks the wrong
nights to disappear. Is that dune buggy of his licensed
for use on roads?"

"Yes."

"Does Joe want an all points bulletin put out on
him?"

"Just a second." Calvin went off the line to talk to
Joe. "I don't think so," he said. "You know, he may
show up. It may be nothing. Let's not panic."

"My neck is getting stretched out very far on this," I
said. "You get that attorney over here fast."

I hung up and dialed the Pasadena police and then
Granville. I gave him the rough details and then walked
back out to the street.

A small group of neighbors had formed a cluster on
the pavement near Rosemary's body. I got them moved

back and then went over to Alma Kramer. She was
leaning back against a car. Beneath her shawl I could
see her hand gripped around the automatic.

"That's going to make the police nervous." I nodded
toward the gun. "And I don't think you have a permit
to carry a concealed weapon."

"Then I'll just hold it right here in my hand, right out
in the open." She brandished it. "Don't tell me about
the police. Where were they when that filth killed my
sister?"

"No one killed Rosemary for her money." I took the
gun out of her hand, removed the clip, and slipped it
into my pocket.

"Well, don't think I'm going to tell them what I was
telling you—about Hollis Brownlee and buying the
baby—because I'm not."

"Why?"

"Because it's shameful and I won't have people talking bad about my sister."

Now that she was dead Rosemary was suddenly
worth something.

"Wouldn't you like to get the people who did this?" I
asked. "You might know a little too much yourself."

"How do you know any of that?" she cried peevishly.
"You don't know anything. Look at her! Someone just
hit her and snatched her purse." Her eyes flashed. "I
don't want the police snooping around my house. I—I
could get into trouble."

"Over what?"

"That baby-selling business," she said weakly.

"That was a quarter of a century ago. The statute of
limitations ran out on it a long time ago."

"Well, the liquor then, you fool," she hissed. "I've
got a whole basement full of home-made liquor. I'm a
bootlegger."

"Oh Jesus," I said. "You mix up peach brandy for
your neighbors. This is murder, Miss Kramer. That's
what the cops are going to care about."

Those were the last words I had with her because the Pasadena police arrived then, followed by some media wagons who'd picked up the call on the police band. The area was lit up and cordoned off, and before you knew it, it was looking like a movie set. Under the lamps, lying on her back, Rosemary Kramer had a garish carnival air; there should have been sawdust coming out of her head instead of dark red blood. You felt she would have been tickled at all the male attention she was getting.

I kept my statement short and simple. A homicide detective took it down. Rosemary had won twenty dollars at bingo in the church hall that night, and the police seemed less interested in me than in finding out whom she'd been playing with. It looked like a straightforward mugging to them, which was fine with a nervous man called Thomas Kyd.

I didn't see Granville until he was standing right next to me. He had the rabbit with him and another character with a blunt, snub-nosed face that included everything but a forehead. He looked like he could pick the pavement up and throw it at me. The rabbit wore a wet yokel smile. It was one of these nervous, mindless smiles which would stay there when he read the evening papers, when he watched the sun go down, and when he kicked you in the spine.

With a murmured grunt and a gleam of police shield they detached me from the throng and walked me back to the Kramer house. They didn't say anything. But they crowded me, the one in front walking too slow, the one behind grazing my heels. They were getting the message across. I was supposed to feel that they wanted something but that any attempt I made to give it to them would only make matters worse. The longer I failed to give it to them, the worse would be their method of dealing with me. They were strictly from Kafka, and you could tell they liked their work.

The one with no forehead opened the front door with

Alma Kramer's keys. We went into the kitchen. Granville sat down at the table by the window, lit a cigar, and said:

"Search that bastard."

Rabbit's partner grabbed my arms from behind, pointed me at the wall, and then threw me. I put out my hands to stop the wall from smacking me in the face, and Rabbit kicked my feet out from under me

"I want you to stand up," Rabbit said. "Didn't you hear the chief? Hands against the wall, feet back and spread apart, and shut up."

I did what I was told. While the tough one searched me, Rabbit kicked my ankles back and hollered at me to stand still. After they found the Mauser and Alma Kramer's automatic, Rabbit drew his hand swiftly up my legs and punched me in the groin. I blacked out.

I was awakened by a loud thudding sound that seemed to be coming from inside my head. The nauseatingly throbbing blur of light and color slowly resolved itself into Alma Kramer's kitchen. The thudding sound was a hand methodically slamming into my cheeks. Connected to the hand was an arm, connected to the arm was a shoulder, and connected to the shoulder was a neck with a face on the end of it that looked like a fist with eyes. I blacked out again.

When I came to they were all three sitting there watching me with calm, cold, patient eyes. From now on, they seemed to say, hitting me was going to be as automatic and inevitable as lighting a cigarette.

"What were you doing in Pasadena, Kyd?" Granville said.

"I want to talk to a lawyer." I got to my knees and then crashed over on my side from the nausea.

"He must mean a doctor, chief, not a lawyer," Rabbit said earnestly.

"I'm protected by an attorney's right to private communication with his client. I don't have to tell you anything. Ever. About anything." I was fighting not to vomit. I felt like someone had run my guts through an electric blender and poured them back down my throat.

"You're impeding a murder investigation. You're running around with guns. I'm going to nail a one-to-five jacket on you."

"Why don't you pick up the croaker, Granville?" I said.

"You're withholding evidence." Rabbit said.

"Guys like you all have one thing in common." I spit out some blood laced with bile. "When they unstrap their guns, their balls drop off."

Granville sighed in disgust.

"You're either too smart, or they left out a screw when they put you together, and both ways you're spitting in the wind. You better get your mind right or you're going to remember me every time you try to take a leak for the rest of your life."

He said it like he meant it and like it bored the hell out of him.

"We know you take a punch good." Granville sighed. "We can see you're one hell of a tough punk. You talk back real good too. Don't be a loser all your life, fellah. Give us your angles and you can walk out of here."

"You better take me in, or let me go," I said. "I haven't got anything else to say to you."

"Cuff him." Granville put out his cigar. "I don't want him playing with himself on the way downtown."

Rabbit's partner hoisted me up by my belt and Rabbit snapped on the cuffs, jamming my hands up my back. A coat was thrown over my head and I was led quickly out of the kitchen and around the side of the house, then thrown into the back seat of a police car.

Chapter NINETEEN

The ride downtown was a long-drawn-out blur of voices and body sickness. Granville kept asking me questions and when I didn't answer the rabbit would say, "Jeez, lighten up, pal," and hit the side of my face with the butt of his hand. It rattled my teeth and sent waves of pain through my head without leaving a mark on my face. Every time Rabbit socked me, his partner would get mad and protest, "Stop shoving, pal," and poke me from the other side.

They weren't imaginative but they were predictable. Like bowel movements.

"I don't know why he isn't talking," Rabbit piped up cheerfully. "Just looking at him, you know this punk would sell his mother to a coon for a quarter."

"You paid one to put it to yours," I said.

"A live one," the partner remarked genially and socked me in the throat.

"You look like you're going to cry, Kyd," Rabbit said. "You aren't going to cry on us, are you?"

"Eat shit," I said.

"What should I do with your bones?" Rabbit grinned.

"Build a cage for your mother."

"I didn't like that," Rabbit said.

"I didn't go for that one much myself." His partner seized my jaw and bent it toward his face. "I think your mouth needs cleaning out, friend," he said, and spit full into it.

It was a pale green office with a desk, wire mesh screens on the windows, and shiny colorless linoleum on the floor. It smelled of machine oil, sweat, and disinfectant. A hard, shadowless light hummed in every corner of the room. Granville was talking to someone behind the desk, someone to whom he deferred, but I could not hear the man's replies.

"I want to throw the book at him," Granville was saying. "He interferes. He gives us false information. He holds back evidence. He talks back. He badmouths my men. He walks around with guns in his pockets. And he knows something but he won't spit it out."

The man behind the desk picked up the ringing phone, listened a moment, and then hung up. Granville walked back and forth in front of his desk. His superior was a tall, cadaverous-looking man with bony limbs and a tired, careworn face. He had deep, round hazel eyes ringed by shadows, and a long sensitive nose, many times broken, that wandered crookedly through his face. Blue smoke issued in periodic streams from his mouth but you could see no cigarette; he kept it concealed by his palm, and his palm stayed under the desk. Every moment or so he would draw his hand across his mouth in a slow wiping gesture, and a few seconds later a thin stream of blue smoke would emerge.

"Take the cuffs off," he said quietly. Then he offered me a white Sherman's Turkish Oval which I took but could not hold because my fingers were dead. There were pale blue and red marks on my wrists where the steel had bitten into the bloodless flesh. I rubbed them and flexed my fingers, and when some feeling had returned, I bent down and picked the cigarette off the floor and laid it on the desk.

"I think we've got some problem of communication here, Kyd," the man said gravely. "This kind of thing doesn't happen much any more. There's cooperation between the force and most agencies."

I didn't say anything to that.

"Granville isn't a bad guy," he said. "But there's no percentage in rubbing him the wrong way. You boys get a pretty free hand on civil cases. You've all got contacts in the Department and we leak plenty of information to you. On criminal actions like this one we expect the same in return. What'd you say?"

"No one's disagreeing." I shrugged and noticed that Granville smirked.

"So talk a little and we'll drop the charges," the man said. "Or be dumb and we'll dream up some more, suspend your license, hold you for questioning. What d'you say?"

"What charges? I removed Alma Kramer's gun from her at the scene of the crime because I thought one of your boys might get nervous. I've got a permit for my own gun. Exactly what charges are you talking about?"

"A mouth," the man commented wearily.

"I've been ready to cooperate from the start. Granville could have had it all on a plate. But Granville prefers shoving people around." I picked up the cigarette and lit it and was glad to see my hands were steady. "One of his witnesses nearly got bumped off this afternoon because he canceled protective custody on her. The same guy who got Charlotte Elevel's address from the Academy, and who probably made the hit on her and Stackman, was waiting in the Academy parking lot this afternoon for the one witness who could identify him."

"He's lying." Granville yawned.

"I've got a guy from White and Rinehart guarding the witness now," I said. "Tonight Granville doesn't bother to question Alma Kramer. He gives her to the Pasadena cops, who are going to treat the murder like a mugging. I could have let it go but instead I call Granville because I'm ready to explain what this Kramer woman has to do with the case. He brings along two ballbreakers. For openers, the one with no chin punches me in the nuts and the one with no forehead spits in my mouth. I guess that's just the new style you were talking about in your little speech on cooperation."

"What a mouth." The man shook his head.

"You say that a lot, don't you," I said. "You think I

hate cops. I don't hate cops. Granville isn't a cop. Granville's just a stain that got up off the floor one day and decided to walk around."

"Get him out of here." The man waved his hand. "His goddamn lawyer's screaming law at me on the phone."

Rabbit and his partner walked me to the door.

"Wait a minute," the man said. He leaned back in his swivel chair and looked at me.

"I don't think you're aware of what you just did, so I'm going to spell it out for you. From now on everything you do is our business. The smallest infraction and we're going to bust your ass. We don't let hippie punks like you get away with anything. Now beat it."

They escorted me down the hall, into an elevator.

Rabbit's partner said, "Why don't you wise up?"

I didn't answer.

"What'd you think, this is some big thrill for us giving you a hard time?" he persisted. "How we going to make a collar if we don't get information?"

"Try the English language," I said.

"What's that?" He scowled.

"Try asking first. If that doesn't work, think of something else. You guys just don't make me feel talkative."

"Five more minutes in the car and you would have talked plenty," Rabbit growled.

"The jerk thinks it was personal," his partner said. "It ain't personal, friend. It's just a job."

"Tell it to Eichmann."

"Don't talk to the fruit," Rabbit said harshly. "You don't have to apologize to a fruit like him."

"Any time you want your lights punched out, Bugs," —I smiled—"you know where I live."

The elevator doors opened. Calvin and Charley LaSalle, Joe's young attorney, were waiting by the desk as we came out. Since I'd never been booked, getting out was a matter of signing a form for my confiscated weapon. As I returned his pen to the desk sergeant, he looked up and said drily, "Thank you for your cooperation, sir." I knew that the L.A. cops had recently been ordered to thank members of the public who cooperated on routine matters.

"Don't mention it," I said. "Have a lovely night shift."

Chapter TWENTY

I sank back into the plush beige seats of the Elevel Bentley and slowly peeled off my shoes and socks. Rabbit had done a job on my ankles. They were a mess of bruised flesh and crusted blood. My kidneys throbbed with a steady ache that became unbearable when I breathed deeply. My jaw and the nerves around my eyes felt like I'd had several hours of root canal work done by an amateur with a corkscrew and a hammer.

Calvin opened the bar in the back seat and a little light came on, illuminating the rich gleam of liquor, sparkling glass, and polished silver. I dropped an ice cube in a tall glass, poured four fingers of Bombay gin over it, and then added a few drops of Angostura bitters. The bitters turned the silvery gin a deep rusty orange, the color of dried blood.

"Sorry we were so long," Calvin said. "But the Pasadena police didn't know where you'd gone."

I poured the gin down my throat, all of it, and gasped at the cold, burning pain. I wanted it to hit fast.

"Where's Tyrone?" I asked.

"He came back," Calvin said quickly. "He'd actually been to Pasadena to visit the old house where he'd lived as a kid. I think all this has churned up a lot of memories in Tyrone."

I decided to put Tyrone on the back burner for a bit. LaSalle and Calvin looked so fresh and young and well-groomed, I felt like making them sweat a bit. They could wait a while to find out whether I'd mentioned Tyrone's trip to Pasadena to the cops.

"I thought Joe was tight with Granville," I said. "I thought the Elevels had Granville house-trained. Someone must have forgotten to give him his doggie biscuit this week."

"There was a certain amout of tension." Calvin cleared his throat. "Because Granville felt you should be dropped from the case and initially Joe was of the same opinion. I understand certain things came up afterward which induced Joe to change his mind. Right now relations could be better with Granville, I'll admit that, certainly."

It killed me the way he talked. Described in that polite rigmarole, a falling out between a millionaire and a bent cop sounded like a meeting of the board, and the systematic torture of a bound man was a failure of communication. I hadn't been punched in the balls at all; I'd only been a peripheral participant in a certain amount of tension between two essentially reasonable parties. Satisfied with my understanding of that distinction, I refilled my glass. I wasn't trying to get loaded. I was merely seeking to alleviate a temporary discomfort consequent on my misunderstanding of the situation wherein I'd got busted in the nuts. I stuck a cigarette between my lips and Calvin and LaSalle both tried to light it with matching gold Dunhill lighters.

"The Bobbsey twins," I said.

"Ordinarily, Mr. Kyd," LaSalle wiped his glasses, "in view of your physical condition we'd have pictures of your ankles and face taken in the presence of a doctor, and we'd press charges."

"It's the clearest case of police brutality I've ever seen," Calvin chimed in virtuously.

"You probably mean the only one," I said.

"But . . . uh . . . right now," LaSalle said, "we don't want to antagonize—you understand—the authorities because, uh . . ."

"Because Tyrone may have beaten in an old lady's skull with a tire iron this evening. I understand." I looked at him and grinned. "You can talk straight to me. You must have gathered I'm not too sensitive about this kind of deal."

"Come on, Mr. Kyd." He flushed. "That's an awfully rash thing to say." He glanced once, quickly, to make sure the glass partition isolating us from the driver was closed. "I understand how you feel and I don't blame you for being mad. You have every right to be. On the other hand, Joe is not unaware of what he owes you. I don't think you're going to be disappointed in his reaction to your loyalty."

"Don't make me cheap, LaSalle," I said softly. "You and I aren't on the same payroll and never will be. When those characters were taking shots at me, it wasn't thinking about money that kept my mouth shut. This is my second ride in a back seat tonight. It's just the sweeter side of the same hype. If Joe *could* buy my silence then you can be damned sure the cops could put in a more convincing bid. But he can't and they couldn't." I paused for breath. "And it's because he can't that they couldn't. And having said that, let's forget it."

"I understand and I'm sorry," LaSalle said.

I lifted my glass to him. "Thanks. I'm glad someone does because I don't."

"Couldn't you have, you know, marginally cooperated with them?"

"Sure. But I've got this allergy to getting punched in the balls. Once it starts you can't do anything with me."

"Is that what they did? Right off?" He grimaced.

"They kicked me a little first to get me in the mood to appreciate the chop in the nuts, but it was the latter which really put the point of disagreement into focus. When they proceded to punch me in the face and kidneys and spit into my mouth I became cognizant that there doubtless did exist a certain amount of tension between Joe and the deputy chief."

"I am very sorry this happened," LaSalle said with real distress.

The liquor had gone to my head and I found myself enjoying talking like a book. It was like looking at the world through a new set of sunglasses.

Calvin leaned toward me. In his black suit and with the dark glasses he looked like an unhealthy ghost.

"Who exactly was this Kramer woman?" he asked.

"What was Tyrone doing in Pasadena?" I said.

Calvin's face tightened. He had a bleached-out, bloodless complexion like someone who had spent his whole life indoors, who'd never had enough to eat, and who was never going to forget it.

"Listen, Kyd," he said softly. "We pay you to find out things. And we expect you to deliver. Who was this Kramer woman?"

"I don't work for you. For all I know you're just the guy who sharpens the pencils and empties the wastepaper baskets."

"You come on so tough," he said harshly, "You're in a hole with the cops. Maybe a complaint from your former client will just put you out of business."

"Yeah, and maybe if I have a little talk with the cops your boss's son is going to get picked up. Don't threaten me with this crap. I'm not in the mood."

There was silence the rest of the way. Getting out of the car, Calvin caught his foot and nearly fell down. He cursed fiercely and without saying anything else walked away to his bungalow.

"I've seen him do that kind of thing before," I said.

LaSalle looked troubled. "He's clumsy. Like an adolescent." He turned and shook my hand. "Again, I'm sorry. I wouldn't have handled things the way Calvin did. I think you're doing a helluva job."

"I appreciate it. Tell Joe I'll have something for him tomorrow."

LaSalle suggested a nightcap but I declined. He was a pleasant guy but I was in an ugly mood. I wanted to do my own drinking in my own house, with my own thoughts. I was feeling a little sick of people.

Chapter TWENTY-ONE

The streets of Bel Air were empty and Sunset had almost no traffic. In the rear-view mirror my face looked swollen. There were shadowlike bruises around my eyes and jaw. Thinking about Granville made me grit my teeth, and that hurt my jaw and throat, and that just made me madder. As for Rabbit, I hoped that one day I could say what an Arab had once said about his enemy: "He kicked me in the back when I wasn't looking, so I kicked him in the face, twice, when he was." After a while I turned on the radio and tried to forget about straightening Rabbit's teeth with my shoe. I got a talk show with a panel of experts discussing gun control. There were guns in over half the homes in America. Some 800,000 Americans had been shot in this century, more than all the Americans lost in all the wars the country had fought since its founding. In the last six years the number of guns had doubled. I switched stations and got a man who could prove with the Book of Revelations that the world was coming to an end. It was all something to do with rising food prices and contraception and the Kennedy assassinations, and if I sent him a check or money order for $7.98 he'd mail me a book that would show me how to escape the coming destruction while making a fortune in desert real estate. He ended his argument by reminding all of us out there that the distance between Sodom and Gomorrah was the same as that between Los Angeles and Las Vegas.

I didn't want to know. I just wanted two more drinks, a hot shower, and bed. I turned off the radio and listened to the smooth, powerful hum of the MG's engine. It could do a hundred without starting to shake and cruised like a glider at seventy-five. If you didn't worry about breaking the law, it could get me anywhere as fast as a Bentley could. I wondered how you could afford a Bentley anyway, without breaking a few laws. Joe Elevel hadn't made his twenty million dollars by watching his pennies and saving food coupons. If he was a prudent, industrious man, he was also, you could be sure, a predator in his business dealings. It had been clear early on that in some way, unknown to me, I was being used by him. He was holding back something. But I didn't believe he was a murderer. I couldn't even glimpse a possible motive connecting him to the case. Calvin might benefit financially from the deaths of Joe's wife and daughter but he looked destined to make his pile anyway, by legitimate means. He didn't strike me as the type to go for long shots unless he was betting with someone else's money. Tyrone, of course, looked like good material for any atrocity, and his trip to Pasadena didn't sound like coincidence. Coronado and Grande I felt sure of. They were in it, and the killer was their main piece on the board. But then somewhere I had to fit in a twenty-five-year-old baby-selling ring, a dead old woman, and a screwy sister who came on like John Wayne. Not to mention peripheral figures like Roth, and Leonardo, and perhaps even Lucy. I was doubly damned there, damned for genuinely liking her, and damned for my secret uneasiness and the moral uncertainty I felt. Does a suspicion of role-playing lie at the heart of every human relationship? Couldn't I keep one corner of my life untouched by ambiguity and doubt? I felt lousy. After three days I had a lot of illegally procured evidence, one suicide, three murders, and a case that had about as much symmetry as a half-digested pizza. The police wanted to put me out of business, and the way I felt, I thought they might be doing me a favor.

A hot wind was blowing as I got out of my car. It crackled the eucalyptus leaves that lay in piles along the street. I walked the ten yards to my front gate, swung it open, and stopped. The flagstone path ahead of me was bathed in the glow of the street lamp. Lying on the grass to the side of the path was a nearly black cigar butt, the long, twisted variety that looks like a braided licorice stick. The main house in front of me concealed my own place from view but the man waiting for me would have heard my car. I backed out of the gate and walked away down the windy street.

Was Gervano really in there waiting in the dark, or had he come and gone? Bundy Drive is a long, winding residential street that curls like a descending stream through the folds of the hills until it straightens out on the flat land below. At my end of the drive the houses nestle at the base of rugged foothills that descend right into their backyards. Farther north these foothills become the Santa Monica Mountains, dividing what is loosely termed Los Angeles from the San Fernando Valley.

I had retreated into these hills before, to escape domestic quarrels, to evade marshals trying to issue summonses, or simply to get a taste of the landscape they had obliterated when they constructed the stucco and neon wilderness of Los Angeles.

When I'd put several hundred yards behind me I cut in between two houses and climbed into the thick brush covering the hillside. From a distance, in daylight, the vegetation looks mild and friendly, washed with dusty pastel colors, and you imagine you could climb up through it with ease. It is in fact a massive, densely woven thicket in which the footing is treacherous. You have to move through it crouched over with your hands in front of your eyes and expect to drop through the dead underbrush at any moment. No gloves, the wrong shoes, and darkness didn't help my progress. By the time I reached the crest of the hill I was soaked with sweat and my skin felt like I'd been rolling in thumb tacks.

I rested for several moments, peering down at the

road below, and then followed the broad fire trail that ran along the summit, until I was directly above my house.

I descended again into the brush, went fifty yards down, and then followed a coyote trail on hands and knees until I came out into a small clearing. It was dominated by a bigger-than-average scrub oak. Looking up into the tangled branches, it took me several moments to pick out the strand of rope. When I found it, I climbed up and undid the knot, letting down the basket-shaped birds' nest I had rigged in the upper branches.

It had been over two years since I'd visited the clearing, and I got a weird flash of the state of mind I must have been in when I went to such lengths to hide something.

Inside the birds' nest was a steel toolbox with everything you'd expect to find in a paranoid's survival kit. It held false identification in the form of a passport and driver's license in the name of Arthur Baker, plus a copy of his birth certificate from the Los Angeles Hall of Records. Arthur Baker and I had been born on the same day but he had died at the age of two weeks. I'd used the birth certificate to get a social security number, and with that, the driver's license and passport were easy to obtain. Stuck between the pages of the passport was a sheaf of twenty one-hundred-dollar bills. The other compartments contained a box of disposable hypos, ampules of morphine, enough speed to keep me awake for a week, and a long-bladed folding knife. In the very bottom, under the upper tray, was a short-barreled Smith & Wesson .38 revolver with six spare rounds.

It was a logical collection of items for someone poised to slip from one identity into another, for a fugitive, for someone whose life was seriously threatened. But two years ago I'd been none of those things. There had been no objective reason for hanging the makings of a new and dangerous life up in that tree. Was it just the old habit of distrust? A premonition that, things being what they were, I was one day bound to abandon my existence as Thomas Kyd?

The gun was in a sealed plastic envelope filled with oil. I took it out, wiped it clean, and put in six shells, then emptied the remaining boxes of ammunition into my pocket. No, I thought, assembling a second identity hadn't been motivated by distrust, or fear. I'd done it very soon after my wife died, in a quiet methodical fury, hoping unconsciously to escape a life in ruins. Being on the run under a false name would have been light relief during that period.

And now I was probably going to have to use the one item in the toolbox I'd hesitated about including: the gun.

I was not happy. But I was ready.

Chapter TWENTY-TWO

It took almost an hour to work my way down the hillside to within a few yards of my back garden. It had to be done on my ass, along narrow passages made by and for coyotes. It was snake country, and it was the hour for rattlers to be out hunting. The hot wind playing with the underbrush masked the sound of my descent, but I wasn't fooling the locals. Every mouse, bird, and insect within fifty yards followed my progress in unnatural hushed silence.

I poised myself in the bushes for a long wait. A spotlight in my neighbor's garden partially illuminated my backyard, but the reflection off the sliding glass windows prevented me from seeing into the living room. It was a quarter after three. In a few hours the light would change enough for me to get a better look.

It was possible the man who smoked the twisted cigars was not inside. While I'd been in the underbrush I'd heard several cars ascend and descend Bundy Drive. There was also a chance he was waiting somewhere between the guest house and the main house, in the bushes like myself.

In the next hour I heard my phone ring at least a dozen times. Someone badly wanted to reach me, either the Elevels, or Lucy. The last time it rang I saw a flash of red light made by a pair of hands cupping a match in the living room. Smoking kills.

I moved around the garden to the kitchen door at the side of the house, and waited. After a few minutes the phone rang again. It rang about ten times. I used each individual ring to cover the noise I made getting through the kitchen into the hallway off the living room. There was enough light to see that my visitor had moved from his original position. That knowledge brought my pulse up a good fifty beats a minute. He was no longer in the living room.

I waited in the dark hallway, feeling the sweat run down my ribs, the breath hardly moving in my lungs.

There was a sound of someone urinating into the toilet bowl, followed by a faint splash and sizzle as he dropped his cigar. Then he glided into the living room and sat down in an armchair. I couldn't see him well. He was just a dark shape in the shadows, as motionless and silent as the furniture.

I was positive he was the man whose scarred fingertips had touched Charlotte's publicity photos at the Academy, who'd put a slug through her brain, who'd been waiting in the parking lot for Lucy. Maybe he'd also done the tire-iron hit on Rosemary Kramer.

I steadied the .38 in both my hands. I was a good enough shot at that close range to wound a man without killing him. I wanted his vocal cords in good shape for the district attorney's office.

I dropped to one knee and took a bead on him, partially protected by the corner of the wall.

"Don't move!" I shouted.

He exploded out of the chair, and hurled himself head first toward the door. My first shot caught him in the leg. I was screaming at him not to move or I'd kill him but he was the wrong kind of animal. He crashed down, rolling and kicking into the table legs. Somehow, from that startled wounded tangle of limbs, came answering fire. Bright orange sheets of light blinded my eyes. He was shooting some heavy automatic fire into the darkness over my head, and I was flat on the ground. That shooting-him-in-the-leg phase was over. I was aiming for the middle of him, anywhere so long as it turned off his trigger finger. It didn't. His gun emptied itself, spraying the walls and ceiling in a last convulsive spurt, the way a person's bowels sometimes erupt in the moment of death.

In the dark I could hear him flopping on the floor and making a retching sound, and the click of his firing pin hitting spent shells.

I switched on the overhead light. The room was full of smoke, white drifting wreaths and clouds that eddied and wavered as I walked through them. He was flat on his back, a look of utter horror and surprise on his face. He was shaking his gun as if he wanted to let go of it but his hand wouldn't do what it was told. It jerked and flopped and rattled the heavy automatic against the floor. I pried his fingers from the gun and took it from him, and he immediately transferred his grip to my hand. I couldn't make out his face. His eyes were so huge, and his face so colorless and distended by the effort to breathe, that I wouldn't have recognized him if he had been my brother.

There were three stains spreading together across the front of his green silk shirt, merging with every breath he took, and one more on his bright yellow slacks above the knee. He kept trying to say something but all that came out of his mouth was blood frothing up pink from his lungs. I wanted it to end. I bent down and touched his chest. It was like touching the quivering skin of a kettledrum. I could feel his heart beating through his body, then nothing, then two powerful protracted thuds. I looked into his eyes. From tiny pinpoints the black pupils swiftly enlarged and engulfed the irises in their shiny blackness, and suddenly everything stopped; his eyes had no more life than a mounted owl's. Abruptly his chest deflated, expelling the air in a querulous rattle like wind through dry leaves.

Time passed. My whole body was trembling and humming like a tuning fork, and the horribly bright room humming along with me. I kept waiting for the dead man's grip on my hand to relax. I don't know how long it took me to realize that his hand was limp and I was the one doing the squeezing.

The phone rang and I remember I screamed involuntarily. It was Lucy but it might as well have been the man on the moon. All I remember of the conversation was having to stop twice to lurch into the bathroom and vomit. Each time, as I stood up from the bowl, I caught a glimpse of my face in the mirror, and each time the hair on the back of my neck shivered erect. I knew I was not in Vietnam. I knew the air did not taste dank and there was no smell of bloated corpses. It was a hallucination. There was no murmuring of Vietnamese voices on the edge of my hearing. It was an acid flashback.

"No, I'm fine," I said into the phone. "Just tired. I have to hang up now. I have to phone the police. Yes, yes, it's the same with me. I do too . . ."

I hung up and went into the kitchen and found a bottle of Johnny Walker Black Label, last year's Christmas present from White and Rinehart. I didn't swig from the bottle. I poured out a deep measure, dropped in a handful of ice cubes, and lightly sprayed it with seltzer. I was back in Los Angeles in my own house. A dawn light was spreading down the mountainside, across my backyard, and into the kitchen.

I walked back into the living room, bringing the bottle with me, and switched off the light. I turned the chair where the dead man had been sitting so that it faced the garden, sat down, and put the phone in my lap.

By the time the first squad cars arrived, the level in the bottle was down several inches, and the birds outside had initiated the first fierce conversation of the day.

I was going to have to get Elevel to reimburse me for the stained rug, shattered windows, and ruined set of clothes. You couldn't charge a client for the other stuff. They hadn't invented the language to write the invoices with.

Chapter TWENTY-THREE

That afternoon's edition of the paper carried a front-page photograph of the Mexican lying on my living room rug with three big ones in his chest. Behind him you could see the coffee table and standard lamp he'd knocked over, and the sliding glass window with a bullet hole near the top. Deputy Chief Granville's white patent leather loafers with the double brass chains were visible in the lower lefthand corner, adding the finishing touch to a very ugly picture.

It was an off day for big stories so the papers were giving the case the full treatment. The inside pages were filled with police shots of Charlotte Elevel, Harlan Stackman, and Rosemary Kramer. You could see their white faces, the wounds that had killed them, and the pools of blood, the kind of graphic details that make a rag worth twenty cents to the man on the street. There was even a picture of the deputy chief standing next to me in my living room, and another of my bullet-ridden wall. Rabbit got into that one somehow. The camera preserved him for history, looking with sullen prejudice at my bookcase as if he were about to arrest it.

Whatever button Elevel had pushed to keep his family out of the news wasn't responding any more. His tragedy was up for grabs, being condensed every hour on the half hour, between the commercials and the latest sports results.

I wouldn't talk to the reporters camped outside my door because I was paid to keep the confidence of my clients. I wouldn't talk to them anyway. They questioned my neighbors and went through my garbage and trampled my garden trying for telephoto shots through the windows. After several hours of it I was ready to go out and fight back but reporters don't fight back, they just take pictures of you throwing punches, and that's good copy too, so you never win like that.

I called my answering service but so many messages had backed up, I gave up after answering the first half a dozen. Most of them were people who'd read about the case in the papers and wanted to hire me to do something for them. What they all really wanted was to talk about the Elevel case so I referred them all to White and Rinehart and told them to ask for Tony Turino.

The big stain on the rug got to bothering me so I covered it with the couch. Somehow the message was getting through to me that I wasn't going to like living in that particular house any more.

Around six Lucy called and asked if I wanted company. We had a long intense conversation in which I tried to explain that I wasn't used to shooting people to death in my living room and I needed a little time to calm down. She understood that. She understood it so sensitively that I had to grit my teeth not to beg her to come over right then. I think I would have done it but there are times you feel so weak that even kindness seems frightening.

"At least it's over," she said. "The worst is over."

"That's what the papers say."

"You don't sound very convinced." Suddenly there was a note of warning, or alarm, in her voice.

"I killed the wrong man, Lucy, that's all."

"Listen, for one thing you didn't kill him. You were defending yourself from someone who was trying to murder you. It was in the papers. It's done, Thomas. *Past* history."

"That's not how I see it."

"Don't tell me you're going on with this!" she cried.

It was always hard for me to take advice, but this time I did. I didn't tell her.

"All I'm going to do," I said, "is take a sleeping pill,

have a few drinks, take the phone off the hook, and go to bed. I have to testify tomorrow at the inquest."

"Good," she said. "You'll feel better in the morning."

We talked a few more minutes and then just before hanging up, she asked casually, "Why did you say you killed the wrong man?"

"Did I say that?"

"You know you said it."

"I don't know. Maybe it always feels like that afterward. The case doesn't really add up yet. That's why it bugs me. It's all solved and it's totally meaningless. It makes it kind of ugly that way."

"You know, if I were you, I would stop thinking that way and be glad you're alive," she said firmly. "Think about it."

I expected her to go on but she didn't, and because of that the call ended on a strange empty note.

In my mind I could assemble a dozen water-tight facts to prove that I was paranoid and that Lucy was as unconnected to the case as the bird hopping across my lawn. But the very fact that I was defending her to myself proved the opposite of what I wanted to believe. And at the same time I knew I was crazy even to suspect her. This case was making me crazy. No one could say anything to me without my detecting a sinister double meaning.

Chapter TWENTY-FOUR

The inquest was a big hit. The only question left was what to call the man stretched out in a refrigerated box in the city morgue. On the original warrant put out on him for the Benedict Canyon slayings, he was identified as an unknown felon under a standard John Doe, Serial Number BL 40040. The other alternative was to call him Gervano, the name he had given at the Academy. For all the heat the Mexican was going to take off the police, I thought the least they could do was let him have a name. The coroner eventually decided to go with Gervano. In the papers it would sound like someone knew who the hell he was.

Not that it mattered a lot. Gervano was a district attorney's dream. When the evidence came in, no one even resented the fact he didn't have any fingerprints. A man from the Ballistic Unit testified that the .22 automatic found in the trunk of Gervano's stolen car was the same weapon that had killed Charlotte and Stackman. Prints Division had lifted scar markings from the pearl handle which matched the particular cracks and ridges on his finger tips. That wiped two unsolved homicides off the books.

Rosemary Kramer was even easier to dispose of. Traces of her blood had been found in Gervano's hair, a few drops having spattered him when he hit her. To clinch it, a few threads from his silk shirt were found lodged under her fingernails.

The medical evidence was even fancier. They knew just about everything you can find out from measuring, weighing, cutting up, and chemically analyzing a dead body. They knew what he'd eaten that day and how well he'd digested it. From his dental work they knew the kind of prisons he'd been in in Mexico and America. They even knew he was from out of town because his lungs lacked certain smog traces common to Los Angeles residents.

Considering all the things police ingenuity and technology had uncovered about the man, it would have been churlish to linger over a minor question like why had he done it, where was he from, whom did he work for. The cops had him cold on three counts of murder, and what was left of him would get a pauper's funeral. Alive he hadn't been a very nice guy, but dead he was solving problems for everyone from Elevel to the police to the people who'd contracted him.

One thing I'd been wrong about: he was lousy at his job. No piece man would use a pearl-handled weapon when he could use a ridged one that takes no prints. No professional worth hiring would hang on to a murder weapon after a hit, or try to take you inside your own house. I was lucky. I led a charmed life. I wondered why I felt like something the dog had coughed up.

In the corridor outside the inquest room the DA was getting ready to give a statement to the press. As I pushed my way through the reporters, a hand caught my arm and detained me. It was Granville. He was wearing the same color-coordinated double-knit outfit he'd had on the other day, only today's was green instead of burgundy. He grinned at me and opened his mouth but nothing came out. Flashbulbs were going off continuously. He was mouthing a pantomime conversation to put the icing on the pantomime inquest.

"This case has more loose ends than a bowl of spaghetti," I said.

"It's on the books," he said through smiling lips. "*Closed.*"

"If I'd known how many asses I was going to save, I would have let Gervano go."

"Lighten up, Kyd," he growled. "Later. We'll talk it over later."

"Just one more, chief," a reporter shouted.

"How'd you get three in his chest, Kyd?"

"Do you think you could have taken him alive?"

"Do you always carry a gun?"

"No comment." I forced myself through the press of bodies and got clear except for a single reporter who pestered me going down the hall. He'd been the worst of the crowd outside my house yesterday. He followed me into the elevator, swinging up his camera as he stepped in and knocking a woman back against the wall.

I put my hand on the lens and said, "Don't."

"Anything you say," he said, and immediately after I dropped my hand, he snapped the picture.

It was a big camera and he had a small mouth but I think I got some of it inside. The flash had blinded me.

I went into a bar on South Hill. It was the kind of place where you could ask the bartender for a spoon to pick a fly out of your beer without anyone thinking you were a fairy. I took my glass to an empty table at the rear. A waitress brought me a bowl of chili and a slice of sour dough without asking and slapped a bill to a stain on the tablecloth. I ate some chili and polished off the beer.

Chili and beer. According to the autopsy, it was the last thing Gervano had eaten.

Chapter TWENTY-FIVE

When I got back to my office, the phone was ringing. I picked up the receiver and a voice said, "You were lucky once. Don't look to get lucky twice." It was a cool, suave voice with a Latin accent.

"I thought I'd done you a favor," I said.

He chuckled lightly. "You saved me some money. Now do yourself a favor. Go back to divorce work."

"Everyone's pretty happy the way things are?"

"Don't push it, Kyd. I don't mind spending that money you saved me."

The line went dead.

I smoked a few cigarettes and thought it over. I got out the bottle from the desk and poured out a few inches of gin. I was going to be needing lots of those inches if I walked away from this one. And I didn't know if I liked the stuff that much.

I put a call through to Ian White.

"You're sending us lots of business, Thomas," he said. "That Beverly Hills blue-rinse crowd likes you so much I'm thinking of making you a partner."

"Thanks, but no thanks."

"Afraid of success, pal?"

"Maybe."

"I knew a call girl like you once," he sighed. "Irish Catholic. She really liked the work but it went against her principles. She charged next to nothing, and half the time she didn't get paid, so she never made a dime out of it. It was her conscience. Her conscience felt better that way."

"What happened to her?" I asked.

"I married her." Ian chuckled. "Now what can I do for you?"

"There's a guy called Hollis Brownlee. He used to be a painter and maybe he still is. He used to live in Pasadena. See if the police have a rap sheet on him."

"This connected with the Elevel case?"

"Is the Pope Catholic?"

"I thought you'd gift-wrapped it for the DA's office."

"I just got a call from Coronado. He wanted to make sure I was going to let the investigation drop. In so many words he told me there were plenty of other guys where Gervano came from."

"I'll call you back in ten minutes," Ian said. "By the way, with all these referrals you're giving us, you're getting to be my business."

"What's that mean?"

"Just say, I'd like to protect a good investment."

"Don't put a backup man on me. I've got enough to think about without that." I put the phone down.

In a little while he called me back.

"Brownlee's a house painter all right. He was a second-story man for a while after the war. One conviction. Served three years. Two years ago he was charged with receiving stolen goods but they couldn't make it stick. His MO is hitting houses in the middle of the afternoon."

"Cat burglars have eyes in the back of their heads. Don't put a backup man on me."

"The police figure Brownlee for maybe four scores last year. Big ones. But no evidence. There's no surveillance on him in L.A. There's a current warrant out on him from Philadelphia but they can't extradite him because he hasn't broken any laws out here. He's very careful. They've tried putting tails on him. He either paints a house, or loses them. The cops can't figure him out. He's an old guy and he juices very hard."

"Thanks."

"I couldn't say whether I'm doing you a favor or not," Ian said. "Coronado isn't a two-bit extortionist. He's a businessman. When he says stay out of my business, he means do it or you're going to open the door one morning and get a bucket of acid in the face."

"I'm not that friendly in the morning myself. I know where he lives. He isn't made out of steel or ferroconcrete. I owe him a knock."

"Hey, take it easy," he chided me.

"Yeah."

"It's their world, Thomas. If you don't like it, become a cop but don't try knocking those guys down with an investigator's license. Play to win. Don't just play cause some pimp rubbed you the wrong way."

"Thanks, Ian."

"If you can't come out of it, don't play." He put the phone down. I put my phone down. Then I poured the gin back into the bottle.

I drove over to Pasadena that night and checked out Brownlee's house. It was an expensive new tract house on a sizable plot with a swimming pool in the rear and several thousand dollars' worth of plants and shrubbery growing up around the walls. The lights were on.

I parked down the street and walked back. When I reached Brownlee's place, I cut across his front lawn, paused to wind up a garden hose, and moved around the side of the house. The curtains were drawn, the windows were barred and wired with the most sophisticated alarm system on the market. The back of the house was equally impregnable, both doors having triple locks. Parked deep in the driveway was a new Lincoln Continental. I peeked through the garage window. Inside was a gleaming Ford pickup, and a small red Alfa Romeo. It was obviously the garage of a painter, with five-gallon paint drums stacked against the walls, and several large spraying rigs visible, but somehow the set-up didn't look right. Everything was as clean and new and unused as the display in a large paint store.

His garbage cans were equally interesting. He drank imported German beer, cave wines by the case, twenty-year-old Scotch, Russian vodka, and the best Hine brandy. Along with potato chips, peanuts, and pretzels, that seemed to be what he lived on.

During the next week I followed him sporadically. I was only interested in what he did between noon and four in the afternoon, his working hours. Usually he'd come out of his house around one, dressed in clean white painter's overalls, and he'd take off in the Ford pickup. His eventual destination was always the Truesdale Estates in Beverly Hills. He usually visited at least one house in an afternoon but he wasn't robbing them, he was giving an estimate on how much it would cost to paint them. It was a very obvious and slick scam. A half-hour visit was enough time to check out everything of interest to a second-story man. If he actually painted the house he would learn all he needed to know about the comings and goings of the people inside. He probably had at least a hundred likely scores from this kind of research and could afford to wait a year or two between giving the estimate and burglarizing the house. Or he could sell that kind of information to other burglars in return for a percentage of their take.

His phone bills were very high. He made long distance calls regularly to Philadelphia, Detroit, New York, and Bakersfield. The New York calls were to a dealer on the diamond exchange, and the Bakersfield number was a pawnbroker. The Philadelphia number was a lawyer's office. The Detroit number was listed under a Monroe Sorel who turned out to have an LAPD rap sheet. Sorel was the young burglar who had used Brownlee as a fence two years ago. The charge had never become a conviction.

It looked to me as if Brownlee were getting ready to move on something. Six days after I started following him he took out the Lincoln and went to Los Angeles Airport. He met Sorel coming in from Detroit. They had a long conversation in the airport bar and Brownlee handed over some papers.

After Brownlee left, I stayed with Sorel. He was a

curvy, copper-skinned fag with big almond eyes and lots of tousled black curls. His clothes were too tight and he dressed a little too flashily for my taste but then he wasn't trying to please me so who cared. He rented a Pinto at the airport and checked in at a nondescript motel on San Vicente in the Wilshire district.

I waited outside the motel until eleven o'clock and then figured he'd gone to bed for the night. I went home.

The next morning I was back outside the motel by eight. Sorel came out at nine and had breakfast across the street at a House of Pies coffee shop. I looked into his car in the parking lot. The Beverly Hills directory was lying on the passenger seat next to a pair of leather driving gloves. It was already nearly eighty degrees outside, so the gloves weren't for keeping his hands warm.

His next stop was an exclusive tennis shop on Melrose where he bought a sweater, racquet, shorts, shoes, socks, and shirt.

I was parked farther down on the opposite side of the street watching him through binoculars. He paid at the cash register, walked out, tossed his purchases into his car, and crossed the street, walking away from me. I got out of my car and followed him.

Two blocks east he came to a medical building and entered its underground garage. I went in after him slowly, keeping close to the wall. At the bottom of the ramp, I moved quickly behind the cover of some cars and surveyed the acre and a half of parked automobiles. I could see Sorel walking casually down a row of cars, past a pillar, and then he was gone, out of sight. I waited a moment and then lay flat on the ground and peered through the wilderness of tires. I could see the lower half of his body kneeling behind a car, then his hand, holding a screwdriver, came into view. A moment later there was a metallic grating sound.

I was back sitting in my car by the time he came out of the garage. He had gone in wearing a leather sports coat but it was now draped over his arm, with two license plates wrapped in its folds.

For the rest of the morning he drifted through the Beverly Hills business district, indistinguishable from the crowds of fashionably dressed shoppers. He bought a twelve-inch heavy-duty screwdriver at a hardware store and booked a flight back to Detroit for that evening.

He ate lunch at a small French restaurant on Wilshire near Canon, where I collected my second ticket of the day for illegal parking.

From there he drove to a gay health club on Santa Monica Boulevard and left his car in its parking lot. Whatever he found there kept him inside for an hour and a half. When he came out he was dressed in the tennis clothes he'd bought and was carrying the racket. In the parking lot he replaced his license plates with the stolen ones and headed west on Santa Monica towards Beverly Hills. On the way he stopped twice at pay phones, probably phoning the house he intended to hit, to verify that no one was home.

From that point on I figured he was going to be watching out for surveillance. The residential streets of Beverly Hills are too deserted to work a successful tail. In the preceding week Brownlee had cased eight houses and five of them were within three or four minutes of each other. I decided to drive from one to the other and was hoping I'd find Sorel's car parked outside one of them.

I found the blue Pinto parked in front of the third house I drove past, a mock Southern plantation mansion set well back from the street. Sorel was somewhere inside. I backed into a neighbor's driveway and waited.

A little while later Sorel came out, looking spruce and sporty in his tennis whites, with his sweater held loosely in his arm, and his free hand swinging his racquet. In that outfit he blended in perfectly with the neighborhood, the time of day, and the Beverly Hills life-style. If anyone in another house had observed his entrance and noted down his license number the clue would lead nowhere.

Sorel headed straight back to the health club, where he had probably rented a locker. In the parking lot he switched plates again and dropped the stolen ones down a storm drain. Forty-five minutes later Brownlee's Ford pickup arrived with the back filled with painting equipment and materials. Brownlee went into the health club carrying a leather toolbag and came out two minutes later followed by Sorel, now in his street clothes again. They parted without signaling that they knew each other.

Sorel would be on his way back to Detroit, probably in the air by the time the theft was discovered.

Chapter TWENTY-SIX

I was waiting for Brownlee when he got home. He had just got the front door open when I stepped from behind a bush and shoved him headfirst through the door. He started to protest but then he saw the gun in my hand and decided he was in a listening mood.

He was a thin, wiry man in his late fifties, dressed in white slacks and a florid Hawaiian shirt. His cheeks and nose were crisscrossed with broken blood vessels, each busted vein testifying to a little corner of his brain that had shut down in protest against a lifetime of being poisoned. His thin lips were drawn back over a set of bright polished dentures. I waved him away from the toolbag.

"You haven't got any search warrant. This is illegal search and seizure."

"In the living room," I said.

"That bastard, Sorel . . ."

"Be quiet, Brownlee." I waved him over to a couch. There was a coffee table with a tray of drinks on it. "Mix yourself a drink."

I dumped the contents of the toolbag onto the rug. There was a box of powdered spackle, and inside, under the paper bag of white powder, a felt jewelry pouch.

I emptied out the pouch onto the coffee table and spread the contents so I could see what I had. It was almost all gold, perhaps three or four pounds of it, cast in bracelets, necklaces, and rings.

"The gold goes to your pawnbroker in Bakersfield," I said.

Brownlee said nothing. He was pouring a highball glass full of Wild Turkey. There was a deeply wronged expression in his bloodshot eyes. It was the other pieces

that had made the score worthwhile: a ruby and diamond necklace with matching bracelet, earrings, and
cluster pin, a double strand of pearls with a platinum
and diamond clasp, and an emerald and diamond necklace as long as my arm.

"We're looking at the rest of your life, Brownlee," I
said. "Drink up. You look like you just bit into a piece
of Death Valley."

He drained his glass and immediately refilled it.

"So what's your story? I know the cops are interested
in me. I don't know you." The booze was giving him
back an edge.

"It's like this. Philadelphia wants you extradited, and
the L.A. cops are now in a position to hand you over.
This little haul here's enough to put you away for the
rest of your life . . . without a drink."

"Maybe," he grunted.

"I think, objectively speaking, Brownlee, that I've got
you cold, with your pants down. If you don't believe
that, you're out to lunch."

"So I believe it." He sipped his drink. "What else is
new?"

"Don't get snotty with me, old man. This isn't your
day. That's what I want you to get through your head.
Otherwise it's all going to come down on you like a blizzard of shit. You're going to die an unhappy old man in
a state pen."

"What do you want, mister?" He said it in a voice as
raspy as a file wearing down an iron bar.

"I want to know where you got that baby you sold to
Rosemary Kramer twenty-five years ago."

Confusion widened his eyes and then he slowly
looked up at me as if I were crazy. "What is this? What
the hell are you talking about?"

"Brownlee, I'm asking the questions. If you come up
with some useful answers, I'll forget the jewels. If you
jive me, you're going back to Philadelphia with bracelets on."

"What's the deal?" He scowled unhappily. "Do I keep the score?"

"You don't keep anything. The stuff goes back but no one pins anything on you. That's the only deal we're talking about."

"It stinks," he said.

I reached for the phone, and he added quickly, "Maybe it doesn't stink so bad." He looked at me warily and then something dawned in his eyes. "I've seen you. You blew away that Mex. What's your name?" He rubbed his chin.

"Talk, Brownlee."

"Sure. Babies. It was just after the war. But first you got to realize I was only marginally involved. Nothing but a runner."

"You're getting on my nerves, old man."

"Okay." He raised his hands. "Most of the babies were illegitimate Mexican kids, from maids working for Americans. They got knocked up and their religion wouldn't let them have an abortion so they had the kid. I never knew most of the people involved. It was done very hush-hush. I know there were people working for the county in the records department and at the coroner's office, but I never knew names. I worked the other end, with the Mexican girls. Usually the kid was delivered in a motel by a quack and then handed over to the adopting parents with a legit birth certificate. Only the doctor's name was phony.

"There was another angle but they didn't work it so much. Some broad would give birth to a kid at home and the sawbones would tell her the kid wasn't made right, or it was going to die, or some cockamamy story. He'd take the kid to the county coroner, get a death certificate, but, see, the kid was perfectly healthy. While one broad is crying her eyes out cause she's given birth to a dead monster, some other lady's weeping for joy cause she's got a kid at last. On this last angle they made the big money cause you could charge more for an American kid than a Mex. That's all there was to it. This Kramer broad worked in a joint I used to patronize, and I did her a favor. I got her a kid cheap. I never knew the name of the doctor I used to deal with. After that they got me on a breaking-and-entering rap and I went down for three years. When I got out I wasn't looking to sell babies. It was never my style, you know, and the money was strictly from hunger. The croakers cleaned up and we got the crumbs. End of story."

"What did Harlan Stackman think of all this?" I watched him closely.

"That penny-ante bum," he said scornfully. "He never got the time of day out of me. I'm no pigeon, pal. If you hadn't busted in here you wouldn't have got nothing out of me either."

"When was the last time you saw Stackman?"

"I don't know. Sometime last month. He was in the Holiday Inn with a wad of five spots. That's the kind of cheapie he was. He thought spending fifteen bucks at the Holiday Inn was the big time. Once the guy tried to shake me down over this baby-selling operation. I just let him know how cheap it was to have someone's kneecaps powdered in this town. He never mentioned the subject again." Brownlee smiled with pleasure at the memory. "He was celebrating that night at the Holiday Inn. 'What are you so happy about?' I ask him. 'I have a lead on a case I've been working on for twenty years,' he says. That was Stackman all over. Most guys who spend twenty years getting nowhere keep quiet about it. Stackman, he celebrates. We went to the same high school. He was class president and look at him now, a stumblebum private dick. . . ."

I played with the jewels, tried on some of the gold rings, and then said, "About five years ago someone else tried to shake you down about the Kramer kid. Tell me about it."

"I don't know what you're talking about."

"You haven't told me anything yet, Brownlee. You're

already halfway downtown." I picked up a handful of gold and jewels and threw them at his chest. "I shot a guy to death already this month, and I sleep fine knowing about it. It wouldn't bother me at all to slap you around."

"I'm cooperating already!" He picked the jewels out of his lap and placed them carefully back on the table. "You want to beat up an old man? With a heart condition?"

"Sure."

"You sound like the other guy," he said.

"What other guy?"

"A maniac. A psycho." He shuddered. "Listen, five years ago a guy calls me up and says he wants his apartment painted. I go over to make an estimate. And the guy punches me in the guts. No questions. No explanation. He just racks me up. On account of him I've got these clackers." Brownlee pointed at his mouth. "He broke my teeth and he would have busted my spine if I hadn't talked. All the guys I knew in the business were dead and I never knew any others. There wasn't nothing I could give the guy except the name of a clinic that was owned by six doctors. It was the Magnum Clinic on Rosedale."

"What did this guy look like?"

"Young," Brownlee said indignantly. "Like some young hippie bum who'd ask for spare change on the street. He had long black hair and a black mustache, with these mean blue eyes—like a Manson. And his skin was real yellow, like a suntan, but it didn't look right, it looked sort of stained. A week later the bastard is waiting for me with a sap glove outside my dentist's office. He's got an old newspaper picture of the mayor officially opening the Magnum Clinic. The medico I dealt with was in the picture. I pointed him out but the bastard still went upside my head. He said if I ever told anyone anything he'd cut my tongue out. A crazy, a psycho—and I don't scare easy."

"This the guy?" I showed him a picture of Tyrone that I'd taken from Mrs. Elevel's purse.

"Around the eyes they look the same," Brownlee said. "The rest of the face, I don't know—this guy had so much hair. Besides, I was hurt bad. I don't know. But I don't like those eyes." He reached for his drink. "I've been seeing those eyes too long in my sleep."

I rang Information and got the number of the Magnum Clinic, dialed it, and asked to speak to Dr. Lester. The receptionist said there was no such doctor connected to the clinic. I said I was an attorney representing the estate of a Miss Nina Langsdale who had bequeathed a sizable amount of securities jointly to Dr. Lester and the clinic. It might have been as much as twenty-five years since Dr. Lester had been connected with the clinic.

"I wasn't even born then," the receptionist said.

"We're talking about upward of a quarter of a million in Coca-Cola and General Motors stock. Coca-Cola is a soda pop. General Motors makes cars. Ever hear of them?"

"If you'll hold," she said frostily, "I'll make an inquiry of the bookkeeper."

A moment later she came back on the line. All the frost had melted out of her voice. "You're absolutely correct, sir. There was a Dr. Samuel Lester here but he sold his interest in the clinic in nineteen fifty-seven. The bookkeeper would very much like to have a word with you. What is your name, please, sir?"

"Dale Evans," I said and put the phone down.

Then I called Dr. Lester's Beverly Hills office and got his nurse. "This is Mr. Irwin Humboldt's secretary speaking," I said briskly. "Mr. Humboldt has an appointment with the mayor this afternoon and his personal physician wasn't able to travel with him from Houston. Would it be at all possible for Mr. Humboldt to have his insulin prescription filled by Dr. Lester?"

"Was Dr. Lester recommended by another physician," the receptionist asked, "or referred by one of the doctor's patients?"

"Could you hold please? I've got the mayor's office on another line." I ran my thumbnail over the receiver and waited several moments. Officious voices had been telling me to *hold please* all my life, and I got a flash of what little power trips you could go on with a switchboard.

"Thank you for waiting," I said after two minutes. "I'm afraid Mr. Humboldt is at a meeting at the Polo Lounge. I don't know *who* recommended Dr. Lester. Probably the attorney general's wife. The *point* is that Mr. Humboldt needs a shot of insulin within the next *hour*. If there's any problem, please, do tell me now as I have a whole *list* of physicians—"

"No, that's fine," she stammered. "The doctor will be delighted to see Mr. Humboldt. That *is* the Mr. Humboldt of the Humboldt Oil Company?"

"Humboldt Oil? Does he own that too? I suppose he does. I hope I've made myself clear as to the urgency . . . it has to be in and out. Not a long wait. He'll be furious if he's late for the mayor."

"The doctor will see him right away."

"Good day." I put the phone down.

Act pushy, self-important, throw a few names around, and you could turn people like her into human doormats. I smiled at Brownlee, reached over, and forced his hand into the gold and jewels, squeezing his fingertips against the surfaces that would take prints.

"I just want people to know they're yours, Brownlee."

"What's going on?" he said miserably.

I took out my Instamatic, fitted a flash into the attachment, and then draped some of the necklaces around Brownlee's neck. "We're going to visit Dr. Lester. All you have to do is walk into his office, look at him, and walk out. I want him to see you. Maybe later I'll want you to tell the cops who he is and how you know him." I was taking pictures as I talked. "You'll turn state's witness on him. He'll go down. You'll walk. As soon as you've testified, you can have these pictures back."

"How do I know you aren't going to burn me after I testify?" he demanded. "You say you'll get me a deal. Who are you to get people deals?"

"Let's go." I hoisted him to his feet.

"I'm not going to do it." He balked. "I don't trust you."

I removed a slipcover from a pillow and scooped it full of the gold and jewelry. "If I was going to rip you off, Brownlee, I wouldn't be standing here talking to you. I'd be long gone with your score and you'd be waking up with a bump on your head."

He started to say something and I took him by the arm and propelled him toward the door.

"You already got your goddamn deal," I said. "You pulled off a score, I got you dead to rights, and you're still walking around. I got pictures of you casing that house, pictures of Sorel busting in. Now do I crack you in the mouth, or are you going to act like a reasonable citizen?"

He came along but he didn't like it. Somewhere he knew it was all a hype but he was too mixed up and scared to think it out clearly. In the first place I wasn't licensed to bust anyone, and even if I were, I hadn't followed the correct procedure for search and seizure of a suspect. Legally, busting old cons like Brownlee is like trying to type with boxing gloves. My only hope now was to play on his fear of being smacked around, of dying in prison.

I locked the jewels and camera in the trunk and forced him into the passenger seat.

"What'd ya say to half?" he asked. "There's maybe thirty-six, thirty-eight grand I can get in New York for that stuff." He waited a moment. "All right, take twenty grand. Twenty grand for nothing."

"Brownlee," I said very softly, *"shut your face!"* I shouted as loud as I could and he collapsed into silence. Every time he tried to talk to me after that I screamed at him and acted like I was ready to pull off the road and pistol-whip him. He could have stepped out of the car at any traffic light and walked away and there wouldn't have been a damn thing I could have done about it. But the screaming and threats kept him too paralyzed to consider that option.

By the time we reached Beverly Hills his shirt was so dark with sweat you could hardly see its pattern of tropical flowers. He smelled like a pool of bourbon lying in a steaming tennis shoe.

I parked on Canon Drive just off Wilshire and marched him into Dr. Lester's building. We took the elevator up with a group of overdressed, emotionally undernourished women whose attachment to jewels constituted Brownlee's living. They had beauty parlor-cooked hair, meticulously painted faces, and a look of repressed hunger for something more than a square meal. In the enclosed elevator Brownlee was as out of place as a dead horse floating in one of their swimming pools.

"They can do all kinds of things with leprosy these days," I said cheerfully, patting Brownlee's shoulder. "We'll get you fixed up in no time, dad."

The elevator doors opened on the third floor and I steered him out.

Dr. Lester's waiting room was empty except for an old gentleman in a yachting blazer and white ducks, poring over a copy of the *Wall Street Journal*. He had minutely wrinkled skin the color of rice paper and two little brown eyes that were all pupil. He looked at us with the flat, impersonal curiosity of a morphine addict contemplating a fly on the wall. Then his head drooped down on his little pigeon chest, and he went on the nod.

A moment later, he lifted his head, blinked his eyes, and remarked in a thin dry voice, "Cancer."

"I'm sorry," I said.

He patted his chest as if it were made out of fragile hand-blown glass. "I'm rotten with it. You're looking at a dead man." For a moment there was a spark in his eyes, a look of perverse pride, as if death were a club which people like me weren't allowed to join. Then he said, "Damn it all to hell," and pushed the magazine off his lap with a childish gesture.

A buxom nurse in a white uniform entered the waiting room. She was all pink, and starched, and face-powdered. When she moved she made a crackling sound like newspapers being balled up. The generous line of her lipstick didn't correspond to her actual lips, which hardly existed. Above her eyes she had drawn two half-moon eyebrows that were meant to suggest astonishment, girlish spirits, and naughty good humor. She was about as astonished, girlish, and good-humored as a pair of handcuffs.

"Mr. Humboldt?" She frowned.

"I hope Dr. Lester's ready to see him." I glanced at my watch.

She surveyed Brownlee with suspicion, trying to reconcile what she saw with her mental image of the Texas oil baron.

"The mayor is waiting." I tapped my watch. "And Mr. Humboldt would like that insulin injection."

"This way, please," she said, leading Brownlee out of the room.

The old gentleman cleared his throat. "You're a big fellow, aren't you?" he muttered. "In my day you could have played football. Today you'd be too small. Eat a lot, don't you? I used to eat. Eat anyone under the table. Drink too. Now it's no use. I don't think about anything but my next injection." His hands fluttered petulantly in his lap. He looked down at them as if they belonged to someone else, to someone he didn't even like. "Awww shit!" He flopped back in his chair and entirely forgot about me.

The door opened a moment later and Brownlee emerged, followed by the nurse.

"He's the croaker," Brownlee said in disgust.

From the open corridor I could hear Dr. Lester's voice raised in anger. The nurse was sputtering, demanding to know the meaning of it all, and how dared we upset Dr. Lester like that.

"Who *are* you?" She took hold of my sleeve.

"You wouldn't know my name," I said. "Come on, Brownlee."

She blocked the door of the waiting room.

"Lady," I said, "don't worry, this fellow and the doctor go back a long ways. They used to sell babies for fun and profit a quarter of a century ago."

"I don't know what you're talking about." She looked from me to Brownlee and back again.

"You work for a bent quack who's just taken a fall. But maybe you didn't know that."

"What do you mean?" There was sweat popping through the thick powder on her face.

"Forget it." I brushed past her and hustled Brownlee into the corridor. "The old fellow's waiting for his fix," I said as I walked out. "Why don't you give him what he wants before the cops shut the place down."

In the elevator going down, Brownlee smiled grudgingly.

"He made me the second I walked in," he said. "I'd forgotten how much I hated his lousy guts. They ought to put quacks like him in the slammer the day they're born."

"Why's that, Brownlee?"

"You're asking me?" He snorted contemptuously. "Cause a guy like Lester isn't a crook, that's why. He's respectable. He's a pillar of the community. And he's beating both sides for a dirty buck. He has no class."

"But it's different when you pretend you're a house painter?"

"No one cares about a lousy house painter. You're just a bum with a brush in your hand. And if you get caught, you go down. I ain't really stealing from people, I'm hurting the big insurance companies. But that son of a bitch is supposed to be a doctor. His whole life, people've been kissing his ass and treating him like the Pope and what is he? A creep who sells babies."

I didn't think I could add much to Brownlee's description of Lester. I just hoped he'd come through as a witness for the prosecution.

"Where're we going?" Brownlee asked as I put him in the car.

"One more stop, old man. You don't have to do anything more than nod your head and remember back five years."

Chapter TWENTY-SEVEN

In the late afternoon sun the leaded windows of the Elevel mansion gleamed like mirrors. Shadows of the encircling trees lengthened across the lawn. A reddish glow came off the chaparral behind and some of that ruddy light seemed to touch the pale Disneyesque spires and turrets of the mansion.

I parked behind Joe's Bentley and briefly considered helping myself to a drink from his back-seat bar. But one drink wouldn't help. It was better to get the damn thing over with.

We walked over the blacktop, past the garages, and approached the pool area. Brownlee wasn't saying anything any more; he was too busy casing the joint, and imagining the kind of loot there had to be inside.

I could see Roth standing on the diving board with a stopwatch. Approaching him, Tyrone's arms churned the water in a strange desperate stroke, dragging the vertical, nearly dead weight of his legs behind him. Every second he looked as if he were going under but then his bronzed, muscled arm would flash up out of the water and split the surface with a powerful chopping stroke.

Tyrone did ten grueling laps like that while Roth crooned encouragement to him. Finally Roth saw us. He leaned down and said something to Tyrone which I couldn't hear, and then Tyrone swam to the side and hoisted himself up. Roth handed him a towel but instead of covering his shoulders, Tyrone laid it over his thin, atrophied thighs. Seen that way, he looked like any other young Adonis sitting with his feet dangling in the pool of a body-building spa.

"Mr. Kyd." Roth came forward beaming, with his hand outstretched. "I think congratulations are in order."

I took his hand, nodded, and said, "Hello, Tyrone."

"What do you want?" Tyrone said glumly.

"You're quite a swimmer," I said.

"We're in training," Roth said. "Tyrone's decided to go out for the wheelchair Olympics. Unofficially he just broke the record for the four-hundred-meter freestyle."

"Well?" I said to Brownlee.

"What?" he said.

"Do you recognize him?"

"Who?" Brownlee asked.

"Don't play games with me, Brownlee." A sick feeling of dread swept through my stomach and chest.

"Have you ever seen this man before?" I pointed at Tyrone.

"Never," Brownlee said emphatically, and then grinned at me. "I suddenly get a feeling you don't know what the hell you're doing.

"What's this all about?" Tyrone asked.

The sun reflected off the surface of the water, glaring into my eyes, and the three men stared at me, waiting for an explanation. I was not only out on a limb in a professional and ethical sense, I was on the wrong tree. I tried to think. My mind was spinning in a panic, as if a hundred different wheels were moving at different speeds but none of them were engaged. I thought back to the first meeting with Joe in my office and the suicide note he'd shown me. And then gradually the wheels slowed down, one by one, clicking into place like symbols on a fruit machine.

There was no breeze but I felt something like a gust of icy air brush the back of my neck. It was like suddenly realizing that a piece of furniture in your room was actually a live intruder, staring at you. It had been there all the time and Mrs. Elevel had said it all in one word: *unspeakable.*

I mumbled an apology to Roth and Tyrone and took Brownlee's arm, leading him back toward the main house. When I reached the top of the stairs, I didn't really feel like ringing the bell, or going in to face the nightmare inside. I understood why Mrs. Elevel had preferred an overdose to playing her role in the tragedy and why Charlotte had been driven to the brink of suicide. But I had no choice. I knew, and knowing in this case was a death sentence. I had to get convictions or else Coronado would have me eliminated.

Maria, the cook, answered the door and asked us to wait in the foyer while she called Joe. After a moment he appeared at the head of the stairs. It was hard to believe this was the same man who had bristled with authority in my office. He looked frightened and old and there was a new hoarse quavering in his voice.

"What is it?" he asked. "Haven't we had enough?"

"I'd like to talk to you in private, Mr. Elevel," I said. "I think this man can clear up a few things." I felt like a bastard putting it that way. Brownlee wasn't going to clear up anything. He was about to unveil a nightmare that anyone with a grain of feeling would prefer not to know.

Joe descended the stairs cautiously, holding the banister and watching his feet.

"Is it Tyrone?" he asked.

"No, it isn't."

"Very well." He shuffled in his bedroom slippers down the central corridor into the library. He had lost weight and you could see the ridge of his stooped spine through his satin dressing gown. He walked over to his desk, and turned to face us. One hand was thrust into his pocket, the other nervously swiveled an onyx penholder on its base. Pointedly, he didn't ask us to sit down.

"A long time ago in Pasadena," I said, "Dr. Lester was connected with the Magnum Clinic. At that time he was your family physician. Is that right?"

"I thought we'd been through this," Joe said irritably.

"This man," I gestured to Brownlee, "was in Pasadena at the same time. He worked for a baby-selling ring."

"What does any of this have to do with me?" Joe's hand shook as he lit a cigarette.

"This man has just positively identified Dr. Lester as one of the ringleaders in that baby-selling business. You told me once, Mr. Elevel, that Dr. Lester had done your family a service but you wouldn't tell me what it was. A common ploy for acquiring babies was for a doctor to inform a mother that her child had been born deformed, or mentally defective. The child was then removed. A false death certificate was obtained from the county coroner and the parents presumably buried a coffin with no corpse inside it. Deformed children upset families. It's something people usually prefer to keep secret. I think I know what the favor was that Dr. Lester did for you."

Joe sat down abruptly. After a long silence, he said, "I have a son. Is that what you want me to admit? A poor idiot, a vegetable who has spent his whole life in diapers. Yes, that's right. I have a twenty-five-year-old monster called Francis Elevel. He's in an institution in Rhode Island. He has been there all his life. Does that satisfy you?"

"I'm sorry, Mr. Elevel."

"Apart from Dr. Lester and myself, you are the only person who knows about him. Quite frankly, Mr. Kyd, I don't see what business it is of yours."

"Have you ever seen him?"

"No, is there any point in seeing him?" He grimaced. "Is there any point in digging this up?"

"I presume Dr. Lester handles all this for you?"

"That's right. Now if there's nothing else, I wish you'd leave me alone."

"How are payments made to this institution in Rhode

Island? Nursing for your son must be expensive, and he's been there for twenty-five years."

"It's done through Lester, damn it!" Joe got to his feet.

"I think you should sit down, Mr. Elevel. I'm going to tell you what really happened, and it's not a pretty story."

Joe remained standing, with something like that challenging glare in his eyes that I remembered from our first meeting. Only his white hand, fluttering over the desktop, wouldn't stay still; it scratched around in search of something to hold onto, to hide its secret trembling.

"Go wait in my car, Brownlee," I said. "And don't even think about taking a hike."

I waited until Brownlee had shuffled out and closed the door. My story was going to win the Ugly Prize of the year. It didn't need an audience.

"Your son wasn't born a monster," I said. "You've been paying Lester for twenty-five years to take care of a cripple who isn't a cripple at all. Maybe Lester conned you. Maybe you knew something. I don't know. One thing I'm sure of. Lester took a perfectly healthy infant and sold it to Rosemary Kramer, through Brownlee."

Joe looked at me queerly. He reached his hand back to locate the chair and then sat down on the edge of it. "He said it was a monster. You can't blame me. I was never . . ."

"Did you ever see the child? Even for an instant?"

"Lester told us it was better if we didn't see it. He offered to get a death certificate saying it was stillborn, and then he placed it in that institution."

"You're up to your neck. You sure you want to keep lying?"

"What do you mean?" Joe said weakly. "I never knew."

"But you suspected something or else you wouldn't

have gone to Rosemary Kramer's to look at the baby. I don't know what she did to the kid. Probably drugged it. It was enough to fool you. Or was it?"

Joe's expression was bleak, rigid, a stoic mask. His voice issued in a frail, defeated whisper.

"It's hard to say how much I knew. My business was nothing in those days. I was in debt. My wife was an emotional wreck from having to give up the baby. She kept pressuring me, asking questions, blaming herself. In the back of her mind was this nagging feeling that it was all wrong, that somehow *we'd* gone wrong. I went for her sake, to put her mind at rest about the child. Christ, how could I tell? I believed what I'd been told. After that I went to see Lester. I remember he was ill-at-ease. He told me it wouldn't live more than a few weeks. I don't know why I did it but I asked him for money that day, a loan. It was two thousand dollars and he just wrote me out a check for it. It was sort of understood that I'd never have to pay him back. After that my business took off. I had one good break after another. That two grand turned into ten, then twenty, then fifty, then a hundred. I should have been a happy man but I wasn't. Every year I'd pay Lester the asylum costs for the boy. I used to wish they were higher. Sometimes I wished I was poor enough that keeping the child there would have been a real sacrifice. But it wasn't. Nothing was a sacrifice any more."

"Why didn't you get rid of Lester?"

"I don't know. I've always loathed the man. But he was the only one who knew. My wife didn't know. She would have been suspicious if I'd let Lester go." Joe's face had broken out into a faint rash and his voice trembled with an almost plaintive whine. "We couldn't—we didn't want people to know—and the longer it lived, the harder it got to do anything. We had Tyrone and Charlotte to think about. We were terrified their children might be deformed. We tried to shelter Charlotte, to make her afraid of boys, to protect her—

and when Tyrone was paralyzed, it almost seemed like a blessing. Lester said he would never have been able to have children that weren't like his brother."

I couldn't look into Joe's face any more. He had distorted his whole life and the lives of his wife and children out of fear of a nonexistent terror. But not quite. There had been that moment twenty-five years ago when he'd stood in Lester's office and asked for two thousand dollars, knowing something was wrong, knowing somehow he would get the money. And then everything had blossomed for him; everything he'd touched had turned to gold: larger and more magnificent homes, a more-and-more-prosperous business, greater social prominence. But he'd just missed being enough of a bastard to enjoy it. The dark little sin of a quarter of a century ago hadn't stopped troubling him. It had been such a successful sin. It was even, he must have thought in his more hopeful moments, not really a sin at all. What did he know? He had no proof. Only that the steadily growing wealth and opulence and power weighed him down, reminded him of something cold and mean he'd done long ago.

"What's going to happen?" he said quietly. You could see he'd digested the whole thing. He was thinking about Lester, wondering how much was going to come out, ready to cut his losses. He'd already retired back into that frozen private region of himself where no one could touch him. He still didn't understand. "I suppose the boy's grown up now." He sighed. "Naturally I'd like to help in any way possible. A trust fund. I don't see how prosecuting Lester at this late stage could help. Just more unpleasantness."

There was a faint click and the oak library door swung open on its hinges. Brownlee stood framed in the entrance with his hands folded on the top of his head. There was a deep livid cut running down from his eyebrow across the bridge of his nose to the side of his mouth. The blood had run in rivulets down his chin and neck. He was grimacing. His teeth were dark with blood. He staggered forward. Then his knees buckled under him and he did a swan dive on the carpet. When his head hit the ground, it bounced, and a fine bloody spray flew up from his mangled face.

Calvin stepped lightly into the room and shut the door behind him. When he turned back there was a .22 long-barreled automatic in his hand.

"What are you doing, Calvin?" Joe came alive, starting forward. "Put that gun away."

A strange gloating smile formed on Calvin's lips. He jabbed the gun forward in a vicious jerking movement, driving Joe backward. He pulled off his tinted glasses with a flourish which seemed entirely out of place, and let them drop on the ground. Then he ground them under his heel. The eyes that surveyed us were no longer glossy and black; they were astonishingly blue and bright with hate.

"Unstrap that harness." Calvin aimed his gun at my midsection. "Leave it on the floor, and step back away from it."

His voice was firm but restrained, his movements sure and careful. There was no strain on his face; it had almost a look of dreamy complacency. I'd seen that kind of look before on other faces. I thought he was looking forward to blowing my brains into my lap. I'd seen prettier smiles on wharf rats.

"Now back up," he said.

I stepped backward until my hands touched the drawn curtains of the French windows lining the end of the room. I could feel a current of air coming through, with a smell of nearby flowers and freshly watered grass. I even thought I heard a distant splash from the swimming pool.

"Now you." Calvin pointed the gun at Joe's face. "Go stand with him."

As Joe came around the back of the desk to join me, Calvin moved forward swiftly to where Joe had been sitting. He opened the top desk drawer, pulled out a small automatic pistol, and slipped it into his pocket. Then he rummaged through another desk drawer and came up with a small pink envelope.

"Why are you doing this?" Joe demanded. His head was cocked to the side, his eyes bulging with emotion. His face was trying to look frightened and outraged and broken-hearted all at once. "Why have you done this?" His hands closed and opened and seemed to claw at the air separating him from Calvin. His breath was coming in gasps. The realization that he was looking at his own son churned through him in raw, sickening waves, held him paralyzed like a man stuck to an electric fence.

"I was curious." Calvin walked over to an oil painting of Mrs. Elevel and pulled it from the wall, revealing a safe with a combination lock. He spoke with a brisk disdain, not looking at Joe, as if he were answering a stupid and irrelevant question. "Everyone is curious about his parents," he said. "It's human nature. I was in lots of homes. I had lots of foster parents. They were people who had nothing to do with me. I didn't like them, if you see what I mean."

"I understand that," Joe cried. "If you only knew how we—"

"Oh shut up." Calvin whirled around. *"You!* You've never understood anything. Don't tell me what you thought, or what you did. You never did anything. *I* found *you."*

"But it was impossible, Calvin."

"It was easy," Calvin said. "All it took was the determination. The records aren't that closely guarded. I was in a car accident and I made a little money from the damages, enough for this bargain-basement plastic job. If I'd had more money I could have been fixed up by a decent doctor. I wouldn't have had to look like this. But I needed the money to pay someone in the records department. I got that Kramer woman's name and address and her sister put me on to Brownlee. She didn't *have*

to put me up for adoption, you know." He smiled un-
pleasantly. "The courts couldn't have taken me away
from her. She signed the papers voluntarily. Maybe she
thought doing that would get her paroled."

"Rosemary Kramer never stopped looking for you."
It was the first thing I'd said. It was a mistake. He
seemed to remember how little liking he had for me.

"You can keep out of it," he said, swinging the gun
from Joe to me. "That bitch gave me away. Like an old
shoe." It was the same term Alma Kramer had used.
"Her own sister told me about it. She also told me
about a little visit from my father."

"Lester said you were . . . you weren't made right,"
Joe whispered. "I went because I had to know. The
Kramer woman said you weren't right. I couldn't tell,
Calvin. I didn't know what to do. They were lying to
me."

"You *sold* me to Lester," Calvin said. "He showed
me the check. Two thousand dollars. I paid for everything you've got. I was the down payment. Do you
know what a foster home is like? Do you know the kind
of bastards who take kids in for the money the state
gives them? And then the money goes on booze or you
get some religious crank who wants to read the Bible to
you while he's sticking it up your ass. And every year
an extra ten grand going into Lester's pocket. I've got
nothing to say to you. There's no way you're ever going
to change any of that."

Calvin had stopped talking but you could tell the
fight wasn't over. He was just starting to get in touch
with the cancerous rage he'd lived with since the day
he'd realized he was an orphan. Joe was still trying to
placate him and justify himself but it wasn't going to
work. Calvin had been out in the cold too long.

"He's tricked you," Joe said. "Lester's tricked you
the same way he tricked me. I swear I never knew."

"You didn't *want* to know." Calvin's lips were
twisted in a disgusted snarl but he wouldn't meet Joe's

eyes. "You wanted to bury the whole thing. When Lester got me the job with you, I was still ready to tell you who I was. I was sure you'd notice something. I couldn't believe bleached hair and a pair of contact lenses would be enough. What a laugh that was! Where've you been all your life? Who *do* you know? Do you think you know your children? Do you think you knew your wife? Do you think anyone gives a shit about your money and your big house? I've had more laughs in the slam than in this dump."

He turned the handle of the safe and swung it open. He seemed to know his way around inside it.

"How could I have recognized you?" Joe said. "With your face like that?"

"What's the matter? Don't you like it?" Calvin sneered. "I'm surprised you kept me around the house. I might have scared your precious kids."

"You tried to kill Tyrone," Joe said suddenly. "You did that. What did Tyrone have to do with any of it?"

"I don't have to explain myself to you or anyone. I don't owe you anything. You owe *me*. All I'm doing is squaring accounts."

"Sleeping with your mother and then blackmailing her?" I said. "That really balanced the books."

"I'm not talking to you." Calvin busied himself counting money.

"Anything you say, Oedipus." I lit a cigarette and tossed the match on the rug. It burned for a moment and then went out.

"It's not the same thing," Calvin said. "He didn't know what he was doing. As you can see, I did."

"You think so?" I steadied Joe with my hand. "You look awfully like a patsy to me."

"You won't know what you look like if you don't shut your mouth." The gun came around and up.

"Why, you little son of a bitch!" Joe hissed. "Who do you think you are? How dare you?"

Calvin laughed nervously. "Listen to him. Just listen

to that. In a minute he's going to send me to my room."

"Don't waste your breath." I kept hold of Joe's arm. "He doesn't know what he's doing. You ought to feel sorry for him. He wanted to blackmail his mother and he was stupid enough to get two bugs like Coronado and Grande to help him. They've taken him to the cleaners."

"I told you to shut up." He lifted the gun and aimed it at my face.

"So shoot me. You're still a chump. You're not blackmailing anyone. Coronado's blackmailing you. If Mrs. Elevel hadn't killed herself you'd have been caught the day Rosemary Kramer told her who you really were. Hell, you had to *ask* Coronado to get rid of Charlotte and Rosemary Kramer so you wouldn't get caught and so they could keep blackmailing you. You never even saw any of that eighteen grand. You don't even get money out of Lester any more. Coronado's got hold of that account too. Your ass belongs to the Mexican, Calvin."

"Just take the money and get out of here," Joe said. "No one's going to follow you. Just get out of my house."

"You'd like that, wouldn't you?" Calvin turned on him. "Sure, beat it. Just pay me off. First you stick me in a nut ward for twenty-five years and now you'd like me to go away."

"You weren't in any nut ward," I said. "You're just heading for one real fast."

But he wasn't listening. He was staring furiously at Joe. Being ordered out of the house, being told no one would even follow him, so little was he appreciated, had plucked the most sensitive chord of his grievance. It wasn't the reaction he'd been looking for at all. He'd expected rage from Joe, or a plea for his life. Instead he was getting nothing but a wall of contemptuous indifference.

"You could trade testimony," I said. "Give Lester

and the Mexicans to the DA and they'd lighten up on you."

"You . . ." he stammered. "You cheap . . ." He suddenly moved forward and lifted the gun to my head. In the silence of the room I could hear the draperies flapping gently in the breeze. Calvin's face was bloodless, covered in a sheen of sweat like a film of oil. In that white glistening face, his blue eyes looked like a blind man's: flat, fixed. He had skin like a polished bone. I could see a scrap of bloody skin on the gun's sight where he'd raked it across Brownlee's face. If I could have fainted at that moment, I wouldn't have minded missing any of what would follow.

"Trade testimony," he hissed in a soft, scornful voice. "Do you think I'm a Coronado, a Brownlee, a sordid little crook who spends his life cheating people?"

"I don't think anything with that gun in my eye."

"All it would have taken was a letter and I could have got money out of him. You think I did this for money?"

"I don't know. I don't know why you're sticking that popgun in my face. I didn't screw up your life."

Behind him Brownlee had come to and was crawling slowly across the floor to my ankle harness. But the safety was on and there was no shell in the chamber. Brownlee would have to unsnap the leather loop from its button, remove the weapon, click off the safety, jack a shell into the breech, and fire it. All very noisy actions. If he was lucky enough to get a shot off, there was as much chance he would shoot Joe or me as that he'd get Calvin.

It was better than nothing. When Brownlee made the noise, Calvin would turn and fire. Then I could jump Calvin. I didn't care about anything so long as the gun barrel wasn't in my face when Calvin squeezed the trigger.

"How about easing off on that a little," I murmured. "It's making me cross-eyed looking at it."

"If you're going to shoot someone, you little lunatic, shoot me," Joe thundered. That sounded like a good suggestion.

"Yeah," I wheezed. I watched Calvin's hand. The second joint of his forefinger went white, pressing back on the trigger. Another fraction of an inch would release the hammer on the shell.

"Not so smart now?" Calvin said.

"I gave up a long time ago, friend. You've proved your point."

Brownlee drew the Mauser out of its holster and grasped it in both hands. He got to his knees and aimed it more or less at Calvin's back. The pistol wavered. Brownlee shut his eyes, and pulled the trigger.

Absolutely nothing happened. It didn't even make a noise.

"Jesus . . ." I swallowed. "Please don't shoot me, Calvin. I've got thirty grand in jewels in my car. I caught Brownlee with them. Take them."

"He's not going to shoot anyone," Joe said.

I didn't know where Elevel was getting his confidence from. Maybe it wasn't even confidence but just rock-bottom indifference. The worst had already happened to him. All he seemed to have left was loathing for Calvin. Some such thoughts must have been going through Calvin's mind: that nothing had been achieved, no relief granted by what he'd done. He'd gone looking for his father. His father was a man who'd rather get shot than spend another minute in his son's company.

"Okay," Calvin said quietly. He stepped back, still covering us with the gun. A light had gone out of his eyes as if someone had pulled a plug. His mouth was slack. I didn't like the look of him at all. He was the type to kill us all and put the gun in his mouth because life didn't mean anything any more. What was going on behind that dazed, sickly, feverish face of his?

Brownlee had discovered the safety catch and was

now pointing the Mauser at Calvin's approaching back. The room was completely silent except for the wind agitating the curtains, and the distant buzz of a lawnmower.

This time when Brownlee pulled the trigger, the hammer clicked audibly against the empty chamber.

Calvin spun around and fired at Brownlee, who was kneeling on the carpet, not understanding why the Mauser hadn't fired. Following the explosion of Calvin's gun there was a booming thud, and the tinkle of shattering glass. Calvin lurched sideways, tottered, and regained his balance. He stood for a moment in the middle of the library, the smoking .22 in his hand, his eyes shut tight in what looked like concentration. Brownlee was crawling toward a neutral corner. Calvin dropped his gun and when it hit the ground it went off like a firecracker. He didn't respond to the explosion at his feet. He took several wobbly steps backward and unbuttoned his navy blue blazer.

"Mother . . ." he said in an awed whisper.

Suddenly he looked too small for his clothes; they hung on him all wrong. His face wrinkled up to say something but no sound came out. He stumbled backward, hit the bookcase, bounced lightly, and slid to the ground like a drunk in an alley.

The French window behind me opened, swelling out the curtains. I could see a small powder burn on the blue velvet material of the draperies and hear someone breathing and cursing as he struggled through the folds. A polished .357 Magnum appeared, held in a compact hairy fist, then a gleaming white cuff, then the arm of a dark blue suit, followed by the rest of Tony Turino.

"Aw shit." He looked disgustedly at Calvin. "I am aiming all the time for the leg and then he moves. What kinda flake is that?" He jerked his thumb at Brownlee.

But I was looking at Calvin. He was lying with his back to the bookcase. His legs were splayed out, and from between them a stream of blood was pouring into the carpet. He held his hands to his groin and in a few seconds they were red.

"It's cold." He shuddered and his eyes filled with tears. When he wiped his eyes, his knuckles left crimson streaks on his face.

Turino had gone to inspect Brownlee. He stood up and said, "He gonna need a sewing machine to put his face back together, but the kid missed him."

I took a pillow and jammed it between Calvin's legs. The bullet had entered his right thigh just below the hip and cut up through his groin. I didn't know if it had hit any vital organs but from the way he was bleeding I knew it hadn't missed a major artery. His body was damp to the touch and his head lolled on his chest. Most people who've been shot look suddenly and pathetically young; you see faces within faces, the vulnerable faces of childhood. Calvin had the sort of pinched, pale face that must have made him look like an old person even as a child.

I don't know how conscious he was of what was happening around him. He moaned softly. When Joe bent down to help stanch his wound his body stiffened in a spasm that made him cry out with pain. Neither of them said anything intelligible to each other. Joe got his trousers loosened and packed the wound with towels. He murmured to the kid as he made him as comfortable as possible. He held the impromptu dressing in place and then gripped Calvin's wrists to prevent him from getting at the wound. I'd like to think Calvin recognized who was holding him.

The library was full of voices and faces but all I could hear was the twilight being torn apart by more and more sirens. A medic touched my shoulder. I rose to my feet and stepped back as he bent over Calvin. There was blood all over my hands and wrists, blood on Joe, on Calvin, on Brownlee. There was the crackle of police radios, the barked commands of ambulance men, the squeal of cars braking on the driveway. And gray bats seemed to be hovering on the edge of my vision, soft hideous flocks of them, waiting.

I found the bar and poured two shots of gin down my throat. They gave me an instant hangover. I was tired and old and the world looked like it should have been scrapped the day Cain sent Abel to the icehouse.

I swallowed the last drops of gin, put my glass down, and edged my way through the crowd toward the door, where Deputy Chief Granville was waiting for my statement.

You always have to make a statement to the police when it's too late. You have to make a statement when there is nothing left to say.

Chapter TWENTY-EIGHT

With appeals and delays on the various trials, it was almost a year before the last participants in the Elevel case received final sentencing.

Dr. Lester's sentence was long enough to insure that he would die in prison. Calvin, Coronado, and Grande received life sentences with dim prospects for early parole.

It was an overcast afternoon in August when I attended the final sentencing, and as the defendants were led away I determined to put the case out of my mind.

Lucy was waiting for me in her Fiat in a NO PARKING zone outside the Los Angeles County Criminal Courts building on Temple Street. For twelve months we'd been seeing each other while keeping our own separate places. She'd done her best to come to terms with my unpredictable working hours and I'd made an effort to get on with her friends. They were almost all people in the entertainment industry. As a result of the Elevel case, I had a certain notoriety and snob value in those circles. At a show business dinner party a real detective was more of an asset than an actor playing a weekly role as a private dick on TV. At least initially he was. In the end I never hit it off with her crowd. They didn't believe I spent most of my working life sitting in a car reading books. They didn't understand that I was paid to keep quiet about the cases I worked on. I never had the knack of turning my clients' troubles into amusing dinner conversation, and I didn't try very hard. A lot of Lucy's friends were actors who played roles supposedly based on the kind of low-life characters who were my friends. I knew investigators, cops, boosters, and paper merchants. She thought most of my friends were a little crude and frightening. I thought most of her friends were a little hollow and phony. We were probably both right. Anyway, we never tried living together. Whatever chemistry there was between us only worked in private.

Having given my final testimony, I was at last free to leave Los Angeles on a vacation. From the courthouse we were driving straight to the airport and catching a flight to Acapulco. Neither of us had mentioned it, but it was going to be something of a dry run to see if we could stand each other's company over an extended period of time. If it worked out, on our return to Los Angeles we'd move in together and play house for real.

On the plane we ran into a film crew flying down to Acapulco to add some locations shots to a cops-and-robbers film. Some of them were friends of Lucy, the others might as well have been because they all had friends in common. We ended up staying at the same hotel and after three days I figured I might as well have gone to Miami Beach. I finally dragged Lucy away to a small fishing village, Punto Muldonado, farther south. My memory of the place is of a beautiful, rugged spot with incredible spear-fishing. Lucy's is of flies, dirt, and boredom. When we got back to L.A. we kept seeing each other on and off, but there wasn't any more talk about living together. Something died in Mexico, the hope of a future, and without that, seeing each other became unreal.

Nearly a year after the trip to Mexico I was retained by an attorney representing a hit-and-run victim who had lost the use of her arm. The guilty party was an elderly furrier who entered a plea of diminished capacity. The plea was based on alleged brain damage suffered by the furrier during a heart attack six months prior to the accident. The case was heard in Beverly Hills Court. The judge sentenced the furrier to a ninety-day observation period in Atascadero Hospital for the Criminally Insane. My client's attorney suspected the furrier's plea was window dressing, a ploy to avoid paying damages to his client.

Late in June of that year I was dispatched to the town of Atascadero in Northern California to see what I could find out about the furrier's condition. He was a wealthy man, and my client's career as a shorthand typist had been ruined as a result of the paralysis of her arm. I was eager to get her some kind of financial compensation.

At the warden's office I identified myself in such a way that the woman in charge of records assumed I was representing the furrier and that he would be willing to see me.

"Let's see." She left her desk. "Averil Morehouse."

"That's him. He was admitted April twenty-ninth." I admired the clean sweep of her thighs and the bunching roundness of her bottom as she strained to remove a file folder from the high shelf. She was a very pretty blonde with wide, frank blue eyes devoid of any sense of humor. A deep little furrow pinched her eyebrows together; her lips were permanently puckered in thought. I could come into her office every day for a year and it would never occur to her that I was a man and she was a woman.

"Here we are." She ran her finger down the names. "Markham . . . Medcalf . . . Molineux . . . Montero . . . Moonhurst . . . Morehouse. Averil Morehouse. Admitted April twenty-ninth. *Oh!*"

"What is it?"

"I'm awfully sorry, sir. I'm afraid Mr. Morehouse isn't with us any more."

"Great." I leaned dejectedly on the counter and thought about the firm, upright contents of her starched white blouse.

"He died two nights ago." She consulted the file. "At eight forty-three, of a heart attack."

"Terrific," I said. "I just drove up from L.A. for nothing."

"I'm real sorry about that, sir." She started to replace the file.

"Wait a minute. Did you say, 'Moonhurst'?"

"Yes." She turned, frowning.

"Calvin Moonhurst?"

She reopened the file catalogue, ran her finger down the names, and stopped. "C. Moonhurst. Alias Lawrence Koontz. Alias James Tripp. He certainly has a lot of names."

"What's he doing here?" I asked. "I sent that guy to San Quentin eighteen months ago."

"He was transferred." She studied his file.

I wondered if Calvin had flipped out in prison, or had faked insanity to get switched into a hospital.

"Eleven months ago," she said. "He has Huntington's chorea."

"What's that?"

"I don't know, sir. But he's in a special ward so it's critical."

I thanked her and left. Instead of driving straight back to Los Angeles I pointed the car north. The land looked more dramatic, with richer, more vivid colors than the dry pastel monotony I was used to. I drove through the Salinas Valley and then on to Monterey and Carmel, where I stopped for a meal. Opposite the restaurant, set back from the pavement, was a public library with a balcony overlooking a well-tended lawn. When I came out I walked across the street to my car, started to open the door, and then turned and entered the library. After several moments of looking I found a medical dictionary with a description of Huntington's chorea and took it to a table.

It was a fatal, nasty disease, one of those eccentric, rare maladies that seem to exist to no purpose. As it progresses, it renders the subject increasingly prone to muscular uncoordination. Sporadic clumsiness, dizziness, and seizures herald its appearance. But what made my blood run cold was that the disease resulted in a backward evolution. With every month that passed Calvin was growing more childlike, simpler, physically more helpless. He was returning to the womb, going backward toward death. Eventually, as the disease ran its course, he would be indistinguishable from the sad mental defective his parents believed they had kept alive for twenty-five years.

I replaced the book on the shelf and headed toward the door. The visit to the library had taken fifteen minutes. I was fifteen minutes older. Somewhere south of me, in a prison hospital ward, a man was fifteen minutes younger.

Outside, the town was motionless under the harsh afternoon sunlight. Only the sound of the nearby ocean seemed alive with an immense and hissing monotony. Emptying and filling, it turned and polished the pebbled shore as inexorably as some great self-winding clock, keeping eternal time for the man in the prison hospital ward who was returning to the dark cradle.

For a while, I sat slumped in my car looking at the ocean, the white sands, the tossing surf, the cloudless sky over the brooding glitter of the water. For a second the scene stunned me and I sat paralyzed and thought about the man who'd broken the oldest law of nature, who'd come from a dark place and was now sinking back into it.

I shaded my eyes against the glare. I turned the ignition key and put on the air conditioner, and slowly steered the car out into the empty street.

Another bestseller from the world's master storyteller

The Top of the Hill

IRWIN SHAW

author of *Rich Man, Poor Man* and *Beggarman, Thief*

He feared nothing... wanted everything. Every thrill. Every danger. Every woman.

"Pure entertainment. Full of excitement."—*N.Y. Daily News*

"You can taste the stale air in the office and the frostbite on your fingertips, smell the wood in his fireplace and the perfume scent behind his mistresses' ears."—*Houston Chronicle*

A Dell Book $2.95 (18976-4)

Dell Bestsellers